The Hair Trunk
or
The Ideal Commonwealth

The Hair Trunk
or
The Ideal Commonwealth

An Extravaganza

by Robert Louis Stevenson

Edited with an Introduction
and Notes
by Roger G. Swearingen

humming earth

Published by

Humming Earth
an imprint of
Zeticula Ltd
The Roan
Kilkerran
KA19 81S
Scotland.

http://www.hummingearth.com
admin@hummingearth.com

First published in 2014

ISBN 978-1-84622-050-0

Contents

Introduction

Robert Louis Stevenson was twenty-six when in May 1877 he announced to his friend and confidante Frances Sitwell that he had drifted away from writing literary essays and had begun writing a comic novel:

> On Leslie Stephen's advice, I gave up the idea of a book of essays. He said he didn't imagine I was rich enough for such an amusement; and moreover whatever was worth publication was worth republication. So the best of those I had ready: 'An Apology for Idlers', is in proof for the *Cornhill.* I have 'Villon' to do for the same magazine, but God knows when I'll get it done, for – drums, trumpets I'm engaged upon – trumpets, drums – a novel! THE HAIR TRUNK; OR, THE IDEAL COMMONWEALTH. It is a most absurd story of a lot of young Cambridge fellows who are going to found a new society, with no ideas on the subject, and nothing but Bohemian tastes in the place of ideas; and who are – well, I can't explain about the trunk – it would take too long – but the trunk is the fun of it – everybody steals it; burglary, marine fight, life on desert island on W. Coast of Scotland, sloops, etc. The first scene where they make their grand schemes and get drunk is supposed to be very funny, by Henley. I really saw him laugh over it until he cried. (Letter 470)

Leslie Stephen (1832–1904) had been the editor of the *Cornhill Magazine* since 1871, during the early 1870s bringing to its pages the work of Thomas Hardy, Henry James, James Payn, and others including RLS. Two years earlier, on 12 February 1875, visiting Edinburgh to give a lecture, Stephen had introduced Stevenson to another of his young contributors, William Ernest Henley (1849–1903), who was then beginning a long convalescence at the Edinburgh Infirmary after surgery there by Joseph Lister to address the tuberculosis in his foot. Stephen's letter to RLS, probably sent to him in Paris and then forwarded to Edinburgh, is dated 1 March 1877 (Yale GEN MSS 664, Box 91, Folder 508, Beinecke 5560), and it chiefly concerns RLS's proposal to write an essay on François Villon, as he did in "François Villon: Student, Poet, Housebreaker" published in the *Cornhill Magazine* in August.

In February and March 1877, Stevenson and Henley were busily trying to get a new weekly called *London* on its feet, RLS by writing four journalistic sketches, three of them on Paris, and two book reviews for the first four issues, 3–24 February 1877, then rewriting for publication as the journal's *feuilleton* a Scottish story of his, "An Old Song," published anonymously in four weekly installments, 24 February–17 March 1877, Stevenson's first published work of fiction. Henley, also in Edinburgh but soon to move to London, was busy meanwhile writing poetry and book and music reviews for the weekly.

It was probably in April or early May of 1877, then, that Stevenson began writing *The Hair Trunk* and shared the first chapter, if not more, with Henley in Edinburgh. He seems to have had a good idea of at least the beginning of the story at the time that he wrote to Mrs. Sitwell in May. And by mid-May 1877, mentioning then to Sidney Colvin that he was "up to the elbows in a Villon for Stephen" and acting "one leading part and one subordinate" in the private theatricals of Professor and Mrs. Fleeming Jenkin in Edinburgh, he commented: "The novel is at a standstill. I do it so damned ill, it's revolting" (Letter 471).

Nevertheless Stevenson came back to *The Hair Trunk* immediately or sometime in the next two years, carrying the story to its present length and sometime in 1879 making a fair copy of it up to that point. This is the manuscript published for the first time in the present edition, a complete but unfinished fair-copy manuscript of slightly more than 30,000 words written throughout in ink by RLS, in two quarto notebooks now in the Huntington Library, San

Marino, California. On the title page, Stevenson identifies himself as the author of *An Inland Voyage*, *Picturesque Notes on Edinburgh* – and of *Travels with a Donkey*, the first two of these published in 1878 and *Travels with a Donkey* rewritten by him from his journal in December and January and in process of publication by the end of February 1879. He had taken up *The Hair Trunk* again, he told Henley in March 1879, upon his return, on 18 February, from a visit to London – a visit during which a major topic of discussion had been the desperate uncertainties in his personal life caused by Fanny Osbourne's return to the United States at the end of the previous summer and his continuing wish to marry her if she could obtain a divorce:

> I am more at sea than ever, quite lost in my mind; quite lost in life like a careless wayfarer. What's to happen, I don't know. In the meantime, I wait another letter which shall clinch things, and go on with – aye, rub your eyes – 'The Hair Trunk'. I read it over the night I got back from weariness, and as I repeatedly laughed, I said I should finish it. I am now in full swing. Mrs Lemesurier and the Major, I am getting well, I think. (Letter 603)

Stevenson's reference to Mrs Lemesurier and the Major as if they were already familiar suggests that Henley had already seen the story through the chapter in which they appear for the first time, Book II, Chapter III, one chapter from the end of the manuscript as it now stands. His work on *The Hair Trunk* during 1879 must have consisted, therefore, chiefly of writing out the fair-copy manuscript, no doubt improving it here and there as he did so, rather than carrying the story much beyond the point where it now breaks off. By August 1879 he was on his way across ocean and continent to California. *The Hair Trunk* was still unfinished and, as it happened, it was never again mentioned in Stevenson's surviving correspondence or that of his friends.

Stevenson was always an author of beginnings, continually making lists of, and even starting, many more works than he ever finished. What is remarkable about *The*

Hair Trunk is not so much that Stevenson never finished it, but that he wrote as much as he did, given how much else he was doing at the same time. The years 1877 to 1879 are a period of extraordinary creative activity for Stevenson. They are the years of his first books, of some of his first lasting and memorable familiar essays, and (above all) of his first substantial successes as an author of fiction. One simple but important reason why Stevenson gave up *The Hair Trunk* may have been that at the very same time as he was beginning it, he was suddenly succeeding as an author of short stories as well. According to Henley in a letter to his future wife Anna Boyle, RLS had been "ashamed" of "An Old Song" and asked that she not tell anyone who wrote it (Letter 464, n.1). But it was far different with "A Lodging for the Night" – an unexpected, happy by-product of RLS's essay on Villon for the *Cornhill.* As RLS wrote to Sidney Colvin in June 1877: "And look here, while I was full of Villon, I wrote a little story, ten or twelve pages, about him. Can you suggest anywhere I could place it; for I want money sorely, not altogether for myself; for I have become the most economical of men. Not Leslie Stephen or Macmillan, as they don't take fiction" (June 1877, Letter 472). "A Lodging for the Night: A Story of Francis Villon," RLS's first signed short story, was published in *Temple Bar* in October. In early August, inspired by this acceptance, he planned to send "The Sire de Malétroit's Mousetrap" (as "The Sire de Malétroit's Door" was then called) to *Temple Bar* as well. He eventually did so in November, and it was published in *Temple Bar* in January (RLS to Sidney Colvin, 2 August 1877, Letter 477; RLS to George Bentley, November 1877, Letter 488). "'Will o'the Mill,'" he wrote to Mrs. Sitwell on 10 August, "I suspect, is bosh. But I sent it, red hot, to Stephen, in a fit of haste" (Letter 478). Despite some concern that the story hovered uncertainly between realism and allegory, Leslie Stephen accepted "Will o'the Mill" on 29 August (Stephen to RLS, Yale GEN MSS 664, Box 91, Folder 508, Beinecke 5561), and it appeared in the *Cornhill* in January 1878.

Stevenson had been writing stories, and projecting collections of his stories, since he was a teenager. But it was not until these works of his mid-twenties, in 1877, that he felt any of them strong enough to submit for publication – and in all three of these instances during the summer and autumn of 1877 he was successful. In January 1878, proud of his new-found success, he wrote to his mother about the two stories that were both in print that month, gently chiding his parents for their skepticism: "I wonder on the whole, whether 'Will' and the 'Sire' have, between them, at all changed your opinion – yours and my father's that I could never write a story? Let me know the ripest of your conclusions on this head" (Letter 502). From then until the end of his life there is hardly a three-month period during which Stevenson does not publish a long or a short work of fiction – and often both. During the last six months of 1877, he is enjoying his first substantial successes as a writer of fiction, and in shorter forms than that of the novel.

Another important factor in Stevenson's leaving *The Hair Trunk* aside in 1877 may have been that his attention was diverted to another new novel of his, "In the Windbound Arethusa," of which the 82 surviving manuscript pages were sold in 1914 (Anderson I, 299), in an earlier part of the same sale at which *The Hair Trunk* first appeared. These pages, unfortunately, are unknown since then, but RLS's cousin and biographer Graham Balfour describes "In the Windbound Arethusa" as "another attempt of the same date" as *The Hair Trunk* and says that it "attained no better result" (Balfour, *1*, 142). *The Hair Trunk* is only one of several new ventures in fiction for Stevenson in 1877 and 1878, and he is active in other directions as well. In December, he remarked to Sidney Colvin that, despite many personal worries, he was still "engaged in the confection of my cheery literature" – in particular, rewriting the journal of the canoe trip that he had taken in Belgium and France with Sir Walter Simpson in September 1876 (Letter 494). He finished it in Dieppe in January, the result being *An Inland Voyage*, RLS's first book, published on 28 April 1878. This, too, would have taken time and attention away from *The Hair Trunk*.

A third important factor in Stevenson's leaving aside *The Hair Trunk* may have been that, as time went on, it may have come to seem in some ways redundant. In his work for *London* in 1878, especially but not only in the stories serialized there as "Latter-Day Arabian Nights" from 8 June to 26 October 1878, Stevenson found a lively alternative vehicle for the same comic, satiric, and philosophic interests that are embodied in the simpler narrative mode of *The Hair Trunk*. Partly from a dislike of the weekly's founding editor Robert Glasgow Brown, RLS had stopped contributing to *London* after the last installment of "An Old Song" appeared in mid-March 1877. But in December Brown resigned, and Henley took over the editorship. Contributors were few, RLS's wife recalled years later, and "[it] often happened that an entire number of *London* was written by Mr. Henley and my husband alone" ("Prefatory Note," *New Arabian Nights*, Biographical Edition, 1905). During the spring and summer of 1878, to fill the pages of *London*, RLS greatly extended his range both as an essayist – in "A Plea for Gas Lamps" (27 April), "Pan's Pipes" (4 May), and "El Dorado" (11 May) – and as a writer of fiction.

Again and again in *The Hair Trunk* one is reminded of characters and jokes and comic paradoxes in the essays and stories that Stevenson was writing and publishing at the same time – as if all of these works originate in the same single inspiration or vision of modern life. "Here am I," the clergyman Mr. Rolles laments in the "Story of the Young Man in Holy Orders," the fifth of the "Latter-Day Arabian Nights" stories, published in *London* on 31 August and 7 September 1878, "with learning enough to be a Bishop, and I positively do not know how to dispose of a stolen diamond. . . . This inspires me with very low ideas of University training." Prince Florizel does offer one suggestion: "You may gather some notions from Gaboriau. . . . He is at least suggestive; and as he is an author much studied by Prince Bismarck, you will, at the worst, lose your time in good society." (In the collection of English translations launched by the London publisher Henry Vizetelly in February 1881, just below the series title "Gaboriau's Sensational Novels" appears the line: "The Favourite Reading of Prince Bismarck." For a reproduction of one such cover see Roger Bonniot, *Émile Gaboriau ou La Naissance du Roman Policier* [1985], facing 385. The source of RLS's earlier reference here must have been one of the French editions.)

"What piping folly all education is!" Turton exclaims in the second chapter of *The Hair Trunk*, in a similar vein: "Here am I, three and twenty . . . and never knew anything about the world until this moment! Here have I spent all my substance on their damned schools and universities; and they turn me out physically incapable of doing anything for an honest livelihood" (16). "Society is proved to be powerless against educated malefactors," says Hardy as they unfold their plans. "And then there's Gaboriau's M Lecocq," adds Turton, "who got into the police by showing them a whole hatful of patent-safety crimes, that anybody might commit . . . and the devil himself wouldn't find out" (65).

"I am sure I would rather be a bargee than occupy any position under Heaven that required attendance at an office," RLS wrote in his own voice in the chapter "On the Willebroek Canal" in *An Inland Voyage*, and in a later chapter he tells of his and Sir Walter Simpson's day-dreaming, during their canoe voyage together, about living on a barge themselves – a plan that was actually begun the following summer, when RLS, Simpson, and others purchased a barge and hired a French carpenter to remodel it. In *The Hair Trunk*, Ratcliffe (nicknamed The Highway) "had moulded himself on the pattern of a Bargee. He declared loudly that he cared for nothing under the sun but beer and tobacco" (6). "We all like the open air," Blackburn says, outlining his plan for them all.

> "Well, here's an obvious course for us: – let us go away from houses. Again . . . we dislike stools, and desks, and Bonuses and, in short, all ways of making money. Second obvious course: let us go where we can do without it. Once more . . . we like sailoring. In God's name, then, let's go to sea! 'Tis an open thoroughfare, and the wind costs nothing. A few fellows in a handy craft may go pretty nearly where they will, and do precisely what they please. Look at Rajah Brooke!" (18)

Here and throughout *The Hair Trunk* one finds the same high-spirited joking – "Look at Rajah Brooke!" – and the same celebration of irresponsible gaiety, absurd schemes, independence of mind, and the open air, that appears also in

Stevenson's travel books, essays, and short stories written at the same time. All of these works are part of the same effort that, in dedicating *Virginibus Puerisque* to Henley in 1881, RLS declared had been his aim in his early essays:

> I was to be the *Advocatus*, not I hope *Diaboli*, but *Juventutis*; I was to state temperately the beliefs of youth as opposed to the contentions of age; to go over all the field where the two differ, and produce at last a little volume of special pleadings which I might call, without misnomer, *Life at Twenty-Five*.

His protagonists in *The Hair Trunk* are indeed "A Pack of Young Fools," as RLS called them in a deleted first version of the title of the first chapter. But this is as it should be. As he put it in "Crabbed Age and Youth," written in July and August 1877 in response to Leslie Stephen's request for another essay in the vein of "An Apology for Idlers," written the year before but first published in the *Cornhill Magazine* in July 1877:

> It is as natural and as right for a young man to be imprudent and exaggerated, to live in swoops and circles, and beat about his cage like any other wild thing newly captured, as it is for old men to turn gray, or mothers to love their offspring, or heroes to die for something worthier than their lives. (*Virginibus Puerisque*, 1881)

"I clung hard to that entrancing age," RLS continued in his Dedication of *Virginibus Puerisque* to Henley: "but with the best will, no man can be twenty-five forever. The old, ruddy convictions deserted me, and, along with them, the style that fits their presentation and defence." As time went on, *The Hair Trunk* may have come to seem a less effective expression and examination of his outlook that did his work in other forms. And, as he himself suggests, probably it was also an outlook that he had, to some degree at least, outgrown. Other forms and views beckoned, and Stevenson was happy to follow them.

The Hair Trunk is an engaging and memorable snapshot of Stevenson in his mid-twenties, enjoying to the fullest the very beginning of his success as a writer of fiction. Stevenson's own frustrated complaint ("I do it so damned ill, it's revolting") notwithstanding, the story really is well and efficiently told, and at a good pace, and there are moments of pure descriptive intensity that look forward as much as a decade in Stevenson's work. The description of the streets of London in the opening pages of Part I, Chapter V – especially that "strange and rather spectral contest of lights and shadows" visible at the ends of streets open to the west (73) – looks ahead to similar descriptions in "Latter-Day Arabian Nights" (1878), *The Dynamiter* (1885), and *Dr. Jekyll and Mr. Hyde* (1886). The descriptions of the Highland landscape in Part II look ahead in their particularity and concreteness to *Travels With a Donkey in the Cevénnes* (1879) and *Kidnapped* (1886).

The Hair Trunk is also unique among Stevenson's literary works, however, in that it shows us a side of his temperament (and details of his outlook) that his friends knew well but that remained visible only in occasional glimpses until the publication of his letters complete by Yale University Press during the 1990s. This is an ironic, joking, skeptical and at times almost cynical Stevenson. *The Hair Trunk* is filled with contemporary references, and almost all of them are the products of Stevenson's casting a knowing, satirical eye on the more pretentious (and ambitious) undertakings of his busiest contemporaries. Blackburn suggests that on their remote island Turton will "never hear the Messiah any more." But Turton replies that this is not so:

> "O yes," returned Turton cheerfully. "I shall be sent back as Plenipotentiary, about the time of the Handel Festival. Egad, I think I see myself, leaning back in an open carriage like Doctor Kenealy, with a beard, and a Sunday hat, and beads round my neck. Plenipotentiary is a very noble word. Doctor Kenealy looks a plenipotentiary every inch of him: so noble and so replete!" (81)

As everyone at the time would have known, the week-long "Triennial Handel Festival" was hardly an instance of high-brow musical art. It featured performances, including of *The Messiah*, in the re-built Crystal Palace, with a gigantic organ, thousands of singers and orchestral musicians, and audiences normally numbering about 20,000. During the early 1870s, Dr. Edward Vaughan Hyde Kenealy had been the chief counsel representing the so-called Tichborne Claimant, Arthur Orton, first in seeking the proceeds of an immense inheritance and then in answering criminal charges of perjury, in trials of what proved to be unprecedented duration. In both of these actions Kenealy was unsuccessful. His client was sent to prison and he was himself disbarred, but during the rest of the 1870s Kenealy travelled the country protesting the verdicts and demanding justice. He wore a full black beard, and not only had he been caricatured during the trial by Leslie Ward ("Spy") in *Vanity Fair* as "The Claimant's Counsel," it is unmistakably a dreaming Kenealy who appears in Henry Holiday's illustration for Fit the Sixth, "The Barrister's Dream," in Lewis Carroll's *The Hunting of the Snark* (1876), published less than year before RLS began *The Hair Trunk*. Mark Twain, too, followed the trial with interest. He had a scrapbook kept for the newspaper accounts, and on his round-the-world tour in 1895 he visited the Claimant's former home in Australia.

Not only is *The Hair Trunk* full of jokes like these, as often as not Stevenson is making fun of interests that he himself shares. It is not only a charming irony, but a sign of his own deep interest, that Samoa, where Stevenson settled and eventually died and was buried, is chosen as the place where The Ideal Commonwealth is to be established. Useless or puzzling though they might seem to outsiders, quaternions and multi-dimensional geometries were not only among the latest topics in advanced mathematics and key in the emergence of modern physics as a science of fields rather than of forces. Stevenson himself had studied them – or at least heard about them – in his engineering classes at the University of Edinburgh, and under one of the pioneers of the new mathematics, Professor Peter Guthrie Tait, who in addition was a close friend of his father's. In London he dined with and was a fellow-member of the Savile

Club with another pioneer, William Kingdon Clifford, whose mathematical brilliance was joined with what Stevenson later called an engaging, "irresponsible boyishness of mind and manner" and "hot fit[s] of the most noisy atheism." "He was a very brilliant fellow and he never grew up," RLS remarked of Clifford; and so much was atheism "the fashion of the hour" that his own "first great social success of the period, not now to be sniffed at, was gained by outdoing poor Clifford in a contest of schoolboy blasphemy" ("Memoirs of Himself," additional material dictated in the 1890s; Vailima Edition, 1923).

In *The Hair Trunk* Stevenson never misses a chance to poke fun: to launch a witty, satirical barb at pretense, enthusiasm, or mere undue seriousness. But there is no malice or anger in his view. He is as amused and skeptical about Herbert Spencer and Jeremy Bentham, about utopias and colonies and missionaries, Greenland's icy mountains and Rajah Brooke, as he is about cockneyfied castles in the Highlands for the newly rich, about the go-ahead spirit of Birmingham and of Thomas Cook's guided travellers, about mechanical pianos and chromolithographs, or about the practical value of geometries in unlimited dimensions and the latest entities in vector calculus. At Tufto Castle, in Scotland, where the founders of the Ideal Commonwealth must go to get the hair trunk, retired Major Cunningham is a wonderful comic creation: "a constant inmate of the castle, on the footing of family friend . . . a fine old pickled Anglo-Indian" (110) for whom the imperious widow Mrs. Lemesurier, another fine creation, has chosen the derisive nickname Heics, for his service in the Honourable East India Company's Service. Son Hugo is suitably vacant, frustrated, and ineffectual, at one point reflecting, when the commotion has subsided somewhat, that "it was obvious that underneath all this, lay one of those mysteries which struck him as so undesirable a feature in the life of a country gentleman" (144).

The truth is that regardless of age or occupation, we are all unable to get outside ourselves, all of us equally as incapable of justifying our enthusiasms (or prejudices) as we are unable not to follow them. As RLS wrote concluding his essay "El Dorado," first published in *London* on 11 May 1878, about a year after he announced the beginning of *The Hair Trunk* to Mrs. Sitwell:

> A strange picture we make on our way to our Chimæras, ceaselessly marching, grudging ourselves the time for rest; indefatigable, adventurous pioneers. It is true that we shall never reach the goal; it is even more than probable that there is no such place; and if we lived for centuries and were endowed with the powers of a god, we should find ourselves not much nearer what we wanted at the end. O toiling hands of mortals! O unwearied feet, travelling ye know not whither. Soon, soon, it seems to you, you must come forth on some conspicuous hilltop, and but a little way farther, against the setting sun, descry the spires of El Dorado. Little do ye know your own blessedness; for to travel hopefully is a better thing than to arrive, and the true success is to labour. (*Virginibus Puerisque*, 1881)

It is this vision of modern life – a vision that is at once skeptical and humorous, gloomy and upbeat, doubtful and loving, serious but only up to a point – that permeates *The Hair Trunk* and accounts for its unique, and uniquely Stevensonian, character. We are fortunate in having so much of it to read and enjoy today.

Manuscripts

This edition presents the text of *The Hair Trunk* as Stevenson left it sometime during the spring or early summer of 1879. Except for four very short quotations in Robert Irwin Hillier, *The South Seas Fiction of Robert Louis Stevenson* (1989), and a French translation by Isabelle Chapman with a completion by Michel LeBris, *La Malle en cuir ou La Société idéale* (2011), *The Hair Trunk* has never before appeared in print. It appears here as Stevenson's own readers might have seen it if, as RLS did with the opening chapters of *The South Seas* (1890), he had decided to print what he then had, incomplete as it stood, as a working fragment to be revisited later.

Stevenson's fair-copy manuscript of *The Hair Trunk* is in the Huntington Library, San Marino, California, HM 2411. It was sold originally to the well-known New York bookdealer George D. Smith, for $1,400, in January 1915 as Lot 360 in Part II of the three-part sale at the Anderson Galleries, New York, 1914–1916, a sale of material consigned by RLS's stepdaughter Isobel Field. The title page is reproduced as the frontispiece in the catalogue of this sale. The manuscript was sold again four and one-half years later as Lot 760a in sale 1430, "English Literature from London," at the Anderson Galleries, New York, 13-14 May 1919. The manuscript occupies two quarto notebooks, slightly more than 30,000 words written throughout in ink by RLS on the right-hand pages, the facing backs of the pages being left blank, with a few changes and comments in pencil as well as other changes in ink, within the text and occasionally on the facing pages. RLS has written catchwords at the foot of every text page. The page number – a single series taking in both notebooks – appears in the top center of each page.

The manuscript is a fair copy: a snapshot of a work in progress created for private circulation and comment. This is apparent from the clarity of Stevenson's handwriting, the fewness of his revisions, and from the fact that in the first notebook volume RLS included a title-page and that both volumes begin with correctly-paged tables of contents. Chapter follows chapter continuously, each chapter beginning on the same page as the end of the previous one, without a gap, rather than at the top of a new page. The first notebook is full – it contains pages 1 through 80 and there are no blank pages – and the text ends in mid-sentence, the continuation appearing on the first page of the second notebook. The second notebook, pages 81 through 145, is likewise continuous. It ends with the title (only) of Chapter V in Part II, "The Dragons in Disorder," and the remaining pages are blank.

On the front fly-leaf of the first notebook is a list in pencil, possibly by someone other than RLS, of page numbers on which brief notes in pencil appear suggesting changes. Inside the front cover of the second notebook RLS has written the titles and the length in number of pages of five of his essays published in the *Cornhill Magazine*, no doubt for a projected collection. The earliest is "Walking Tours" (June 1876), the latest is "Crabbed Age and Youth" (March 1878). On a page at the very back of the same notebook he has written a few words, possibly of dialogue, and a list of six untitled scenes and the names of the characters in each scene in Act I of an untitled play. The characters are those in "An April Day; or Autolycus in Service" (MSS., Folger Shakespeare Library, Washington D. C.), a farce possibly based on a earlier story or idea of RLS's that he and Henley were re-working as a play during the early months of 1879.

Eight pages of a version (or versions) of *The Hair Trunk* earlier than the version in the Huntington Library notebooks are in the Beinecke Rare Book and Manuscript Library, Yale University (Yale GEN MSS 664, Box 106, Folder 2029, Beinecke 6271). This fragment, the only portion of *The Hair Trunk* known other than in the Huntington notebooks, is written in ink on both sides of four faintly ruled folio leaves, 12⅜ in high by 8¾ in wide, probably two four-page folders originally. The first three leaves are watermarked with a seated figure of Britannia; the last is watermarked STOWFORD | MILLS | 1876. Six of the pages are numbered in the top left-hand corner, possibly by Stevenson: 3–8. The second of the remaining two pages is numbered 2; the first of these is not numbered, or is possibly numbered 4 at the foot of the page. The text in these eight pages is consecutive and consists of about 3,000 words corresponding to Book I, Chapter IV of the notebook version, from Strutt's comment, "Now, if we can raise funds to go; why not raise them and stay where we are?" (50), through Blackburn's and Strutt's private discussion walking around the quadrangle (65). There are more first thoughts and other changes in the Yale draft than in the notebook version, but the wording that Stevenson finally arrives at is usually so close to the notebook version as to suggest that these draft pages were its immediate source.

Three paragraphs of dialogue appear twice, in two different versions, in the Yale draft. This occurs at the foot of the page numbered 8 and at the top of the un-numbered page. In the second of the two versions, the first duplicated paragraph begins, "Shall we wear masques?" and the last ends, "I could shed tears!" (62). This second version is followed in the notebook version. In the earlier version, however, the word *masques* is spelled *masks*, and the paragraph itself originally began: "So much the better!" cried Turton. This suggests that the first version of these three paragraphs, at the foot of page 8, is a version that Stevenson wrote, but then – some time later, rather than immediately – changed his mind about. When he returned to the draft, he started anew at the top of a new page but forgot to delete the first version at the foot of page 8. Details on this change, and on a few other first thoughts and differences between the pages that make up the Yale draft and the Huntington Library notebook version are included in the Textual Notes to this edition.

Text and Annotations

In the version of *The Hair Trunk* that is presented here, changes that Stevenson made in the course of writing out the manuscript, or afterwards, have almost always been assimilated without comment. Only the final version is given, as if the manuscript were being set in type for publication. Only when a change has seemed to me clearly a change of intention or desired effect, or in some other way to shed light on Stevenson's intentions or his actual or potential satiric targets, is notice taken of it in the Textual Notes. Also made without comment are corrections of spelling errors and of inconsistencies or omissions in details such as capitalization, the spelling of proper names, and in the hyphenation of compound words.

Stevenson writes, for example, *appartment(s)*, *dependancy(ies)* *dwellt*, *excentric*, *excercise*, *Isoceles*, *nieghbourhood*, *niether*, *rythm*, *smellt*, and *wiegh*, and although not meant to be printed in this way, in his way of writing them a connector much like a hyphen appears in words in which the prefix *dis-* is used, among these *dis-ciples*, *dis-cipline*, *dis-closed*, *dis-cord*, *dis-credited*, and *undis-covered*. He carries this into French, writing *soi dis-ant*, and he also writes *mis-understandings*. He invariably omits the hyphen from numerical compounds such as *thirty-six, forty-eight, and sixty-five*. He writes as two words compounds such as *dark-haired*, *free-tongued*, *half-pay*, *jog-trot*, *old-high*, and *pot-house*. He omits, or sometimes omits, the initial capital letter in *Bible*, *Chippendale*, *Colonies*, *Creigh*, and *Southdown*. He is inconsistent in spelling the surnames *Urquhart* and *Thomson*, sometimes including and sometimes omitting the *h* or the *p*; and he represents Major Cunningham's pronunciation of *extraordinary* in several ways, among which *extr'or'nary* has been chosen for this edition only because it is the most common. Whenever a correction removes what seems clearly an unintended distraction, I have made it, just as would have been done if *The Hair Trunk* had been set in type for publication.

Stevenson's own occasional capitalization of words not usually or not always capitalized – among them, *Bargee*, *Summer*, *Island*, and *Spring* – has, however, been followed, as it seems possible that by this practice he wishes to emphasize or to give an abstract categorical status to the words by so doing. I have also followed his highly idiosyncratic (and not always consistent) use of commas, semicolons, dashes, parentheses, and ellipses – this because the eccentricities of his usage often seem intended to render the actual rhythms of speech or the logic of what is being presented. To change or standardize RLS's punctuation – for example, to delete the commas and semicolons that so often introduce a sudden break or hitch in the otherwise easy, rapid flow of sentences, or to use ellipses only to indicate pauses in speech, semicolons only to indicate grammatical or logical divisions – might make the text somewhat easier to read, but only at the cost of other effects that Stevenson may have been anxious to retain despite their difficulty. As he wrote in 1887 to the proofreader of "A Chapter on Dreams" for *Scribner's Magazine* about the numerous improvements that were being made: "If I receive another proof of this sort, I shall return it at once with the general direction: 'See MS.' I must suppose my system of punctuation to be very bad; but it is mine; and it shall be adhered to with punctual exactness, by every created printer who shall print for me" (RLS to James B. Carrington, *ca.* 4 November 1887, Letter 1933).

Stevenson's own manuscript page numbers have also been kept. These appear, in square brackets, after the last word of text that appears on the manuscript page so numbered. Doing so keeps alive the idea that this edition presents the text of a manuscript that Stevenson prepared for his own use and for his friends, not a work that he also saw through to publication. In addition, as the explanatory and textual notes are linked to these original manuscript page numbers rather than to the physical page and line numbers in this edition, the links remain correct no matter what the actual page and line number (if any) may be in this or any future edition, printed or electronic.

Explanatory and Textual Notes

In addition to the text of *The Hair Trunk*, this edition also offers Explanatory Notes and Textual Notes, both sets of notes keyed to the original manuscript page numbers provided in square brackets in the text. Because so much of the humor in *The Hair Trunk* depends on references to the now-forgotten here and now of the 1870s in Britain – and because so much of its literary interest, today, lies in its connections with Stevenson's published works then and later – the Explanatory Notes often provide much more than is needed merely for identification. As Martin Gardner remarked in the Introduction to his pioneering edition, *The Annotated Alice* (1960): "No joke is funny unless you see the point of it, and sometimes a point has to be explained." In *The Hair Trunk*, as in *Alice in Wonderland*, in Gardner's words, "we are dealing with a very curious, complicated kind of nonsense, written for British readers of another century, and we need to know a great many things that are not part of the text if we wish to capture its full wit and flavor" (7). For this reason, I have summarized, not only cited, little-known novels and stories; I have quoted little-known and forgotten songs, hymns, and verses; and I have given the best account I can of the contemporary philosophic and scientific references that occur throughout, from Jeremy Bentham and Herbert Spencer to quaternions. To convey a sense of how facts and personalities were regarded at the time – again, to restore as much as possible of the satiric and allusive context – I have sometimes quoted from the eleventh edition of the *Encyclopædia Britannica* (1911) in preference to later sources. A few references are still untraced. These are indicated in the Explanatory Notes and await the penetration of readers more alert or learned (or perhaps just luckier) than I. No doubt there are also a few other jokes and references that I have simply failed to realize are there.

Textual Notes give earlier wordings of the text whenever a change has seemed to me clearly a change of intention or desired effect. Lesser variants have been passed over, an exercise of editorial discretion that makes the apparatus less than all-inclusive (if such a term even has meaning in reproducing manuscripts in print) in order to reduce clutter and to keep the focus on variants that really are of interest. Differences between the Yale fragment and the Huntington Library fair-copy version are also given, to show the relations that exist between them.

References

The following short forms of reference have been used in this Introduction and in the Explanatory and Textual Notes. Stevenson's works are identified by title and the date of first publication, or the date of composition if not published during his lifetime, followed by the title and date of the collection in which the work was collected if it was collected during his lifetime.

Details on the composition and publication of all of Stevenson's prose works appear in my detailed guide, *The Prose Writings of Robert Louis Stevenson: A Guide* (1980). Other works are identified at the point of citation with author, title, and date of publication.

Anderson

Items consigned by Stevenson's stepdaughter Isobel Field after the death of her mother in 1914 and offered in the three-part sale at the Anderson Galleries, New York, 1914–1916, are identified as Anderson, followed by the part and item number in the catalogues of this sale.

Balfour

References to Graham Balfour's biography of his cousin are to the English edition, *The Life of Robert Louis Stevenson,* 2 vols. London: Methuen, 1901.

Beinecke 0000, Yale

Manuscripts in the Beinecke Rare Book and Manuscript Library, Yale University, are identified by the new catalogue number and, if they are also listed in the catalogue by George L. McKay, *A Stevenson Library . . .* 6 vols. New Haven: Yale University Press, 1951–1964, by the item number in that catalogue. For example, RLS's play *Monmouth* is identified as Yale GEN MSS 664, Box 33, Folder 34, Beinecke 6587. Printed books at Yale are identified simply as Yale or, when there is such an entry, by the label Beinecke and the item number in the same catalogue.

Brewer

E. Cobham Brewer, *Dictionary of Phrase and Fable.* New and Enlarged Edition. London: Cassell and Company, 1894.

DNB

The Dictionary of National Biography, ed. Leslie Stephen and Sidney Lee. 22 vols. Oxford: Oxford University Press, 1885–1901; reprinted, 1921–1922.

Encyclopædia Britannica

The Encyclopædia Britannica. 11th ed. 29 vols. New York: Encyclopædia Britannica Company, 1910–1911.

Letter 0000

Stevenson's letters are quoted from and are identified by recipient, date, and letter number in the authoritative edition, *The Letters of Robert Louis Stevenson,* ed. Bradford A. Booth and Ernest J. Mehew. 8 vols. New Haven: Yale University Press, 1994–1995.

OED

The Oxford English Dictionary, ed. James A. H. Murray, *et al.* 1884-1928, 1933; online edition accessed June 2014

The Hair Trunk.

or

The Ideal Commonwealth

An Extravaganza.

by Robert Louis Stevenson

author of "An Inland Voyage", "Picturesque Notes on Edinburgh,"
"Travels with a donkey".

(I)

"Sir", said Doctor Johnson, let us make a Society."

Wo fehlt's nicht irgendwo auf dieser Welt?
Dem dies, dem das, hier aber fehlt das Geld.
. . . .
Im ~~Bergund~~ Berges adern, Mauergründen
Ist Gold gemünzt und ungemünzt zu finden;
Und fragt ihr mich, wer es zu Tage schafft:
Begabten Manns Natur- und Geisteskraft.

Mephistopheles

The Hair Trunk
or
The Ideal Commonwealth

An Extravaganza

by Robert Louis Stevenson
author of “An Inland Voyage”,
“Picturesque Notes on Edinburgh”,
“Travels with a Donkey”

(I)

Sir, said Doctor Johnson, let us make a society.

Wo fehlt’s nicht irgendwo auf dieser Welt?
Dem dies, dem das, hier aber fehlt das Geld.
. . . .
In Bergesadern, Mauergründen
Ist Gold gemünzt und ungemünzt zu finden,
Und fragt ihr mich, wer es zutage schafft:
Begabten Manns Natur- und Geisteskraft.
Mephistopheles

The Hair Trunk; or The Ideal Commonwealth

The Hair Trunk;

or, The Ideal Commonwealth.

Book I – The Prophet Blackburn

Chapter I

The Disciples

If there is any one manifestation of the human spirit more out of credit than another in these days of Mr Spencer, it is the good old fashioned quality of youthfulness. People make haste to be rid of it, as if it were an unpleasant malady; they travel past, for two and forty and a bank parlour; they regard life through the disenchanting spectacles of middle age. And yet even in the bald-head generation, there are instances of youth in its most acute form; and although the victims labour under serious social disability, they are none the less for that good fellows all, and may perhaps furnish the matter for a story out of their headlong and unwise existences. [1]

Some years ago, in a certain College of the University of Cambridge, which shall here be nameless, a party of gay and fantastic striplings sought out more hardships, pursued more absurd adventures, ran more unnecessary risks, and generally excelled their contemporaries in this respect of youthfulness. Their monkey or donkey tricks, it is proper to mention, engrossed those hours of the day which should have been set apart for study, and often enough the best part of those hours of the night which should have been sacred to sleep. They believed in the accomplishment of their preposterous adventures, as fanatics believe in a mission. They were fools with all the seriousness in the world. A canoe voyage in mid-winter, a journey of some hundred miles on foot without purse or knapsack, a bold infringement of College or University discipline, seemed to them matters of a far higher order of importance than a degree, a place in a tripos, or even a comfortable fellowship for life. I am not prepared to say that they were altogether wrong in this opinion; for every man is the best judge of his own affairs; and a degree, a place in a tripos or a fellowship, is worth no more, when all is said than [2] the amount of gratification it can minister to the successful candidate. Some would throw the chagrin of all the disappointed ones into the bargain; but this is an ill-natured and ungentlemanly doctrine, devoutly to be renounced. At any rate, there is one thing certain enough: that those who prefer canoe voyages in the present to chancellorships in the blue and dubious future, and suffer their footsteps to be conducted by the vagabond and shameless Spirit of Escapade instead of the Benthamite Angel of Prudence – however right and noble they may be from a high-philosophical point of view – are exceedingly unlikely to come to honours or riches in this huckstering and debilitated age. This was well illustrated by the University career of the young fellows in question; for though they were most of them capable enough, they all, with one exception, ended in the mud.

The exception, Hardy by name, had somehow or other, it would appear, found time for reading amidst his other and more apparent occupations; and when he was put to the proof, came out a high Wrangler and was made a fellow of the college. Hardy, therefore, remained in evidence at the University, as one of its educational pinnacles; while his companions, who had enjoyed three [3] years of notoriety along with him, disappeared promptly and forever out of public view. And yet some of them were as much worth looking at as Hardy; and if this great nation should ever awaken to a sense of its true interests with regard to the eccentric and the partially insane, I have no doubt that more than one of them will be fished up out of the dark, anonymous strata of Society, and installed in some fitting situation. As things are, however, these fellows were for no use. They were all fatally incomplete, intellectually deformed, shortsighted with one eye and longsighted with the other, totally lacking any sense of proportion in conduct, unable to distinguish between a heroism and an absurdity – and in short, just such another as yourself, dear reader, if you are the man I take you for. To all their excellences, some neglected fairy godmother had added a damning ingredient. They saw things wrong-side-up, in a sublime confusion; and they were gifted with a strange instinct for the impracticable and the useless. Even their one successful man was tarred with the same stick, although not so intolerably as the others. He was an accomplished mathematician, and solved many difficult and curious problems; but then they were all problems belonging to an imaginary order of things; and [4] he never condescended to employ his y's and x's on a universe of less than half a dozen dimensions at the least. Another of the crew, who had shown some little talent for stringing verses, instead of following in the wake of Mr Swinburne and venting his passions in sanguinary, anapestic rhapsodies, struck out on an entirely new track for himself, or rather found an old track so entirely discredited and deserted, that he might walk therein with all the isolation of a pioneer. What do you think he took upon himself to revive? Why, the most barren and dry of all poetic heresies. He set himself to concoct a poem of some dimensions, from which the unoffending first letter of the alphabet was to be rigorously excluded. It is true that he soon wearied of the enterprise.

Hardy, the oldest of the party by some years, had possibly enjoyed all their pranks from a point of view rather different from that of the others; and stood best with the authorities, even before his unexpected degree.

Dick Turton, commonly called *Turpin*, was the opposite of Hardy in that particular; he spent his whole curriculum within an ace of being sent down; and after the most showy beginnings, and much talk of Kant and Hegel he had ended with a full degree in Botany, to the merriment of his acquaintances. [5]

Ratcliffe (nicknamed The Highway) had done a great deal to form the manners of his companions. It was difficult to understand how he had obtained his influence; for he was very silent; and when he did offer a remark, it was vastly like anybody else's. But his silence seemed to make disciples. He was an athletic fellow, and had moulded himself on the pattern of a Bargee. He declared loudly that he cared for nothing under the sun but beer and tobacco. He boxed, and refused to fence; characterising the latter exercise as too full of airs for the like of him. He wore a pea-jacket in the warmest weather, refused to clean his nails, and cultivated a heavy slouch in his carriage and a great brutality of manner. It was odd enough to see The Highway while he was thus fooling himself to the top of his bent; but Turton made a still more comical figure. He was a light weight, and very elegant and slender; and yet he mimicked his companion to the echo and could never get his shoulders round enough, or his face sufficiently heavy and vacant. They were a pair of conscientious performers all over.

Hartley Strutt was of a different order of man, and tried to keep up a tradition of refinement in the band. He was a tall, slim fellow, with a blonde, ordinary face, an eyeglass, and irreproachable tweed clothes, in the English Gentleman on the Continent style of architecture, [6] which were half the time brushed and comely, and half the time in a pitiful pickle from the exploits in which he was obliged to share. He knew a vast deal about the mysterious backward parts of London Theatres, was full of cynical prudence in his speech, and had always to be pushed and hauled into an adventure by the united encouragements of the others. Occasionally Strutt would leave his usual associates, and consort with other men in the colleges for a day or two. Amid these more congenial surroundings, the original Strutt revived and blossomed forth in gloves and neckties and a mincing 'haviour of the body! But there seemed to be a fatality upon the man; and he always returned to his wallowing in the mire. He had taken the degree he meant to take from the first; a humble one, but not abject like Turton's.

Urquhart was a short, sturdy, vigorous fellow; underhung, which gave him an air of determination; and with a general look of intentness and capability, which was misleading in the highest degree. He was the maddest of the lot, by a great way. He had fits of everything, and everything by fits. His rooms were a kind of museum, and illustrated the phases [7] of the man. There you would find canary birds, dogs, cats and land tortoises, trumpets and pianos, easels and paintboxes, basket-sticks, boxing gloves and canoe paddles, all very carefully arranged on the historical system, with the latest hobby nearest hand. In some one corner or other, there was sure to be a whiskey bottle; but he was faithful to that – at least until it was empty: the rest were his visits but this was his home. Poor Urquhart! All his desultory talents and accomplishments lay loose and higgledy-piggledy, like so many spelicans upon a table, and the whole man was nervous, wrong-headed and doleful, for lack of that one sunny gift of self-approval which keeps people in a good humour with themselves and the world at large. He could never believe that anybody liked him without some reserve; indeed it was only with a great deal of abatement, that he could tolerate himself; and so he would too often take refuge from the friends he mistrusted, and consequently misused, with guinea-pigs and whiskey punch. Whether it was the pigs or the punch or the piano, or all of them, he had made the one flagrant disaster of the party; he had been gently ploughed.

There had been others who took part in the perilous and illegal diversions already characterised, some to a greater [8] extent than Strutt, many to a greater degree than Urquhart; but it is with those I have named that our business lies. They it was who formed the party for colonising Inchmagarrie, and who undertook the Strange Adventure of the Hair Trunk.

Chapter II

Urquhart's Island

In the recess immediately following on the fatal occasion when Turton and Ratcliffe took their infamous degrees in Botany, and Urquhart failed to take any degree whatever, the whole party returned to Cambridge on a visit. Hardy, not yet a fellow, but holding some interim appointment as a lecturer had rooms of his own in College; and the rest were accommodated for the occasion.

Turton, in the course of his wanderings, had picked up an odd companion, answering to the name of Ralph Blackburn, and had brought him down to Cambridge in a third class carriage, with the aid of a flask of Spiers and Pond's Amontillado and a pair of clay pipes. This Blackburn was small, spare and agile; clean shaven; not specially well-looking in the face; with a complexion both sun-burnt and blotchy, a nose like a truncheon, a pair of shining, berry-brown eyes and a big, sensual, humourous mouth. His dress told no tales as to his position, character or habits; indeed, [9] so far as that goes, he might as well have been naked. But he was a man of easy intercourse, who seemed to have done pretty well everything and been pretty well everywhere from the bottom of a coalpit to the highest flight of Æronauts, within a trifle of our white-faced neighbour, the Moon. I do not know which of his many qualifications had first endeared him to Turton; whether it was his dexterity at all manner of physical exercises, or his delight in the society of humble, not to say blackguard, acquaintances; or whether, after all, they were not brought together by the simple gravitation of one idle man towards another, in the comparative vacuum of this busy world. They had grown fast friends, at least; and upon Turton's introduction, the new-comer speedily took a lead in the little coterie, and began to decide questions, and put down objectors, with a decided and yet conciliatory manner that belonged to himself.

If it had not been for Blackburn, it would have been a mighty dismal visit for all concerned. It is not for nothing that a man deracinates his character out of the bed where it has grown and prospered for any considerable interval of years. To say farewell to the past, and go forth into the bleak world with no friend but the one below your own hat, and no object [10] but the vague abstraction called Success – is something of the nature of a surgical operation even for the pluckiest of men. And Cambridge, emptied of all its jolly companions, swept by a fitful wind and dabbled with Spring showers, struck cold and heavy on their hearts. This was the last bivouac before the battle. Tomorrow, they would be down in the heart of the enemy's country, among bawling Q. C.'s and obscene financiers; tomorrow, youth with all its agreeable dallyings about the brink, would be forever at an end, and they must take up life with its solemn absurdities and run, with hunger at their heels, in the great race for a bald head and a bedeviled conscience. Nor was it merely a certain natural chill, before entering on the unpleasant Babel of Society; there was also a touch of something not unlike remorse among their feelings. For we cannot take away our own rich, vital and benificent personalities from any place we have long honoured by our presence, without unfeigned pity for what we leave behind us. How solitary will be our morning's walk, with nothing moving in it all forenoon but birds and shadows! How will even the oldest inhabitant support the burthen of his existence, when he lacks our animating countenance? It seems really sad to snuff out the [11] life and light from a whole unoffending countryside – to take away the many coloured lanthorn by which it saw itself, the brains by which it had an intelligent knowledge of its own existence, the centrepoint about which it turned, the admirable being for whom it sang, and shone, and decked itself in Spring Novelties at Easter!

With these various feelings on their shoulders, the party required to be more than usually gay, not to be altogether wretched. And pretty early on the first evening, as they sat smoking in Hardy's rooms, a sort of raw, uncivil atmosphere seemed to envelope the smokers; and talk languished, or was only carried on by fits and dashes. Urquhart retired to bed; but he had addressed himself so exclusively to his glass all evening, that his absence was comparatively unimportant. The others drew about the fire early; Blackburn began to fancy himself one too many, and was preparing to say good night; there was not even spirit enough in the company to recharge their pipes, and when they were smoked out, they held them empty in their hands. Suddenly Turton, who had been silent a while, broke out into speech; it was obviously the out-cropping of a long train of subterranean meditation. [12]

"It's all very well for you fellows," he said; "but it's a deuced blue look out for me. Hardy has his fellowship. Strutt and The Highway are rolling in coins. Urquhart's drunk . . . and besides he has an estate in the West Highlands. You're right enough, it's plain. But look at me . . . what am I to do?"

"You've got to work, my bo-ay," said Hardy brutally.

"Work? What at? I don't want to become a mere banker. I can't be a tailor. I've no vocation for the Church, and they would be sure to defrock me with every circumstance of ignominy, before I had worked once round the Psalms. I might," he added, a pallid gleam of hope irradiating his countenance, "I might turn Bargee, of course."

"Not strong enough," said Ratcliffe, hoarsely.

"Why not try the Colonies?" asked Blackburn. "There are nice open parts . . . plenty of elbow room . . . and air. Nobody about but the Aborigines. And you may do what you like with them; shoot, rob, baptise . . . or put them in the way of unlimited fire-water, and look on with your arms folded, until the run is cleared. Then, of course, you substitute a respectable breed of sheep and begin to make your fortune. You might do worse than try the Colonies." [13]

"You remember the touching missionary hymn?" suggested Strutt. "'There every prospect pleases, and only man is vile.'"

"If I had a wife, I would go to the Colonies tomorrow. But you won't catch me spending my best years alone with a pack of sheep and kangaroos. I'm not particular, either; I would marry a milkmaid – a blonde milkmaid. But then I have no one in my eye . . . and a real wife is so expensive."

"Look here," said Strutt, "You seem very sorry for yourself, Dick Turpin. Far be it from me to interfere with you in that. . . you are a legitimate object of pity, I admit. But I have the pleasure of presenting two other candidates in the persons" – fixing his eyeglass – "of Mr Ratcliffe and myself. Speaking theoretically, I have a modest competence. Speaking practically . . . my dear boy, I am a beggar."

"I'm a beggar too," added Ratcliffe. "I have scarcely enough to keep myself in beer and tobacco."

"I thought that was all you wanted," returned Turton.

"I want boats," replied Ratcliffe.

"You see," said Strutt, "Ratcliffe is after boats. I should like a commodious family mansion with a billiard room and a line of legitimate descendants . . . not to mention [14] the partner of my joys. You can't do that style of thing, you will admit, at three hundred a year. You ask what are you to do? I haven't the ghost of an idea. What am I to do?"

"What the devil am I fit for, I should like to know," rumbled Ratcliffe. "I'm stupid. . . and damned ignorant."

A flash of educational interest came over Hardy; the latent Don stirred in his bosom.

"I suppose you fellows have forgotten all your Botany by this time?" he asked.

"I never knew any," answered Turton.

Hardy laughed. "The fact is," he said, returning to the original subject, "we have all ruined ourselves for ordinary life. We have learned idle, easy, open-air habits, and turned ourselves bodily into amateur savages. And when they come and ask us to leave all this, and walk into an office, why, the fact is, we can't. It's not possible. Flesh and Blood [15] cannot support so Violent a change."

"I could no more go to an office than to my grave," said Turton, dejectedly.

"That's an office we all have to go to, some day or other."

"True . . . but only once," returned Blackburn. "And that makes a famous difference."

"As for me," Turton continued, ". . . there's no use mincing matters . . . I'm not fit for human food. I'm a cumberer of the ground; I'll never make the price of an ounce of tobacco; I'm a shirk and a coward; I don't pull my weight; and the sooner I'm shovelled out of the boat, the better for all concerned. What piping folly all education is! Here am I, three and twenty . . . and never knew anything about the world until this moment! Here have I spent all my substance on their damned schools and universities; and they turn me out physically incapable of doing anything for an honest livelihood. [16]

"Listen to this degraded being," said Strutt, "and observe the consequence of wearing flannel shirts. I always told you your Bohemian game wouldn't fight."

"Society is not constituted with a view to Bohemianism," observed Blackburn. "That, I believe, is where the shoe pinches. Now, how about a radical cure? If the world is not worthy of you. . . or you not fit for the world, that's all one . . . cut the world. If you don't suit the Society in which you were born, form a Society of your own. How else was Rome begun? Begin another Rome."

"I vote we begin with the decadence then," said Turton.

"I speak seriously," continued Blackburn. "I would join you myself with pleasure. I'm tired of all these Bagmen and Bishops. I want a change of air and circumstances. Let us make the change together."

"Explain yourself," said Hardy.

"Gentlemen, fill your glasses. You seem to me the sort of men who will understand a plain proposal. You are not fellows who require to grow *in* [17] *situ* like a toadstool, or feel lost to find themselves a hundred miles from the nearest umbrella. You wouldn't blink at a sweeping change in your lives. You could face round the other way and start fresh – could you not? I am going to propose a *coup de tête*. My programme will sound a little visionary, I give you fair warning . . . like all programmes that are purely logical. I am a great friend to the straight way. Half a moment's thought, in nine cases out of ten, shows you the root of the evil. And when he knows the root, any man can use a spud. For instance . . . We all like the open air. Well, here's an obvious course for us: – let us go away from houses. Again . . . we dislike stools, and desks, and Bonuses and, in short, all ways of making money. Second obvious course: let us go where we can do without it. Once more . . . we like sailoring. In God's name, then, let's go to sea! 'Tis an open thoroughfare, and the wind costs nothing. A few fellows in a handy craft may go pretty nearly where they will, and do precisely what they please. Look at Rajah Brooke!"

"Our Rome," observed Strutt primly, "is apparently to be a Rome 'pon the rolling deep."

"Wait a bit," answered Blackburn. "I am coming to [18] dry land. There is one point in what I have said that looks ugly. And you may ask pertinently enough – Is there any place where people can do without money? There is, by the Lord! What sort of place is it? Why, gentlemen, it's a paradise . . . an ideal climate, ideal inhabitants, ideal products . . . the best place in the world . . . the pick of the whole globe . . . and not yet colonised! Already people are beginning to prick their ears; already you may see a few emigrants with their nose in that direction; in a year or so, it will be a stampede. Are we to let the occasion slip? Let me tell you my honest opinion . . . a young man is simply Not Sane, who stays to dry-rot here in beggarly England, when he has only to step aboard the first ship, and find Happiness ready-made in Navigator Islands."

"Navigator Islands," came the echo.

"The word is out," said Blackburn. "Navigator's Isles! The South Sea is the true home of mankind . . . Gold, vines, tobacco, eternal summer and a handsome race . . . An easy, rudimentary civilisation already afoot . . . People with no clothes, and flowers in their hair! . . . Scenery and sunsets for those who like them. . . . And the first comer, who feels the want of them and [19] has nothing else to do, free to fill a whole Island with children, mossy waterwheels and drawing-masters' cottages! If you have imagined anything better for Heaven, gentlemen, I will give up the scheme."

"They have leprosy in the South Sea Islands, have they not?" inquired Hardy.

"Not in Navigator," replied Blackburn. "In the Sandwich group I believe they have something of the kind, but not in Navigator."

"It might transplant," said Hardy, doubtfully.

"I think you mean," asked Ratcliffe, laboriously, "that we should go and colonise some place . . . the lot of us . . . in a ship of our own? It's a big excursion, that's all. . . . And I'm your man."

"We might found Society on some different basis," said Hardy thoughtfully. "It would probably collapse . . . I can see that . . . owing to imperfect adaptation. But it would always be an interesting and critical experiment while it lasted." And a vision of a very thick volume passed before his eyes, a volume fortified with maps and tables and a portrait of the Author after a photograph by Sarony & Co and labelled on the back: "An Experiment in Sociology by Thomas Hardy." [20]

Turton rose to his feet in an apotheosis of generous enthusiasm. He held his glass higher than his shoulder; his face was resplendent, his eyes shone with an unnatural lustre.

"My Lords and gentlemen," he said, "we have just listened to the sunniest, smilingest proposal ever made to mortal men. It is the realisation of all our schoolboy dreams. It combines Dumas, and The Coming Race, and Herbert Spencer . . . along with plenty of yachting, eating, drinking, smoking and living in the open air. I will not detain you, my Lords and Gentlemen, by dwelling on the fact that I am unaccustomed to Public Speaking. Suffice it to say . . . in the unavoidable absence of her majesty Queen Victoria . . . who would have said it so much better . . . that the voice of my friend and father, Mr Blackburn, is the voice of a God. (Shake hands with me, Blackburn!)" – Applause, Sensation – "Gentlemen . . . Here's His Health . . . and prosperity to *The Ideal Commonwealth*!"

Imitating the pleasing modesty of the Newspaper Reporter, I decline to attempt any description of the enthusiasm with which the toast was received. The whole party, Blackburn included, drained their tumblers with a readiness and a ruffling and heroical demeanour, that would have done [21] honour to Prince Rupert's cavaliers. The night was already old, and the grog (as grog will) had been growing stiffer as the hours went on; So that this last *rasade*, or Willie-waucht, made the room go round the table and staggered the whole party to the heart. Some of them stared reproachfully into their empty glasses; Turton winked very hard and looked down sideways on the floor; and Hardy hid his face in his hands, as if he were about to burst into tears.

"That took me by the throat," observed Blackburn.

Alone of the party, Strutt preserved an appearance of calm. His person must have been formed of Dutch clay, or some particularly bleached and plastic putty, or perhaps a damp papier-mâché of eighteenth century blank verse. It was impossible [22] to inaugurate a tremor in the fellow's nerves; and his soul dwelt complacently in this unapproachable tabernacle, like a rat in a river bank. Finding therefore a difference between himself and all his companions, Strutt not unnaturally explained it on the theory that he was sober and the rest were drunk. Smiling in a phantom manner, he took up the last words of the toast.

"Ideal Commonwealth?" he repeated. "Think I've heard the phrase before."

"Did you ever hear of El Dorado?" demanded Turton, flinging round upon him in heroic exaltation.

"I have had that pleasure."

"Well, Raleigh went in search of El Dorado . . ."

"And didn't find it," put in Strutt.

". . . And brought home tobacco," concluded Turton.

"I have no desire to be wiser than my company," returned Strutt, with a shrug. "If you all go to Penang or wherever it is, I suppose I must go to Penang along with you. It's folly. But it may be amusing for a while."

"Folly!" remonstrated Blackburn. "It's not folly. It's merely a *coup de tête*." And he opened his hands in a highly [23] expository manner, and beamed upon Strutt with the countenance of one inspired.

"Another toast!" began Turton.

"O for God's sake, no!" said Ratcliffe, heartily.

"Sociologically speaking," began Hardy, ". . . the tendency . . . sociologically speaking . . ."

"Look here," said Blackburn. "One word more. We require three things. We require to study each other . . . as we are doing at the present moment; we require to learn more seamanship; we require recruits. Now, here is my proposal. I pick up a sloop . . . for an old song. We go yachting together all Summer. In Winter we learn trades and find other men to join. And in Spring, we fit out the real vessel . . . and to Sea."

"That's the sort of thing I like to hear," cried Turton. "Fellows' lives laid out for them with the wave of a hand! It's so spurious . . . and so noble."

"It's capital sense too . . . mind you that," said Hardy cloudily. "I shake hands upon the scheme."

"And so do I."

"And I."

And the party went through the ceremony with unction. [24]

"I note we have a shore-station all the same," said Strutt. "We are to play at sailoring; we may as well play at being colonists, while our hands are in. And for my part, I shall confine myself strictly to that department of Art. I am often unaccountably melancholy upon the deep."

"By all means," said Blackburn. "Let us find some quiet bit of coast with an anchorage at hand, and pitch our camp. It will be a charming Summer . . . even if it leads no farther."

"It must be an Island," cried Turton. "Don't forget that."

"Why?" from Ratcliffe.

"Damn it, Ratcliffe, you haven't the feelings of a human being."

"An island, to be sure."

"And uninhabited . . . no untutored savages."

"I'll tell you!" cried Turton, rising to his feet. "Urquhart's place is on the West Coast of Scotland, which is all uninhabited islands together. He's sure to have the very thing for us. Let's go and wake him at once."

They were like one man and proceeded in [25] open order towards the rooms inhabited by the unconscious Urquhart, lapped hours ago in dreamless slumber. Turton mixed a stiff grog and carried it along with him, with exaggerated ceremony, as a bribe or a reward, according to the dispositions of the highland laird in question. The procession was headed by the wavering Hardy, bearing a candle and making interminable apologies for going before his guests; and it was brought up by Strutt, still supercilious, with his hands under his coat tails, and his face screwed up around his eye glass and totally obliterated with grog and slumber.

Arrived upon the scene of action, Turton deposited the glass upon the floor, took off his coat, folded it ostentatiously, rolled up his shirt sleeves, made an acrobatic bow to the company, and proceeded to knock at Urquhart's door, in the most florid and figurative style of execution, now piano on the frame, now thundering fortissimo on the panels, and now covering the whole surface with kicks and buffets in a paroxysm of unbridled violence.

"Symphony expressive of an Ideal Commonwealth," he explained.

"The others looked on, half in feeble merriment, half in stupidity. Hardy, who was swaying like a reed, introduced the flame of the candle into Ratcliffe's whisker. Ratcliffe [26] started, swore, and then apologised to Blackburn with gloomy penitence. All three who took part in this little interlude, felt dimly that it was susceptible of some elucidation; but none cared to pursue the subject.

"Complicated passage for the Drums," cried Turton, redoubling in fury on the door.

It was no use. The Performer stopped; he was covered with honourable sweat; the symphony expressive of an Ideal Commonwealth was an exacting work for the virtuoso.

"Hey! you! Urquhart!" he cried. "Don't you hear? I've liquor, liquor, liquor, don't you hear?"

There was a noise from within. The door was cautiously opened; and Urquhart, in the correct nocturnal costume of the period, presented himself in the opening with unfriendly looks.

“What do you want?” he asked sourly.

“An island! An island!” cried the band.

“A what?” demanded Urquhart.

“An Island of course,” replied Turton.

Urquhart thought he recognised a mere mystification; and with an evil smile, prepared himself to regain his [27] entrenchments. “You can’t have an Island at this time of night,” he said, and tried to close the door. But Turton was too quick for him. Urquhart’s face became dark. “Where’s that liquor?” he said; and for some minutes he would say nothing else.

“Mr Urquhart,” said Blackburn at last, advancing with the glass in his hand, “you shall get this at once, if you answer one question. Is there an uninhabited islet with an anchorage on your estate?”

“Yes, there is,” said Urquhart, “Inchmagarrie!”

The terms of the treaty were honourably implemented; the grog was administered; and while Urquhart barricaded his door, the procession of would-be colonists moved away along the corridor on the return voyage, led by Turton, dancing extravagantly and singing original verses in honour of Anaconda Island; – for so he appeared to have taken up the name. At the head of the stairs, he brought up and directed attention to himself with dignity. Then, when the others – Hardy with the wavering candle, Strutt with the obliterated countenance, Ratcliffe and Blackburn full of cackling and crapulous hilarity – when the others were duly collected and duly attentive – [28] “Portrait of the King of Anaconda!” he cried; and taking a lion-spring over the bannisters, he landed on all fours in the hall below, to the destruction of his best trousers and the detriment of his knees.

The others cheered feebly; and, feebly following, overtook the hero of this last exploit, stopping in the middle of the quad to contemplate the heavens. It was a beautiful night of stars; the zenith was powdered with a diamond dust of worlds and systems; lower down and to windward, the great constellations burned with a more mild and liquid lustre. At the spectacle, a frosty tingle passed along the blood;

the heart expanded underneath the ribs; and a man felt proud of himself and glad to be alive. So – when the others mechanically drew up behind Turton and proceeded to look over his shoulder (as if there was something in the point of view) – they were all thrilled into a momentary silence, and he was himself the first to speak.

"You may smile," he said, turning upon them and smiting his bosom theatrically, "but there's something Here which Responds to these Orbs!"

And he went on his way across the quad [29] with wandering footsteps.

Chapter III

Constructive Sociology

The next morning was just what a Spring morning ought to be; and everyone, as he rose and smelt the wind and looked out into the gay sunshine, had his pulses steadied and all his pegs screwed up, like those of Quarles' Theorbo, from notes higher. There was something inspiriting in the air that was fatal to the repose of slug-a-beds. They felt as if all the world were up and about, except themselves; and the feeling shook them out of their accustomed apathy. Their minds were in an agreeable confusion, and their hearts beat with vague and changeful aspirations. Visions came to them of Summer and Travel; hill-tops and great forests; lilied rivers to bathe in, or the green, tumbling sea. And if there was a drop of gipsy blood in a man's whole constitution, it came to the top, on a morning of this sort, and ran all over him like wildfire.

It was no wonder if the colonists were up betimes for breakfast, which they were to take in Urquhart's rooms, and all in the most adventurous disposition and aspiring noisily after sloops and uninhabited islands. And [30] yet the earliest of the lot was Urquhart; whom Strutt discovered compounding a mess of eggs and sherry for his morning meal; and to whom, over his own tea and toast and bacon, he disclosed the splendid projects of the night. Strutt set forth the adventure in no very glowing terms, and spared none of his peculiar humour, which (as the reader may have remarked) was of a disenchanting and denigratory character.

And Urquhart listened with a shrewd, unfathomable look which was one of his greatest talents, and committed himself by neither word nor sign until the tale was ended.

"Will they pay me a rent for the Island?"

"How charmingly national!" said Strutt.

Urquhart grinned. "I don't care, he said, stirring his mess, ". . . no rent, no island . . . that's flat. They wouldn't let me come in and squat in their rooms, would they? Well, I won't let them squat on my island. It's principle."

Strutt whistled a little air in a low tone but with great precision. "They won't think it friendly," he observed, in rather a more serious tone than was common to him.

"I don't care," repeated Urquhart, ". . . no rent, no island. I don't care for open air and exercise, mind you that. And [31] if I join in their precious tomfoolery at all, they must make it worth my while. There." And he began to dispose of the eggs and sherry with a sort of suspicious deliberation.

Ratcliffe entered, grunted a salutation, and was soon immersed in rare cold roast beef and mustard, which he ate without bread or any qualification whatever, solid or liquid. This seemed to him, and indeed to his associates, a habit of imposing manliness. It was probably with an eye to the same class of effect, that he sat far back from the table on the edge of his chair, and served himself almost exclusively with his knife. Urquhart cherished a particular dislike for Ratcliffe, a dislike of which the athletic man was sunnily unconscious.

"I wish you wouldn't make such a noise when you eat," said the proprietor of Inchmagarrie venemously.

"By George," was the only reply, "there's nothing like beef!"

"I thought the mustard was your particular weakness, observed Strutt. "My dear boy, you push your taste for that condiment almost to the proportions of a vice."

Ratcliffe laughed with his mouth full. "It makes some fellows sneeze," he said. "It almost kills Turton, [32] by George!" And he broke out into a snatch of singing; for like all obtrusively healthy persons, Ratcliffe enjoyed famous spirits in the morning.

Blackburn and Turton appeared together, the latter in his shirt sleeves, and both laughing.

“How about that Ideal Commonwealth?” cried Turton, striking a heroic attitude in the doorway.

“Here’s your coat,” said Urquhart. “You left it outside my diggings last night. You had all been consulting the bowl, you know. You were disgustingly drunk.”

“I’ve a bad knee this morning,” admitted Turton, “and my eyes are full of straws. But I’m fit as a fiddle for all that. Have you heard about your Island, Urquhart? and the great career that’s opening before you among generations yet unborn?”

“I broke the glad tidings to him gently,” answered Strutt.

“Is the Island any size?” asked Blackburn, helping himself to tea.

“It’s four miles round,” answered Urquhart, “with a bay and a druidic stone, and worth about as nearly nothing as possible. And there’s nothing on it.” [33]

“Not even a church?” inquired Strutt. “What Spiritual Destitution!”

“Nothing but heather . . . and granite boulders . . . sheep . . . O! and splendid views, if you count that.”

“What kind of views?” asked Strutt. “Not religious views, I fear?”

“Sea views,” answered Urquhart; and he devoted himself to the mess.

“A bay,” repeated Blackburn. “Could a small craft lie there in any wind?”

“O, I know nothing about boats,” returned Urquhart, bitterly. “The bay’s a big hole in the Island, full of water . . . I’m sure I wish to God it was all dry land to fatten sheep with . . . and there’s sand and sea-weed at the bottom of it . . . and I’ve seen fish.”

“Don’t concern yourself about this Summer,” said Turton airily. “A month or two in a smack . . . a few shanties run up on a desert island . . . plenty boards and tarpaulins . . . plenty Harvey’s Sauce for culinary purposes . . . plenty tobacco . . . all child’s play. What I care about is the Great Scheme. And while we’re on that, I may as well define my position. I’m going to be the Sieyès of the Ideal Commonwealth. I shall dash off [34] the Constitution some morning, whilst shaving. I feel I have the soul of a Publicist.”

"I'll be Minister of Secret Police," said Urquhart.

"And I'll be First Lord of the Admiralty," added Ratcliffe.

"Gentlemen," said Strutt, "the touching unanimity with which you assure me of my own fitness for the position . . . et cetera. Department of Religion, please."

"No!" cried Turton, "here's the man for that!" And he pointed to Hardy, who just then entered the room, and proceeded to shake hands gravely and politely with Blackburn.

"Hardy? Why?" asked Strutt.

"Because he's a man of unostentatious piety," answered Turton. "Let me tell you my tale. Once when we were up in town together, he inveigled me into a prolonged and ponderous luncheon on a Sunday; and while I lay gasping with brown sherry, he shamefully abused the situation and swept me off to Evening Service. I was sometimes asleep and sometimes awake . . . now on the seat, now on the hassock. I was covered with an unnatural dew; I was sewn up and knocked over. And there was Hardy finding all the places . . . and looking so cool and venerable! It was like a cheap print, or something in a novel, don't you [35] know?"

"This seems to demand an explanation," said Strutt.

"I am very fond of children's voices in the choir," admitted Hardy, sentimentally.

"But you don't mean to say that you're religious?" demanded Ratcliffe.

"I suppose I am a little," answered the culprit, with a blush. "I like going to Church. It is good for the health and temper. I find it a capital tonic . . . like sea air. And depend upon it, there must be something to recommend a practice common to the vast majority of the human race. However you may reassure yourself, Ratcliffe . . . I am not moral in the least." And Hardy visibly plumed himself upon his attitude.

"I'm sure I've heard you say the opposite of all that," [36] said Ratcliffe.

"How did this subject turn up?" asked Hardy.

"Ask the Abbé Turpin," answered Strutt. "He was about to rapidly sketch a constitution for the Colony."

"O – O!" said Hardy. "That will require a little thought. We must be careful to avoid the errors of the Phalanstères. A constitution for the Colony is not a thing to be decided before breakfast."

"No, I should think it would come in better after dinner," remarked Strutt.

"You may rely on me, Hardy," said Turton. "You know I'm a sweeping fellow . . . and logical. Here's a gigantic piece of machinery which has been at work for centuries. And what's the outcome? Nobody allowed to do what he likes . . . young men languishing in clammy offices . . . the fine, manly instincts of the criminal classes thwarted at every corner . . . and the whole place crawling with policemen and indignant citizens! Civilisation is up a tree. Civilisation is a hopeless, wholesale, ungodly failure . . . a *blague*, an imposition, a joke and a damned bad joke! – You will doubtless point to the Pyramids of Egypt. Well . . . they are very good Pyramids. Steam is a capital invention. Printing, Gunpowder, Representative Government [37] . . . I know all your catchwords. And this is my answer. Here am I . . . an educated man . . . acquainted with history and science . . . an Englishman . . . in the nineteenth century . . . prepared by ages of development and years of study, sir . . . and I protest against the entire Concern and vote for General Smash. You may say I'm an exception . . . yes, but I'm a burning one! And so long as I exist, Civilisation is a failure. Q. E. D."

"Certainly there can be only one decision," observed Hardy, "when we compare life in nineteenth-century Europe with the healthy existence of a savage. The difficulty . . . it was overlooked by Rousseau . . . comes in on the question of supplies. How are we to combine the extraordinary productive powers of civilisation with the freedom and purity of barbarism? There must plainly be a change of basis."

"Let us signalise the inauguration of our Commonwealth by something practical," remarked Strutt. "Say, the Abolition of Bad Weather. We shall thus avoid the errors of the Phalanstères," he added, with dignity.

"You want a change of basis?" asked Turton, disregarding the ribaldry of Strutt. "I'll give you one. I begin with a Redistribution of the Sexes."

"God bless me, how very interesting!" said Strutt. [38] "Are there to be more or fewer?"

"More," replied Turton. "I begin by a division of Society. . . not by money or birth, which are quite beside the question . . . but by Temperament. Of course, I could put this into Herbert Spencer language; but you wouldn't follow me half so well, and I'm no charlatan. There are to be four classes. First, the Artist Class, comprising artists, fellows who keep coffee stalls, and generally those who have heard the chimes at midnight. Second, the Clergyman Class, comprising natural science men, whitehaired clergymen and Deacons. Colonial Bishops, being men of a high fancy, come in among the artists. Third, the Banker Class. Fourth, the Beast of the Field Class, comprising Ratcliffe . . . and other agricultural labourers. The women are similarly divided. All Bankers marry Bankeresses; no *connubium* between the different classes; the different classes taught to think of each other as different species; and for each class, a special conception of the married state and special marriage laws, adapted to the exingencies of the temperament and the habits of life. In some, it would be indissoluble; in others, very soluble indeed. Among the Beasts of the Field, it could hardly be said to exist; and its place would be taken practically by a [39] graduated poll-tax for the support of a National Nursery. There!" added Turton " . . . there's width of views for you . . . there's grasp. That's what they call a statesmanlike measure!"

"How would you effect the division?" asked Blackburn. "I foresee some malcontents in your Ideal Commonwealth."

"Nothing easier," replied Turton. "At thirteen or fourteen, the children are brought by their parents to a large public building with a portico where they are received by bald-headed acolytes. For a week, they are supplied with a small handbook of Vice and Virtue in the form of a catechism, which I shall draw up for that purpose. Then they are introduced, one by one, into a hall, occupied by Hardy in a hierophantic dressing gown and several medical men, all baronets, with their broughams waiting in front of the portico. The doctors decide on the temperament. Hardy advises the postulants with a sort of patriarchal dignity, and finally receives their decision and forwards it to the Prefect of Police for registration."

"And suppose they all go wrong. Hardy, and his medical baronets, and the postulant himself," suggested Strutt, ". . . and an unprotected clergyman is shot into the thick of the Artists . . . or a Beast of the Field (as you elegantly term it) among the divines. . . What then, my lovely [40] friend?"

"No trifling with an Ideal Commonwealth! . . . A Painless Death!" cried Turton, with an imposing wave of the hand.

"That's awful nonsense," said Ratcliffe.

"What I like about all this," said Strutt, "is the unaffected poetry of Turton's nature."

"Envy . . . envy and Ignorance," said Turton. "The time will come when you will remember all this, and gnash your teeth to see your own temples deserted, and all the world crowding to honour the tomb of the Redistribution of the Sexes. We shall all be worshipped, of course . . . more or less. But the serious fellows . . . who would have been social reformers, if I hadn't settled the whole thing out of hand and left them nothing to do but make commentaries on my Introduction to Vice . . . and the happy people who have just been married, or divorced, or something, will keep trooping in and out of that temple of mine with the most costly offerings, to a degree that defies qualification."

"If I'm to be worshipped, it shall be in my own way," said Urquhart. "Fifty of the most beautiful virgins shall be immured every year in the catacombs below my Holy Sepulchre . . . immured for life. The priests all dumb . . . horrid fellows playing on gongs. Several thousand squalling cats about the temple. Parents coming to [41] weep; virgins heard weeping from below. And if anyone tried to escape," added Urquhart, with gusto, "I would have her buried alive."

"Our little Utopia," observed Strutt, "appears to present a remarkable opening for Hangmen."

Nobody took up this innuendo. They were all a little damped by this outline of Urquhart-Worship; and both Blackburn and Hardy felt keenly that the author of this cheerful cult was not precisely the ideal citizen for an Ideal Commonwealth. Everyone rose and began moving about, filling and lighting pipes, and installing themselves luxuriously in comfortable chairs. Hardy called over the window for some ale; and in a minute or two, they were all devoutly piping, while, in Cambridge fashion, the loving tankard went round from mouth to mouth. Hardy, with one of his movements of politeness, had tried to pass it to the stranger first; but the unconscious Ratcliffe intercepted the liquor and carried it simply to his own lips. The salutary influence of tobacco declared itself at once. Faces relaxed into a permanent expression of beatitude. The dry, fevered eye of the breakfast eater, became moist and blinking. There was not an attitude in the room but might have been chosen by an actor – that sculptor of the nineteenth century – as the supreme embodiment of some agreeable and indolent humour. Tea – the temperance Blue Ruin – [42] with all its baleful consequences, began to relax its hold upon men's brains and bodies. Contemplation and Digestion claimed the company as their own.

"It's a pity to talk bosh about a matter in which we are seriously interested," said Hardy to Turton. "Rigmarole is all very well in its way; but what we require at present are lucid, practical ideas for the reconstitution of society."

"It's easy to say rigmarole," returned the Redistribution of the Sexes. "If I had posted myself up with a lot of long words, you would have been my first disciple. I can tell you, there's a deal of truth in all I said."

"Much in the same way," observed Blackburn, smiling, "as there is a deal of art in a hobby horse."

"We must take out a Brewer," said Ratcliffe, wiping his mouth with the back of his hand.

"And hops."

"I'll take lessons from the college Butler."

"I'll make out a list of everything necessary for a colony," said Turton. "You just leave that to me."

"How did you find out about these Islands?" asked Hardy.

"Principally in a New Zealand Blue Book," answered Blackburn.

"A Blue Book about Paradise!" cried Turton.

"Look at the March of Civilisation," added Strutt. [43]

"The Geological formation is an important condition," said Hardy. "Can you recall the principal features of the Navigator Group?"

"Look here," Strutt broke in, "I've had about enough of castles in the air. Let us play at not being damned fools for a minute or two, and think about the Sinews of War."

"Aha! said Blackburn, "there is a great deal to be said with regard to that." And he rose and put his back against the chimney with a meditative air, as if he were not quite resolved where he should begin his statement, and attached great importance to the effect he might produce. The others settled themselves in their chairs, and prepared for a sermon. Sloops and uninhabited islands, Ideal Commonwealths and cheap tobacco, the rhythm of the Ocean below the moving deck, the smell of salt sea air, the swift and final disappearance out of their lives of all hard work and social discommodity, the realisation of all that a young Bohemian ever dreamed in his most ruddy hours, and a thousand pleasant memories and imaginations prepared the audience to listen in no very critical spirit to the [44] Budget of the New Society.

Chapter IV

A Case of Conscience

"Money," began Blackburn, raising an expository forefinger, "Money is Freedom. Now, we are all of opinion that this should not be. We are all of opinion that the measure of each man's liberty should be something intrinsic and proper to himself. Hence we are going to a country where the favours of nature render money unnecessary, and liberty is a natural birthright of man. I do not look for a Utopia. I think we shall better our position . . . not make it perfect. It rains, even in the South Seas. We cannot get away from sickness, misunderstandings and death. It is my firm belief that we can get rid of our consciences; but nothing can ever free a man from his liver. And remember this: we have a better chance with the Devil himself, than with our own intestines. Moreover, just as surely as each one of us lands on Navigator Islands, just so surely does there land along with him some of what I may call the contraband of an Ideal Commonwealth . . . some of the feelings and prejudices suited to other systems of political organisation, and for [45] that very reason, radically inconsistent with the Fresh Start that we desire to make. One thing . . . and one thing only . . . can we leave behind us finally. And that is, Money. But by an odd incongruity, it is only by means of the devil, that this devil can be cast out . . . only by means of money, and plenty of money, that we can escape from our serfdom to the Golden Calf. We require money for a ship; money for stores; money for our interim studies; money to attract the right sort of active, enterprising and unprejudiced young fellows to throw in their lot with us and become citizens in the Ideal Commonwealth. In short, as I said already, we require money, and plenty of it. Let us see what we can say for ourselves, as we stand. I myself could put three or four hundred pounds into a common fund. Some of you may perhaps do as much . . . or more."

He looked about him, with the air of a chairman taking votes.

"I can't," said Urquhart. "I've nothing but land, and it's entailed . . . besides being mortgaged."

"I could give a hundred or so," said Strutt. [46]

"And you may put me down for three," said Ratcliffe.

"Nothing," said Turton. "I have just about enough to live on till the ship is ready. I've liquidated my resources on a first rate education . . . the results of which I place at the disposal of government."

When it came to Hardy's turn, he coloured deeply; for he had always been rather open-handed, and posed for the young man of fortune, in his undergraduate days.

"I am in Turton's position," he said. "I have nothing left to speak of, but what I get, or what I expect, from the College. I am afraid it is not in my power to help forward our enterprise financially."

"Say, Eight hundred," concluded Blackburn. "Say, a thousand, if you like. It's plain we must have three or four times that. Mess[rs] Strutt, Ratcliffe, Urquhart and myself will continue to receive our incomes; so that the state will enjoy a comparatively large revenue. But the outfit stops the way. This is no case for wilful roughing it. We may rough it as we please, this Summer, on Mr Urquhart's Island. But when we set sail for the South Seas, we must be well found in every sense . . . for war as well as peace . . . nay, and for ostentation, also. [47] For we must make a figure in the eyes of our fellow colonists, and impress them with an idea of our power and wisdom. In short, we must begin things largely or not at all. Now, how to get a capital? There is our question. How to get a capital," he repeated, scanning the syllables, two thousand, or three, or five . . . the more better, but a capital!"

"Gamble on the Stock Exchange," suggested Hardy.

"About which none of us knows anything."

"I beg your pardon," replied Hardy, warmly. "I lost a fortune in stocks before I came up to the University."

"Your experience is hardly encouraging, you will admit," said Blackburn, smiling.

"Well, no," admitted Hardy. "But the gaming table is a different matter. There, all the elements are well known; the probabilities may be calculated with perfect exactitude; and a mathematician, even in a small way, could easily prepare an infallible system in the course of a forenoon. I will undertake that part of it myself; and we can send someone to Monaco or Saxon with a small capital and complete directions."

"Why hasn't it been done before?" demanded [48]
Urquhart. "And why aren't all the tables bankrupt?"

"So few mathematicians apply their science to real life," replied Hardy. "But I mean to set a better example; and our little Experiment in Sociology shall be based on irrefragable calculation. You will be governed by Quaternions."

"Parable of the Quaternion's Servants," said Turton, with a splutter of merriment.

"With your permission," said Strutt, "I should like to describe the result of this Monaco escapade. Our young friend lives like a fighting cock at the Hotel de Paris . . . and has a charming time. He then borrows five francs from a Polish nobleman, and telegraphs to us for another small capital (as Hardy quaintly puts it) to come home with. We send it him; and he returns . . . full of interesting anecdote . . . but" – fixing his eyeglass – "penniless. I think I see myself paying our young friend's cab from the station."

"You're supposing the fellow to be a fool," cried Hardy.

Strutt made no answer.

"Couldn't we borrow?" asked Turton. "I am sure, [49]
there were always droves of fellows wanting to lend on my personal security."

"It's well seen, ye never tried them," remarked Urquhart.

"No," acquiesced Turton. "Where was the use, as long as I had any money of my own? Besides, it was business, which I hate worse than poison . . . and besides, I used to borrow from Hardy."

"One more reflection," resumed Strutt. "One reason for decamping to these Islands of the Blest, was precisely the want of funds. Now, if we can raise funds to go; why not raise them and stay where we are? I only ask for information."

"My dear Mr Strutt," said Blackburn, "why do half-pay captains go to Dinan and the Touraine? With a certain capital, we might perhaps start a firm of pennywise hucksters in England, and by diligent attention to business and palming off inferior articles upon the poor . . . why, we might perhaps retire at sixty . . . to New Cross! With the same amount, we can live like kings and gentlemen in Navigator Islands." [50]

"Besides, there's the fun of the thing," cried Turton.

"And the new society," added Hardy.

"A society of six," said Strutt, ". . . a whale in a tea-pot!"

"We form a nucleus," replied Hardy.

"We begin as pioneers . . ." began Blackburn.

". . . to end as Dictators!" echoed Turton.

"Gentlemen," cried Strutt. "I am silenced. If we are all to be dictators, of course there's no more to be said. Any further cavilling from a man of defective imagination like myself, would be simply unfeeling. Our land will at least enjoy the blessings of liberty," he added.

"In the mean time," said Blackburn, "the Monaco scheme is not approved of . . . nor the money lenders. Mr Ratcliffe, have you any proposal? No? Or you, Mr Urquhart?"

"I don't see why you fellows shouldn't give your capital," replied Urquhart. "If you want to go to the South Sea, you should be ready to pay for your whistle. And it's not entailed, I suppose, like my land."

This sally of Urquhart's was remarkably effective among the capitalists. Blackburn, indeed, broke out [51] laughing; but the countenances of Strutt and Ratcliffe were visibly dis-composed; and the former dropped his eyeglass with a gentlemanly oath. A Bohemian of a hundred horse power, like Turton, spends his capital exactly as he spends his revenue – on himself or others, on a yacht, a horse, a statue or a dinner with a billiard marker – as if there were no such thing as a science of Economics in this sophisticated world. But the case is very different with amateur Bohemians like Strutt, or sham Bohemians like the inept and athletic Ratcliffe. The prudence of the first was not altogether affected; and the second was an example of the law that a man may have too few brains to be a fool. He was still swayed by many salutary superstitions; and in the curious creed which had been worked out for him by his inclinations, his companions and his opportunities, without a single intellectual effort on his part, there was still an article unabrogated which declared the Inviolability of Capital as one of the original dicta of the human mind. Both he and Strutt, at least, regarded Urquhart's proposal with an unfeigned consternation, which grieved the singleminded Turton and vastly tickled the remainder [52] of the party.

Blackburn had studied the disposition of his young companions with some care, and knew them to a nicety. He saw that they had been thoroughly unsettled, and nowise edified, by modern theories. From these, they had learned nothing positive but a taste for theorising. They had given up their old ideas without faithfully embracing any others; and now hung in the wind, a cock-shot for enterprising dogmatists. Indeed the combination of Bohemianism with what are called modern ideas, produces quite a remarkable immunity from all convictions. The morality of current unbelief, suitable enough for highly respectable Professors, is promptly repudiated by the whole army of social free-lances. Its virtues are not their virtues; and where they have need of indulgence, the atheistic rabbi meets them with uncompromising words and a countenance of iron. I can imagine almost any number of consecutive vestrymen falling in tears upon the neck of Mr Herbert Spencer; but I cannot for the life of me imagine a single landscape painter in the same graceful attitude. A Gospel which may be said to consist of equal parts of teak-wood and compound arithmetic, [53] will never have much vogue among the slums and studios. Whether for good or evil, it will remain a dead letter for the outcast and the insubordinate. Its missionaries may succeed, for a time, in destroying other systems, but they will never be men enough to substitute their own.

It was to this moral blank that Blackburn proceeded to address himself.

"Well," said he, "I think I have a more agreeable nostrum. The simplest way to get a fortune in a hurry, is to take one ready made. Now . . . how about a treasure?"

"A treasure?" cried Turton. "What do you mean? What sort of treasure?"

"A treasure in the respectable old story-book sense," replied Blackburn, ". . . a treasure like Monte Cristo's . . . a treasure like that in the Gold Bug . . . or like the treasures of St Mark in Facino Cane."

Turton shook his head with every symptom of discouragement. "No, no, " he said, "it won't do. Don't trifle with a man's best feelings. There's not spirit [54] enough left in the world for that sort of thing. It has gone out along with secret societies and fellows in black masques. I daresay you might find a bundle of railway vouchers, or a damned bank book . . . some of the abstract signs and substitutes of opulence, but not opulence itself . . . not carnal gold . . . not a real, glowing, gaudy, old-high treasure!"

"A real, glowing, gaudy, old-high treasure!" repeated Blackburn. "Carnal Gold. Neither more nor less. Old gold sequins, old gold bracelets, old gold candlesticks and platters . . . some of them carved by Benvenuto and worth a fortune in themselves . . . some of them precious with encrustations . . . some of them enriched with strange inscriptions . . . some of them mere appetising masses of brute metal, heavy and yellow . . . ; and all these crammed away together in an old hair trunk in a forgotten lumber-room, and ready, at a touch, to take new shape as a clever sea-boat and an Ideal Commonwealth in Navigator Islands. Do you think I am romancing? I am not. I give you my word, in three day's time, we may be tumbling out this treasure into the sun upon a heathery hill-top. [55] It is to take or leave. A Big Hair Trunk Full of Old Gold," he repeated savourily, ". . . and to take or leave! Gentlemen, you have the world before you!"

Turton drew a long breath.

"But look here . . . " began Strutt.

"Allow me," interrupted the Prophet. "I am not yet done. There is a little point to be considered."

Here Blackburn paused a moment; and from the expression of his face, it was plain that he was thinking deeply and not altogether pleasantly. From the movement of his right hand, and the faint jingling that accompanied the movement, he seemed to be making a series of cascades with the loose change in his trouser pocket; and he contemplated the rug with remarkable fixity. At last, breaking out into a laugh and smiting the chimney shelf with his left palm, he resumed the thread of his notion.

"The point is ethical. When people start a new society . . . above all a society on a new basis . . . they break with old traditions. You will admit that. You cannot keep your new wine in your old bottles . . . for reasons best known to the bottles. In a *coup de tête,* such as [56] we now propose, there must be no timidity, no superstition, no inconsistent prejudice. As the whole thing is dashing, so will all the parts and parcels of it look extravagant. Mark you . . . that is to be expected. If you wish common sense and common morality, stay by your highly respectable domestic hearths, and leave adventure to others. Or . . . if you choose adventure . . . take the bit in your teeth and go blindly. There are only two ways: either be a lump of putty between Mrs Grundy's thumb and forefinger . . . or a headlong, red-hot cannon ball. If we are to break with society . . . in God's name, let us break with it at once!"

"Hear, hear!" cried Turton.

"For my part," added Hardy, in high approval, "I cannot see why we should carry forward any débris from the unsuccessful past; I cannot see why we should not start with the negation of ethics, alike as a system and a sentiment, and begin the new world unfettered and pure-minded."

"Ethics are so ornamental," objected Turton. "There is the respect for the aged – " [57]

"Herbert Spencer has incidentally exposed that prejudice," replied Hardy. "It is the young who ought to be considered . . . the coming generation who should be treated with respect."

"Damn Herbert Spencer!" cried Turton.

"Order, gentlemen, order," said Strutt.

"Above all, let us avoid the errors of the Phalanstères – You were advising us," he continued, addressing Blackburn, "to stick at nothing (if I may paraphrase your eloquent remarks) from pitch-and-toss to manslaughter. It is really very bracing to the mind. Pray continue."

Blackburn regarded the speaker with a smile of some finesse.

"Let us look at the history of all colonists," he resumed. "As soon as they arrive . . . with their guns and hymn-books, their missionaries and their new diseases . . . they take possession of the land around them; and in the old civil law formula, 'by force or fraud or on an insufficient grant' . . . *vi, clami vel precario* . . . they steadily extrude the inoffensive aborigines. If these prove refractory, the settler shoulders his gun and passes round his rum bottle. And what with lead, and fire-water, and [58] imported epidemics, civilisation advances with gigantic strides. Missionaries look on smiling. M. P.'s, vested in their integrity, compliment each other on our Colonial Empire. Christian manufacturers turn out the deadliest rum and the most imperfect hand-mirrors, literally by the ship load. 'Tis a vast conspiracy; theft and midnight murder are the ingredients of the bowl. Now, this civilised and civilising process is immoral. And yet we cannot charge civilisation with too much immorality in general. Plainly, this is a special case. And how? Because it is International. International policy has been, is, will be, and must be, treacherous in council, ruthless and deadly in execution. There is no quarter and no faith between rival religions, rival races or rival polities. As soon as a city hoists an independent flag, its relations to its neighbours become, in bulk, of a new order: morality vanishes, war succeeds. Morality, even in the most moral communities, is civil and never international."

Strutt emitted a long whistle. "I conclude," he began, "that this portmanteau of gold – "

"Allow me one moment, Mr Strutt. I am almost [59] done. – Last night, gentlemen, we signed our Declaration of

Independence. Today, our attitude to our fellow countrymen is no longer civic but international. They are no more to us . . . and no less . . . than any tribe of painted cannibals on a coral island. A new society, struggling into birth, must do what it can do . . . and take what it can get. It was so that Rome behaved. The social organism (I am sure Mr Hardy will bear me out) has higher rights and more imperious needs than any of the personal organisms that go to swell its composite existence. I take the case in point, to save trouble. If we find this treasure, in the Scotch phrase, where Alan Gregor found the tongs . . . detained, that is, by some *soi-disant* proprietor . . . we must lay aside all superstition, and regard the matter widely, and philosophically, and by the light of naked logic. So judging, we shall treat the trousered proprietor in England exactly as we should treat the nude proprietor in Queensland or on the Gold Coast. And how is that? Why, with an entire and imperturbable disregard of his rights . . . which are civic but not international . . . which affect his fellow citizens but not us . . . which are [60] valid against the subjects of England, but not against the members of an Ideal Commonwealth in Navigator Islands. That, gentlemen, is the theory of the matter. But, in practice, we are not purely logical animals; we are troubled by many elegant but incommodious sentiments. And for these, I add a few words. This treasure is being used by nobody, and can be used by nobody, unless by us . . . Nobody . . . even in the legal or civil sense . . . has a better right to it than we ourselves. From the point of view of the strictest morality, I give you my word as a gentleman, there is nothing mean, dishonest or ungentlemanly in the whole transaction. But I add frankly that it will look very like all these things; that an inhabited house will have to be entered under cover of night; that pistols may be fired, and that the police may be called in."

The prophet looked about him with a grand air, and prepared himself for the reception of difficulties, as a king might prepare himself for the opinion of insubordinate ministers in the purple, old days of prerogative. The whole party was plunged in abstraction, whether from the charm of Blackburn's eloquence, or the difficulties which [61] he had indicated. Ratcliffe was lighting another pipe; Hardy seemed to nourish heavy and important thoughts; Urquhart had a dull and mysterious appearance. As for Strutt, we shall come to that imperturbable gentleman anon. Turton alone broke the silence.

"Shall we wear masques?" he asked.

"I had not thought of it," answered Blackburn; "but upon my life I think we had better."

"I have tried wearing masques at school . . . where there was no need for it, except an imaginative need . . . a thirst that from the soul doth rise," answered Turton. "I've worn a mask to steal green apples in, so strong was my vocation. And now . . . O lord! I could shed tears!"

"One!" cried Blackburn, preparing to check off his recruits upon his fingers. "And you, Mr Ratcliffe?"

"Who? Me? What?" asked Ratcliffe.

"Have you any taste for moonlight adventure . . . or for gold? May I count on you?"

"I've an aunt in Gloucester," answered the athletic one with apparent irrelevancy, ". . . an awful decent old girl, I can tell you. I don't mind for myself; but I [62] shouldn't like to get run in, because of Aunt Jane." The speaker blushed healthily. "Not that I mind about anybody, if it comes to that," he added. "Why a man's aunt, you know, is always . . ."

"Always a man's aunt," supplied Blackburn. "Reassure yourself. This will not cost your aunt a moment's sleep."

"I couldn't work a false name," objected Ratcliffe. "I'm so well known. I've been in the 'Varsity Boat."

"You will never be asked your name, Mr Ratcliffe," answered Blackburn. "We shall take our measures too skilfully for such an accident. I give you my guarantee for that."

"And I will indorse the document," added Hardy. "You know my opinions, all of you. I am an enemy to the doctrine of property; all our most powerful thinkers incline that way; and I am pleased to remember that I have never disguised my adhesion. I look upon this as a manifesto at the outset of our career. And as for Ratcliffe's aunt, why, we know the opinion of all the finest minds of the century. The police is powerful as against brutal and unintelligent crime; [63] but for young men of education and courage, banded together in sufficient numbers and with an adequate provision of ready money, the police is an empty word and nothing more."

"Nothing more," echoed Blackburn. "Look at Balzac's conspiracy of thirteen."

"I was going to refer to that," said Hardy. "In real life, it was not successful . . . for obvious and quite extrinsic reasons. But the theory is absolute. Society is proved to be powerless against educated malefactors."

"And then there's Gaboriau's M Lecocq," added Turton, "who got into the police by showing them a whole hatful of patent-safety crimes, that anybody might commit . . . and the devil himself wouldn't find out."

"I don't know anything about Balzac," answered Ratcliffe; "but if Hardy's in, so am I. Hardy's deep."

"Two. Three," reckoned Blackburn. "Mr Urquhart?"

"I'll not commit myself," replied the laird. "I'm biddable . . . but I'm dry."

"Mr Strutt?"

There was a perceptible change in Blackburn's voice, as if he anticipated a rebuff. Strutt had been quite impassible all [64] this while, regarding the different speakers through his eyeglass. At Blackburn's question, he seemed to awaken out of a deep musing, and dropped his glass.

"I know it's very commonplace of me," he said; "but I draw the line at prigging."

"And as he uttered the last word (which he did with some emphasis) he succeeded in readjusting his eyeglass, and looked about the room with a great appearance of simplicity.

Blackburn laughed aloud.

"Will you do me the favour to walk twice or thrice round the quadrangle with me, Mr Strutt?" he asked.

"My dear Mr Blackburn! As often as you please! I admit I am taking up a puritanic attitude. But walking round a quadrangle . . . O dear no, not the least." And Strutt rose, found his hat and put himself at the prophet's disposal with every exhibition of politeness and good will.

“Gentlemen,” said Blackburn, “give us a little grace. “I shall bring back Mr Strutt in the character of convert.” [65] The pair left the apartment, not without a contest as to precedence which was too unlike the truly English rigidity of Strutt’s ordinary manners, not to be ironical on his part. For indeed there is nothing so profoundly wounding as an excess of politeness. The other four, like the followers of Cortez, “Looked at each other with a wild surmise.”

“It’s a damned pity,” said Ratcliffe. It’s all off, I suppose.”

“Off?” repeated Turton. “Why? What should it be off for. Strutt may play the fool if he chooses . . . it’s a free country . . . but I imagine we may still decide for ourselves. Or rather stick to our decisions. For we had decided, you know.”

There was something appealing, almost querulous, in Turton’s voice. He had seen so many bright illusions fade into the light of common day; he had outlived so many romantic credulities; he had travelled some years in this world of ours, falling daily from the dizzy peaks and roaring cataracts towards the good, fat level, where there is nothing but macadamised roads, and canals, and poplar alleys, and good fat merchants and peasantry, and everything good and flat and profoundly wearisome; and now, after a glimpse [66] of paradise, he began to see his new gods fading like the old, and the treasure, with the masques and other adventurous concomitants, rejoining many other touching and beautiful conceptions in the cloudland of the unfulfilled. All persons of aspiring soul will feel keenly with the Redistributor of the Sexes. But Hardy was not to be moved.

“Decided as to the feasibility of the enterprise,” he distinguished, “but as to nothing else. From a personal point of view, the thing was still to be considered. I am not the sort of man to arrive rapidly at any important decision. I weigh a project long. I was a hundred miles from giving any pledge.”

“It’s a pity you didn’t say so,” returned Urquhart. “I’m the only one who refused.”

“The fact is,” continued Hardy, “that Strutt is in the right, and we are all in the wrong. Strutt has no head for mathematics or any abstract thought; indeed he is remarkably destitute of the qualities that go to make up a philosopher; but he has some practical wisdom. And in the present case, he puts us all to shame. This fellow Blackburn may be a swell mobsman, for all we know."

"You know as well as I do that he isn't," answered Turton. "He's quite a gentleman, and as honest a fellow as [67] ever I saw."

"I don't think honesty is his forte."

"He's an enemy to the doctrine of property," retorted Turton ". . . that's all."

"My dear fellow," said Hardy, "surely you are sufficiently philosophical to understand the difference between theory and practise. Damn it, you know, there *is* such a thing as speculation."

"All right. You're a humbug," answered Turton.

Hardy turned green.

"Come and look at them," cried Urquhart, from the window.

Strutt and Blackburn were walking to and fro in the Quadrangle, Strutt with an appearance of great attention, Blackburn speaking vigourously and volubly, and gesticulating, from time to time, with both his hands. Occasionally, they halted and looked each other between the eyes. Although Strutt said nothing, it was obvious, even from the window of Hardy's room, that the skirmish was hot. One half of their promenade was in the sun and the other in shadow; and a sharp observer might have detected a change in their demeanour as they passed between the two. In the sunlight, Strutt was more on his [68] guard and Blackburn seemed more eloquent. It is possible that this was merely on the face of things and resulted from the difference of illumination. From time to time, Strutt kicked a pebble out of his path; and he once stooped and picked a blade of grass from the lawn which occupied the centre of the quad. The discussion seemed to create no small sensation in the minds of certain academical sparrows, who peered at them over the cornice and twittered occasional comments like the chorus in a Greek Play.

"I wonder what he's saying to him," said Urquhart.

"It's of no use whatever it is. I know Strutt well enough for that."

"Let's pitch a pipe at them," said Ratcliffe.

"No, don't. Let 'em have it out."

"He won't let Strutt speak."

And indeed, just then Blackburn seemed to silence his companion by a gesture.

"He's not far wrong in that."

"Look here, if Strutt is converted, will you be on again, Hardy?"

"Blindly," said Hardy.

"Hulloah! what's this?" [69]

Blackburn had produced a letter and handed it to Strutt; and the pair resumed their promenade, Strutt reading and Blackburn smoking a cigar which he had just lit. The latter carried his head in the air, held one hand open behind his back and displayed some affectation, the least shadow of a swagger, in his gait. He looked like a man who has had something not altogether easy to do, and has done it to his own satisfaction. This was not unnoticed from Hardy's window, but the change was so delicate that nobody liked to speak of it, lest the result should bring him in guilty of finding a mare's nest.

"What the devil can a letter have to do with it?"

"It may be the opinion of a great divine."

"Or a great philosopher."

"It's a woman's letter," said Urquhart. "I can see the crossing."

"Wily, wily Urquhart!"

"It seems to be devilish ill written, anyway. Will he never be done with it?"

"He might read it aloud pro bono publico."

"Pro bono sparroworum."

"What does Strutt mean when he drops his eyeglass? I know he does it on purpose."

"It's a way to gain time. No man can be a wit [70] without a snuff-box, an eyeglass or a stammer. Poor, naked, unprotected devils have to blurt out their good things unlicked and all of a heap. These fellows drop an eyeglass, trip over a consonant or take a pinch of snuff with the most natural air in the world; and out comes an epigram, by George! It makes all the difference between speaking and writing."

"Hulloah! look here!"

There was some cause for this ejaculation. Strutt and Blackburn were shaking hands! The very sparrows seemed to feel the gravity of the occasion, for they came tumbling in a vortex into the middle of the quadrangle and, describing an admirable curve, flew up again and perched among some sunny chimney-pots in a fine flutter of parliamentary agitation. At the same time the wind pounced round the corner and sent a sheet of paper flying into Hardy's window. During the momentary discomfiture produced by this unexpected visitant, Strutt and Blackburn disappeared from below; and their steps were audible almost immediately after, in the stair. The four fellows looked at each other with the expression of persons about to whistle. [71]

"Well!" cried Hardy. "If Strutt has changed his mind, I begin to question Newton's three laws."

"Not in the least, my dear Strutt, not in the least," said Blackburn in the stair.

It was the first time he had ever addressed any of the party except Turton, without the ceremonious prefix of Mister. Plainly things were marching.

"Gentlemen," said Strutt, pausing in the doorway, "I am a new creature. I am one of yourselves. I am a Bold Bandit. All my fancy is set upon deeds of rapine and violence. And I am prepared, in the stirring words of, I believe, Milton, to follow you 'till the red flag by inches is torn from the mast.'"

Chapter V

The Prophet's Chamber

On the evening of the next day, Turton and Blackburn might have been seen threading their way in a hansom from Bishopsgate Station towards the wilds of Chelsea and the howling, undiscovered west. It was already night; the lamps were lit along the gutters; the shop windows flared across the sidewalks; the usual nocturnal population moved to and fro under the usual [72] staring and garish illumination. A deep, clear lustre, colourless as water, filled the western sky; and the streets which had an open end towards that point of the compass presented a strange and rather spectral contest of lights and shadows. Against the pure after-glow, the houses stood out in gray parallelograms, the lamps in yellow and vivid ovals; while the pavements, which had been watered and burnished by some passing showers, reproduced the splendour of the sky with almost unimpaired intensity. On the wet and lucid sidewalks, solitary wanderers walked double, wanderer and shadow. Between the transparent heavens and the shining streets, the concourse of passers by astonished you by strength of tone and richness and opacity of colour; and when, by one of those tricks of illumination of which Hassad is the only master, the gas picked out a single face in a whole street, or far away, at a corner, a shopfront was brought into immediate juxtaposition with the lighted heavens, there was something sublime and infernal, a sort of Birmingham majesty, about the scene, that impressed the mind quite as forcibly, if not quite so nobly, as the wildest prospect among prodigious mountains and unfathomable valleys.

The hansom tacked and dived, in the enchanted [73] twilight, from roaring thoroughfare to cool and silent square. Now, a group of raddled women and half drunk men were crudely lit up in front of a gin palace; now a lone policeman was seen skirting under shadowy gardens. Here and there, a gang of street musicians splashed their brazen melodies abroad upon the night; an organ ground dismally in a corner; or one of those new mechanical pianos trampled through "Spring, Gentle Spring," with a horrid mimicry of dashing execution. All the sights and sounds and smells of the city; the succession of one street to another without end or issue; the sense of inexhaustible millions of fellow creatures and inexhaustible possibilities of adventure; the wretchedness and gaiety, the labour and the shame, that make up London: all these took possession of Turton's mind like an intoxicating drink. He leaned forward over the apron. He drank in every particular with greed. There was a noise in his ears, a manicoloured confusion before his eyes. His heart sang in his breast. He was reminded of the thousand and one pleasures and wants and aspirations, which we discount so lightly when we lay out our future by the fireside; he felt new life stirring [74] in all his veins; he felt himself a man, in every weakness and strength, every passion and sympathy, that the word implies.

"By George," he said, "there's nothing like a great city!"

"Why go to Navigator Islands? why not stay here?"

"A fellow would need to be a millionaire. A city is one vast chorus of voices requesting you to spend coin."

"The *coup d'œil* costs nothing," answered Blackburn, lightly, "and is the best of it."

"Where's the fun of looking into a shop window . . . even for a penniless man . . . unless he has some wish to buy? A city is a shop window; and unless you're just dancing with desire, unless you're full of all the lusts of the flesh and all the pride of life, and in a climax of health and viciousness, you care no more for your *coup d'œil* than a sparrow for an exhibition of agricultural implements. Look at invalids!

Pallid people with a sad, beautiful smile and a bath chair, always vote for the country and rose gardens. But when a man's suffocating with youth and health, O by George, just let him see a town!"

"Aye, there's a good deal of youth in it," said Blackburn drily. "What about the play?" [75]

"The Play? O, well, that's different. But it's only by a great contention of spirit that people can sit it out. The interest is too impersonal; the audience have to indemnify themselves by stealing away between the acts and drinking."

"Here we are," said Blackburn, as the cab drew up before a small two storied house in an empty by street. "Here we are, *chez moi.*"

He opened the door with a latch key and, telling the cabman to bring in the two portmanteaus, led the way upstairs to the first floor, and ushered Turton into a large room with three windows on the street. By the dull and partial firelight, it seemed encumbered with much nondescript and unnecessary furniture; and when Blackburn lit a candle, the impression was only strengthened. A museum had been tumbled bodily into an ordinary lodging house room, without the least attempt to harmonise the discord. There the things lay, in a garish and absurd disorder. At one end stood a large cabinet of oak, with niches, and fluted pillarettes, and a cornice on which nymphs and cupids danced the round and old Silenus swayed upon his donkey. Just opposite was a sideboard, covered with sticky veneer, which [76] was quite a little model of vulgarity and disproportion. The one piece of furniture produced like a mushroom on the decay of upholstery; dropped ready made like a hen's egg on the same morning with a thousand others identically like it, to a vast deal of crowing on hoardings and the outside sheets of newspapers: the other elaborated by some deliberate, bespectacled old workman, who stepped often backward to contemplate the touches of his chisel and took a pleasure in the nymphs and cupids and the whorls of Triton's tail. The cabinet and the sideboard were types of the opposition that reigned throughout the room. In one corner, tumbled books bestrewed the carpet; in another, empty soda-water bottles lay together in a wisp of wires, like the ruins of a small system of telegraphy. Chromo-lithographs, gaudy and egregious; coloured supplements to the illustrated papers representing young persons gathering apples and feeding poultry; an original Manet in the last stage of impressionalism; two or three etchings by good modern etchers, and not a few unframed sketches by indifferent modern art-students; - all these hung, in irregular squadrons, against the infamous lodging-house wall paper. A skull, a lot [77] of compresses, a Dutch clock, a large mahogany wine-cooler and a Chippendale card table spoke to some dim instincts, on the part of the Blackburn, for those higher and clearer zones where Mr Pater occupies the summit of Olympus in company with some aesthetic objects and the works of Paul de St Victor. And yet there, on the mantle shelf, were the original lodging-house flower glasses with the original lodging-house paper flowers: ghastly survivals, like the manacles and thumbscrews preserved in antique castles, to give Cook's tourists a sense of historical continuity and their own peculiar blessedness as Englishmen of the nineteenth century.

The real aesthetic soul would have suffered acutely from these incongruities. But it is to be noted that a truly aesthetic soul is not usually to be found in a Bohemian. The trick of looking upon things and apartments, as a whole, instead of seeing them in spots by the focus of a man's natural eyes, is one only to be acquired after some trouble and by a considerable exercise of the will. It is usually found in combination with some [78] particular notions about the destiny of humankind, and a distaste for bitter beer. To a fellow who goes running about the world with a crop for all corn, who likes green fields and slums at about an equal rate and can enjoy the society of that least and lowest of mankind, the billiard-marker, such a faculty is unnecessary and would end by being vastly disagreeable. Research in pleasures is not in his way, and research in furniture tenfold less. The man who can contentedly wear a fine coat along with a pair of ragged trousers, will not wince at a little discord between chairs and tables. Such people swallow the bad along with the good; they are more pleased than displeased; they can take out a great deal of pleasure in the contemplation of the mediæval wine cooler in one corner of the room, and quietly pass over the deformed chiffonier in the other. In short, they have no moral indignation in the æsthetic kingdom; and must count rather as private saints than as great apostles, in the goodly fellowship of those who adore the beautiful and the Apollo Belvedere. Nay, we may go farther, and say that theirs is, in a mild way, the same tolerant topsy-turvy [79] habit of soul, as enables the Sicilian bandit to enjoy the practical advantages of robbery and murder, side by side with the comforts of religion.

A piano stood open beside the fireplace; and Turton, sitting down to this, thrummed a little Beethoven, while his host settled with the cabman and arranged with his landlady about supper.

The landlady was an active little woman about fifty, with a general look of having originally come from Westmoreland. She treated Blackburn with great deference and affection, as a lodger of old standing and unquestionable solvency.

"Yes, sir, there had been gentlem here," she said. "Mr. Purray, he had your bed two nights ago; and Mr Armstrong, he was in this morning. I told them both as you were expected 'ome sir."

The Prophet and the Redistributor were soon installed over a cold supper at the Chippendale table; for the large centre table was permanently occupied by one of the meanest devices of modern art – a portable billiard board.

"There's nothing like music after all," said [80] Turton, his mind still occupied with his own thrummings.

"You are leaving Music," answered Blackburn, sadly. "You will never hear the Messiah any more."

"O yes," returned Turton cheerfully. "I shall be sent back as Plenipotentiary, about the time of the Handel Festival. Egad, I think I see myself, leaning back in an open carriage like Doctor Kenealy, with a beard, and a Sunday hat, and beads round my neck. Plenipotentiary is a very noble word. Doctor Kenealy looks a plenipotentiary every inch of him: so noble and so replete!"

“On your own showing, you would hardly be the figure for it.”

“It’s not the figure, it’s the grace. I should adopt a plenipotent gait; a sort of *pas de plênipotentiare*: the affable archangel: like this” – and he arose and illustrated his words with suitable deportment. “Plenipotentiary being presented to the Queen: sad but noble. Ditto in consultation with Secretary of State: engaging, diplomatic but grand. Ditto acknowledging applause from open four-wheeler: not to be described in words. Ditto in private life, eating cold [81] ham.” And he resumed his supper. “It’s all in the turn of the hand, you see,” he added, “and a sort of stiff swing on the hips. A child could manage it.”

There was a pause.

“About that portmanteau,” Blackburn began. “I dare say you have some scruples still unsatisfied.”

“Not I!” said Turton heartily. “I’m going to break into a house with a black masque on. I’m as pleased as I can be . . . that’s all.”

“Pardon me, returned Blackburn, “but you take this a little cavalierly. The thing is grave. I have given you my word, of course; and yet I can imagine you demanding something more. I do not say I should be displeased. Intelligent trust is one thing: credulous levity another. You may very well ask how a man is to steal a portmanteau, and still remain a gentleman . . .”

“Jack Sheppard was a thief but he never told a lie,” broke in Turton. “He had the advantage of me there. I’ve told heaps.”

Blackburn seemed a little nettled; his face became graver by several shades.

“I only wished to repeat my assurances,” he said.

“O, never mind me! I’m a credulous-levity fellow. [82] I’m quite dead to morality. I don’t give a damn for anything but sport,” said Turton.

Blackburn was considerably less than pleased; it is always hard to repress a vein of sermonising, and overzealous disciples are perhaps the most mortifying accident in life to discreet Prophets with a taste for making a distinction. Poor

Luther, poor Calvin, ground, all their lives long, under such calamities. The latter, indeed, was reluctantly compelled to burn some of his fellow creatures in the interests of moderation. But Blackburn had neither the stake nor the thumb-screw at command; so it was rather a relief when the door burst open, and a wisp of a dog tumbled into the room at a sidelong, prancing canter, and proceeded to wallow on his boots with odd cries and whimperings.

"Your hound?" asked Turton.

"Yes, it's a beast of mine."

"Fond of you?"

"Yes; he is. I believe he prefers me to most things, except food and sitting in chairs. He is amiable, but an idiot; and I hate stupid dogs . . . a great deal worse than stupid men. But this is a poor world, [83] dogs and all. We have to take our pets in the twig, as we have to take our friends . . . or our wives, when we're fools enough to take any."

"The great thing is, that they shan't bite," said Turton.

"This one doesn't. He is as good as gold; like a dog out of a Sunday School Story Book, if they had any such things for what they call the lower animals. One peculiarity, I notice in him . . . although it's common enough in men. He is fonder of being spoken to than any other dog I ever knew . . . and understands less of what's said to him."

"I bet we try to communicate with dogs on some wrong principle," said Turton. "Speech is obviously not their line. No more's music; they draw the line at music; they howl so horrid."

"People propose geometry on a large scale for the inhabitants of the moon," suggested Blackburn.

"Won't do with dogs," said Turton. "You may show them the illustrations to Euclid till you're blue in the face; it doesn't seem to come home to them. And I'm sure I can't see why it should. It's quite a put-up interest with men; there's no basis of pleasure, no sport about geometry. What do I care [84] about the angles at the base of a Isosceles triangle? We should appeal to some honest animal appetite. If we made an art of eating now? They would rise to that, I think; and we might exchange ideas with them by means of different viands, about all sorts of fundamental principles."

"They know most about the affections," said Blackburn, caressing the terrier's ear; "and the affections are naturally dumb."

"O come!" cried Turton. "This is sentiment."

"A man may surely talk sentiment about a dog," answered Blackburn.

"Well, you know, you said yourself his great game was food."

"Are you really asking me to be logical?" said Blackburn, looking up. "It comes a little lefty-handedly from you."

"Why?" asked Turton.

"Well, after all . . . why?" returned the other, with a nasty laugh. "We may not steal from a thief!"

"He's in a beastly temper," thought Turton to himself; and he strolled back to the piano stool, and began picking chords out of one of Beethoven's sonatas. From time to time he would hit on some turn that greatly delighted him. This [85] he would repeat with nauseous iteration, commenting ecstatically the while. "Listen to that!" he would cry. "By George, it's the finest thing in the world! There's dignity for you! It's an extraordinary thing, there are only two arts in which dignity can be worked off: music and deportment. You may see them together at the opera." Blackburn answered with grunts and continued to caress the terrier. He was still irritated against the Redistributor; still smarting inwardly in the character of the overshot prophet; but his temper was beginning to settle; and by the time the landlady had brought tea, he was smoking a pipe in great good will to all men.

"What an awful lot of rubbish you have kicking about," said Turton. "I hope you came by them honestly."

"They're heir-looms," answered Blackburn, with a touch of a sneer.

"By Jupiter, what a jolly snuff-box!"

"Yes, it's not bad. If you care for that kind of thing, open any of the drawers; I have quite a curiosity shop. That's an odd thing now; I can't think where the devil the fellow got it. It is a piece of a crozier. Some old Saint may have belaboured Satan with it in his [86] day."

“What a heap of gold there is!” cried Turton, who was now rummaging in the cabinet, with Blackburn at his shoulder.

“Yes; my father had a craze for gold. It went between him and everything . . . even wealth. I think it must have been the female of his species.”

“Well, there’s something fine about a *pose* of that sort,” said Turton. “It’s an artistic form of vice. It’s gratifying an appetite, and I always sympathise with that . . . it’s so genuine. There’s a kind of grandeur about the merest bald-headed person eating pickles; it’s natural, it’s durable, it’s as old as the sea; it’s true; it’s a protest against Members of Parliament and Isosceles triangles. No man can stand up, before his maker, and pretend that he prefers the angles at the base of an Isosceles triangle to pickles! The lie would stick in his throat; he would become the despicablest humbug in the world; the very brute beasts, sir, would regard him with contempt. . . . But look here,” he added, turning upon Blackburn, “you leave all your jugs and snuff-boxes lying around loose. It appears you and your [87] landlady are not on international terms?”

The Prophet blushed deeply.

“Don’t bother any more with these confounded things,” he said, abruptly shutting up a drawer which he had just opened. “Come and smoke a pipe.”

“They’re all humbugs,” thought Turton to himself, “. . . all humbugs but me!”

And over the shoulders of the unconscious Prophet, he makes a knowing grimace to the reader of these pages.

End of Book I

[88]

Book II – The Dragons of the Hesperides

Chapter I

Across the Forest

Six active young fellows were making their way on foot with their knapsacks on their shoulders, over a certain wild ridge of mountains in the west of Scotland. It was past midnight; and they had been mounting for more than two hours and were already near the summit of the range. The July nights are short and bright up there in the north. Only a few of the larger planets were visible in the clear sky; and the world was all as distinct as by day in the semi-arctic twilight. Away below and behind them, the travellers could see stage after stage of falling mountain; and then alternate strips of bright sea and bars of dark chersonese; and then the open water sprinkled with islands; and over all a stain of dusky rose and purple on the horizon where the sun had gone down. All around were tumbled heathery hilltops strewn with boulders. Here and there some birches clustered in a hollow; and a few white vapours roosted here and there along the mountain wall.

The road turned and wound and doubled on itself, through a thousand varieties of inclination and direction; and the six fellows pushed along at a good, round, steady, ringing pace. Two of them brought up the rear whistling [89] a march; and their feet fell in time with each other like those of soldiers on parade. Turton and Hardy led the way, being both professed walkers. Blackburn followed a little behind with Urquhart, who had jibbed at first and demanded a halt about twice in the half mile, but had long ago fallen into a dogged, silent, purgatorial jog-trot with clenched fists and chin stuck out. Strutt and Ratcliffe formed the rear guard of the little regiment. They were just then striking up the march of the Connaught Rangers with shrill melodious pipes that sounded far away upon the darkling moors.

"Where are we, Capting?" shouted Turton from the front.

"More than two thirds across the deer forest," answered Blackburn.

"Very little forest and no deer," cried Turton in the same high key.

"Plenty deer when you know how to find 'em," shouted Blackburn back.

And they fell again into the same silent, cheerful swing, swallowing the miles. The short night was already far spent; and the day coming up over Russia and the Baltic. Already the stars were paling and the north beginning to brighten. A little wind ran among the brackens with a shiver. The great [90] vault of heaven and all the tumbled hills were strange and inspiring to behold. The blood raced gladly in the young men's veins; the road rang below their consonant feet; and a solemn exhilaration grew up within them as they thus met the peep of day upon the hilltops.

Suddenly Turton and Hardy came to a halt; and the former threw up his stick and broke into a lusty view hulloah. They had reached the highest point of the road, with all the seaboard and the sea spread out behind them, and all the inland hills and valleys at their feet.

"Three miles more," cried Blackburn.

"Double, you lubbers!" shouted Turton.

And with a scattered cheer, Urquhart internally cursing, the whole half dozen broke into a run and went rattling down the hill at twelve miles an hour. The whistling came to an end, and the order of march was speedily changed; Ratcliffe taking the lead by a foot or two and Urquhart going plump into the rear and tailing away back into the distance, until he fairly gave up and returned to his jog-trot walk, like a fat terrier in the huff. Turton also dropped astern pretty rapidly; but his spirits rose for all that, and he kept cheering and inciting the others like a man coaching a University boat. [91]

The road went headlong down hill, not doubling and tacking as upon the other slope; and it soon led them among plantations of fir; old natural patriarchs standing here and there in an undergrowth of young ones that a man might have stuck in his hat by way of feather. Thence they came into a zone where the plantation was older and better grown and shut out the view on either hand. A little farther, and the road made a sharp dip and rose as sharply on the other side. In the bottom of this hollow, a little modern cottage stood by the way, with a stable and coach house at its back. It was separated from the road by a patch of kitchen garden; and the firs grew so close about the offices, that their branches rested on the roof. The hoarse roaring of a waterfall was audible from somewhere near at hand in the plantations. It was almost broad day; but there was a light in one window of the cottage and a long feather of white smoke at the chimney top, which had a hospitable meaning for the adventurers.

Blackburn brought the party up.

"This is Mulagh Creigh," he said, "my little place I told you of; you can hear the waterfall now we've stopped running. Now, gentlemen, for the reign of discretion. No noise, nothing but business. The whole party keeps to the cover; and no one either gives or asks information [92] from a living soul. Silence, Secrecy, Despatch . . . that is your watchword." And the speaker led the way through the garden to the cottage door.

"Where's Urquhart?"

"Somewhere away behind; he loathes running."

"Let's go back for him in a body," cried Turton.

"O bosh," said Strutt.

"I'll wait on the road for him," said the patient Ratcliffe; and no one offering an objection, he sat down upon the garden gate and began to whistle.

The door was opened by a nice old body in a cap. Blackburn kissed her with a "How d'ye do, Lizzie?" and then turned to the others with "This is Mrs Cameron, my old nurse, one of the best women in the world. Lizzie," he went on, "these are the fellows I wrote you about."

"Come in, laddies," said Mrs Cameron. "Ye'll be tired I'm thinking. Come in by. It's no verra grand; but what's better, it's caller and clean and young folk shuldna be ill to please."

So speaking she ushered the young men into a large, plain kitchen, with a peat fire, comfortable to the eye and very grateful to the nostrils. Clean dishes shone all round upon the walls; the table was laid for six; scones toasted on the hearth; something spluttered in a pan upon the peats; and a range of pint bottles [93] stood along the wall, purporting to contain Dublin stout; and another range, this time of quarts, displayed green whiskey labels on the dresser.

A stifled cheer of satisfaction rose from the party in the house, and was answered by a halloa from the road. Urquhart had begin to feel eerie alone among the pine plantations, had put on the pace again and arrived on the heels of his companions, very much out of breath and temper. But no sooner was he also ushered into the house, than the aspect of the bright kitchen and the preparations visible for a late but welcome supper, smoothed all the wrinkles out of his face and awakened a genial twinkle in his eye. Soon they were all gleefully seated about a dish of stewed fowls, fat and full of eggs, savoury and tender, and melting in savoury brown sauce. It is a dish to which a gastronomist cannot be trusted to refer without hyperbole, and of which hungry young men can scarcely partake without excess. And when it thus meets them at the end of a long night walk in the clear air of the mountains, and stands worthily flanked by piles of smoking cakes and scones, and long sticks of golden butter, and ready to be washed down with pensive porter and whiskey which occupies over other liquids a somewhat similar preeminence of purity to that of mountain atmosphere over all other and [94] meaner sorts of air – why who is there of the dead heart and perverted digestion, who would not cry with Burns that it was worthy of a grace as long as my arm?

Whatever might be its claims in this direction, they were somewhat cavalierly passed over by the Ideal Commonwealthers. Mrs Cameron was shocked at the precipitation of the conslaught.

“Hoots, hoots,” she said. “Ye maun ask a blessing.” And she supplied the oversight at some length.

“Thank you, Lizzie,” said Blackburn. “Hungry men will be hasty men, you know.”

“You've given me no eggs with my stuffing,” complained Urquhart.

“You can have mine. I don't care for them much,” said Ratcliffe.

“Is this dinner, supper or breakfast,” asked Strutt.

“O don't enquire!” cried Turton, “don't spoil the mystery.”

“I could demonstrate it to be lunch . . . by quaternions,” said Hardy.

“By the by, Lizzie, where are we to sleep?”

“Aweel ye ken yoursell there's but ae bed, forbye mines.”

“That shall be for Urquhart the laird.”

“But I've put a wheen strae in the attic. It'll no be verra grand, but it's soft and it's halesome.” [95]

“That'll do famously, old lady.”

“Mrs Cameron,” said Strutt, “you are the best cook in England, Scotland, Wales or Ireland. Stewed fowl is a dish that you have reinvented.”

“And look here, Mrs Cameron,” added Turton, “if it was you that made that butter, you're an angel from Heaven.”

“Na, na, laddie,” returned the old woman, “it was neither me nor ony ither that made that butter. The kye made it when they chowed the bonny green grass in the haugh; and the wright made it when he made the kirn; and over a' it was God that made it; to him be praise and blessing! And as for angels and heaven, the least said may be's the sunest mended; we ken haw an' little aboot them; God grant we may a' ken mair some fine morn. And noo, Master Ralph, I'll awa' to my bed. And if ye'll just excuse my freedom, laddies, see and dinna tak' ower muckle to drink, and see ye and dinnae forget your prayers!”

And she made them a prim salutation, and was gone.

“She's a rum old party,” said Turton.

“She's one of the best women in the world,” said Blackburn.

“I was particularly gratified by her theology,” observed [96] Strutt. “Couldn't we take her to the Ideal shop with us; and make her a kind of arch-druidess? You say I take no interest in your interesting little political stranger; but there's a practical suggestion for you at last."

"She was wrong in her argument about the butter," said Hardy.

"Not at all," said Turton. "I know what she was after. If you were to invent some mathematics . . . something to knock all the rest into a cocked hat . . . something to supersede the whole lot of calculuses . . . a calculus calculorum . . . a double bi-quaternion . . . what you please . . . it wouldn't be you who had done it, but all the mathematicians of the world, from old Egyptian fellows with peaked hats down to the 'varsity tutor who coached you."

"My dear boy," said Strutt, "the old lady had turned your head. At that rate, it would not be we who were going to steal the hair trunk, but the eminently respectable journeyman who made it; and if a fellow commits a murder, we should hang his oldest living ancestor, the man who varnished the walking stick with which the rash act was done, and above all the father and mother of the victim. If you are going to put this into your new constitution, the Commonwealth will be even gayer that I have been led to anticipate already."

"You are all right after a fashion," said Blackburn. [97] "We live in the middle of a string. We speak, and it's only Montaigne or Doctor Johnson speaking out of our mouths. We have a bright thought and think ourselves mighty clever, and it's only Guinness who can brew good stout. We call our souls our own, and we don't know where they begin or end, or whether we have any. We think we are in love with a girl, and it's only because one of our ancestors had a taste for dark-haired women with blue eyes. We are the sails of a mill clattering in the wind, and God knows where the wind blows from and who fills the corn into the hopper. I sometimes get sick at the sound of my own chatter when I think of it. Am I an automaton with a chronic hallucination? Am I only an organ in an organism, a joint in a monstrous animal's tail, a bit of somebody or something else? You fellows think you are going to steal a hair trunk; are you? is that all? I think I am going to found an ideal commonwealth . . . or turn my life into one long picnic party, if you like; am I? is that all, there also? Or are we not all dummies, ducking our heads about to machinery, and with nothing in the world but so much sawdust in our stomachs?"

"I think I'll put a little whiskey into mine," said Urquhart. [98]

"I want to go to bed. I'm sleepy," added Ratcliffe.

"Aye," cried the prophet, "there's good sense! a little whiskey and to bed! There can be no doubt about who tastes the whiskey anyway; it's ourselves and not the mighty dead."

"That's where animal life is so much grander!" cried Turton. "No damned theories . . . no nonsense. I don't care whether it's I or my great-grandfather who's to steal the treasure, so long as I have the fun of it. I don't care if I am a windmill . . . I like being one."

"The unwearied sun is about to rise," said Strutt. "It is now, gentlemen, the witching hour of half past three in the morning or to speak more correctly, five and twenty minutes to four. Do you know I think there was a good deal of philosophy in a remark which fell a little ago from my friend, The Highway. I do not remember the exact terms."

"I said I wished to go to bed, if that's what you mean," said Ratcliffe. "And I do."

The garret occupied the whole size of the little cottage; it was without a ceiling; and through a single dormer window, it was now full of the new daylight. Plenty of clean straw and shearers blankets, a large washing tub full of cold water, a basin or two, soap, and a heap of towels, were the [99] somewhat rude preparations made by Mrs Cameron. But when the window had been thrown wide open, to admit the sweet and busy airs of the morning, the fine fellows threw themselves down upon the straw with great physical satisfaction and were soon drowned in well-earned slumber and all unconscious of the rising sun. Urquhart snored steadily in the little room downstairs; Ratcliffe and Blackburn snored with vigour in the attic; the others took their rest in silence. The peats blinked away by themselves in the kitchen and shone among the empty plates and glasses.

The firs tapped and rustled over the stable roof. The voice of the waterfall became gradually less distinct, as though it were a creature of the night like the bats and owls, and only dozed all day to waken up at evening and rave among the pine trees to the frosty stars. Out in the court, a cock proclaimed his prowess to the Heavens, and paced among his brides with the air of a most accomplished hidalgo. His voice, sometimes as clear as a trumpet, sometimes hoarse like the richest tenor, seemed the very expression of earthly pride and glory. There was "no sorrow in his song"; although perhaps the stewed fowl had once been dear to his heart. But jolly chanticleer, and some persons of transcendent genius, have an immunity from vain repinings; and when dame Partlet finds her way into the kettle, enjoy their own improvisations and the beauty of God's world with an [100] unimpaired and healthful appetite.

Mrs Cameron was the first afoot, and was soon out in the court, in her white mutch and bright steel spectacles, with broken meat and vegetables for chanticleer and his family. And not long after, she was joined by Blackburn, who had a long talk with her in the empty stable. Before it was done, there was a fine bustle in the cottage; splashing of water, peals of laughter, shouts to awaken Urquhart "the Beddist," as he was immediately dubbed by Turton, and other signs of a general awakening among the company.

Chapter II

Tufto Castle

The neighbourhood of Mulagh Creigh was varied and romantic. The hollow in which it stood, was a sort of pocket at the top of the last brisk descent of the mountain into a wide valley watered by a tumultuous highland river. This valley was perhaps a score of miles in length, and contained several mean hamlets and two or three ornamental shooting boxes. The upper end was closed by many rugged mountain summits, thin with distance, as if they had been woven out of air; at the lower, on bright afternoons, might be seen the shining waters of a loch. Often the mountain tops [101] were dappled with sun and shadow; oftener still, they were veiled in heavy clouds; and the rain and the red thunderbolt splashed and fell among their steeps. We speak of the everlasting hills; and indeed these blue peaks looked as if they were throned above calamity, and would continue to gloom and glimmer in the changeful phases of a highland climate, until time was no more and all the stars rolled together in the abyss of space. And yet their coexistence was one long battle, in which they were continually losing ground. The forces of the air waged war against these giants of the earth, as in a kind of antitype of the old myth of the escalcade of Heaven and the resounding ruin of the Titans. The outline of the hills against the sky was all broken and gnawed away by the eating weather; the boulder toppled, the rattling gravel fell, the flanks of the mountain ran down with every rivulet; and day by day, the brawling river in the valley was charioting fresh ruins toward the loch.

The waterfall which made a noise in the ears of the sleepers at Mulagh Creigh, was made by one of the feeders of this river leaping over a steep gap in the mountain side into a narrow and winding valley full of firs. At the bottom of this, the water raged and chafed through a chaos of fallen boulders, until the glen was hemmed in and almost [102] entirely closed by a spur or promontory of the hill. Behind this, the tributary spread out into something too large to be called a pool and not large enough to be called a loch; and on the summit, looking with its front upon the valley and turning its back upon the glen and the waterfall, stood a large and handsome modern edifice called Tufto Castle. A series of terraces descended from the windows to the level of the plain; glittering with balustrades and statues and conspicuous for miles away by bright parterres. The tributary, quite sobered after it left the loch, meandered through the grounds in front with almost as much deliberation as an English brook. Stucco bridges crossed its waters; and clumps of civilized shrubbery had been craftily disposed along its banks. Rustic summerhouses stood in nooks; a range of vineries glittered in an angle of the hill; forest trees, of recent and somewhat weedy growth, made a poor figure on the knolls; bracken and heather had been laboriously exterminated; the park shone green in the sunlight with smooth and park-like turf; and it was surrounded by a stone fence and entered through costly iron gates between two pretentious lodges. Nothing could be imagined much more out of keeping with the waterfall in the fir woods, the deer forest that lay behind the waterfall, or the [103] bald and awful peaks that closed the valley; nothing could be more smart and cocknified, than this desirable residence and its dependencies. There are probably few more hideous instincts in our imperfect nature, than that which leads us to bedabble the face of God's world with what are called tasteful villas. It is not so reprobate, but it has something in common, with that other instinct which leads blinded vulgarians to chisel their initials upon statues. The hills of Xanadu would look none the better, you may take your oath, for the stately pleasure dome of Kubla Khan. But with an architect of Coleridge's good instinct at his elbow, he would not have made quite so deplorable an impertinence, quite so unsightly a wart upon the face of surrounding nature, as had been managed by the projector and architect of Tufto Castle. It was like a Swiss clock in a druidic circle, or a piano in a cavern, or a young gentleman in evening dress upon the Mountains of the Moon. It was as though Antony should be played in a cocked hat and feathers, or Macbeth with a gingham umbrella. It positively gave an air of respectability, if not of fashion, to the rude highland valley, closed by stern hills, full of the noise of waters and often swept by driving rain. Artists looked [104] another way; and mild-eyed, ruminating tourists were shocked and pained, and could not rightly make out why. Tufto Castle was the pride and scandal of the district.

The neighbourhood of the waterfall was perhaps in most flagrant contrast to the bedizened and coquettish policies of the great house. A turbulent burn came suddenly on the edge of the precipice from round a corner; shot over in a thick porter-coloured spout; and was shattered into thin spray before reaching the bottom of a sort of devil's punch bowl that yawned to receive it, among broken rocks, seams of red clay, and fir trees clinging desperately to the slope. Standing just in the throat of the fall, it was possible to follow for some distance the windings of the stream between the steep banks, here black with hanging foliage and there denuded by a recent landslip or the outcropping of the rock from underneath; and though Tufto Castle and the valley of the main river were entirely hidden, the view embraced the more distant hill-tops standing naked and blue along the sky. It was perhaps the absence of any middle distance that gave a peculiar character to the scene; or perhaps it lay in the contrast between the darkness of the glen and the continued roar of the falling water in the foreground, with the ætherial distance and seemingly [105] unbroken stillness of the mountains. Certainly, and however you may choose to explain it, the place was well-suited for reverie; and sentimental people who wished themselves in love, would be tempted to return to it again and again, in search of what are called congenial surroundings. Tufto Castle is not the sort of house in which we should expect to find a Werther; but wherever there are lazy people, there will be sluggish livers; and wherever there are sluggish livers, sad thoughts and melancholy aspirations are sure to be in vogue. Some such person at least, had evidently once inhabited the castle; or perhaps it was only a patient water-colour amateur, the gentlest of mankind! For behold, through all the asperities of the glen, a solid footpath joined the grounds of Tufto to the summit of the waterfall; and there, within a stone's throw of the vent, an elegant iron garden seat painted emerald green had been set down below a tuft of firs. From above, the firs covered it as well as they could with their coarse and hardy arms; the heather had grown up and swollen its purple cushions round it, from below; but there it was, a little cockney dependency of the cockney castle, the last outpost of Birmingham; there it stood, like a piece of newspaper left behind a picnic, or [106] or an umbrella leaning against the base of the Great Pyramid.

It was down this pathway in the glen that Blackburn led his little troop to reconnoitre in the sunny breezy morning. He himself carried a knapsack on his shoulders; for he was to leave them as soon as everybody knew his station for the night, and making a precautionary detour, put up at the little inn beside Tufto Castle gates. The object of this separation was known to no one but himself and Strutt, who was now his great confidant; the others obeyed implicitly, in a frame of mind between discontent and amusement. The whole story of the Hair Trunk they had long ago given up trying to understand; and many believed it would turn out a swindle at the last moment.

Their advance was circumspect. At the sound of a footfall, or the merest sign of gamekeeper or gardener, the whole party had orders to take to the bush and separate. Each had a different story at his tongue's end, in case he should be separately apprehended. Turton was in the liveliest spirits; the fun of the business was beginning at last; and he took the lead and stole round the corners with an elaborate pantomime of caution which was amusing enough to witness. Simply out [107] of the spirit of his part he had taken off his shoes and stockings and crept barefoot over the turf and pine tassel. It did not fit very well with the fiction he was to stop the mouths of enquiring gamekeepers withal; but what did he care for that?

"By George, I should like to see them lay their hands on me," he cried. "I feel as fleet as a hare; this robber business is so splendid for the nerves!"

Indeed they were all excited, with shining eyes, with light and active footsteps, braced from top to toe, and full of zeal and glee. Urquhart himself had thawed amid the general enthusiasm, and was keenly in the spirit.

"We have all decivilised," cried the exulting Hardy. "It was easy – easy!"

"A top-coat to take off!" said Blackburn.

"I feel ashamed of my eyeglass," added Strutt. "It seems to mar the harmony of the evening."

"Attention!" said the leader, "here we are at the skirts of the wood. The field of battle is before us!"

A steep green bank led down to the margin of the river just where it flowed out of the loch below the back of Tufto Castle; and from where they halted, the Commonwealthers could see [108] the course of a road, which led with a wide sweep from the park gates to the kitchen entrance, crossing the stream on its way by a rustic bridge. It was well hidden, for the most part, among thick clumps of rhododendron; and the wood, in several piney promontories, ran almost down to it.

"At one o'clock tomorrow morning," said Blackburn, "Ratcliffe will be on guard at the point of the wood below us. Turton –"

"Present, Capting."

"Turton will be posted among the rhododendrons at the first corner. A single whistle will call the sentries to each other; two will concentrate the party on the point of danger; three will be the signal for dispersion. So much for the outposts; the other four will lie in that great clump beside the bridge. I join you by the road. You see an isolated door, a sort of postern, at the foot of the tower? It is by that we enter. Now then . . . is all understood?"

It was; but Hardy, in his character of a thoughtful man, had a suggestion to make.

“Are we not too much massed?” said he. “We must guard against surprises. I should be inclined to place a few more sentries.”

“And who’s to carry the trunk?” asked Blackburn “. . . full of gold!”

“I say,” cried Turton, “This is life! Let us pray!”

“Now then . . . back to Mulagh Criegh,” said Blackburn. [109] “And keep dark until the hour for action. Remember the watchword . . . Silence, secrecy, dispatch!”

And they separated, Blackburn to skulk down towards the village by the borders of the wood, the others to regain the cottage on the hill.

Chapter III

The Garrison of Tufto

Hugo Lemesurier, of Tufto as he was called (although that was in pure courtesy, for the estate belonged to his mother and not to him) sat after dinner that night with Major Albert Cunningham, H. E. I. C. S., a constant inmate of the castle, on the footing of family friend. Hugo was a handsome, cross, gentlemanly looking fellow, with a highly British moustache and whiskers; the Major, a fine, old, pickled Anglo-Indian, with an appearance suggestive of nothing but a good conscience and brandy and water. On this particular evening, Hugo seemed in a worse temper than usual, and the door had hardly closed behind his mother, ere he broke forth into an ejaculation that sounded like an oath.

"What, in heaven's name, is wrong with her now?" he cried.

"Doosid remarkable woman," said the Major lighting a cheroot.

"Deuced remarkable temper," echoed Hugo. "Why, what can ail the woman? I'm used to contradiction; I can bear that; [110] but what I will not stand is personalities before the servants. She said . . ." And there he paused, not caring apparently to recall the remark to his companion's memory. "Hang me," he went on, "it's too much for flesh and blood."

"When your father married her, Hugo," said the Major – ". . . he was a fine man, your father . . . Lemesurier of ours . . . but she must have been a doosid fine woman for a widow. I saw her first in eighteen hundred and forty-eight. You were a doosid small fellow then, Hugo. I came home on Furlough that year, with Bennet of the Buffs, I remember, and Mrs Major Milligan. Bennet exchanged into the 80th, and gad, they said it was the white feather: most extr'or'nary thing! I never could bear Bennet; hated him worse than Napoleon Buonaparty, egad."

Hugo broke out again upon the former topic, from which the Major had drifted onto the history of Bennet of the Buffs.

"Why is she mad tonight? – that's what beats me!" he cried. "I've been behaving like an angel; I've let her contradict me, and snub me, and insult me; and so have you, if you come to that . . . but then you always do. I let her talk nonsense about machinery, and nonsense about weather and the birds, and nonsense high and low about everything God made; and nothing pacifies her! It's heart-breaking, [111] Major! If she weren't my mother, I'd say she was the devil and be happy!"

"Speaking about machinery," said the Major, "I remember when I came home in the *Gwalior* in eighteen hundred and thirty-six, there was a barometer in the cuddy, and it was doosid ingenious . . . the fellow had put some mercury in . . . to steady it, don't you understand? when the ship was pitching. It was doosid ingenious," added the Major, with a sigh.

"I have it!" cried Hugo, who had not been listening. "That Fellow has been here again!"

"Who's that?" inquired the Major.

"Why, that . . . Fellow, don't you know?"

"Oh ah! Him. I saw him the last time he came; that was in November; most remarkable fellow! Has he been again?"

"That's what I'm going to see," said Hugo. "Ring the bell, Major."

To ring the bell was one of the duties of the family friend at Tufto. The Major rose reluctantly, his cheroot in hand, and did as he was told; and the summons was answered by the awful form of a butler.

"Thomson, has That Fellow been here again today?" demanded Hugo, unabashed by the being's presence.

"He was, Mr Hugo." [112]

"By George, I guessed as much! . . . No name again?"

"No name, Mr. Hugo. He sent in a letter as usual, and then Mrs Lemesurier had him up, and then, sir" – lowering his voice – "they had luncheon together in the morning room!"

"O by Jupiter!" cried Hugo. "And how did she treat him? Like a gentleman?"

"Well, Mr Hugo, it's a little difficult to say with Mrs Lemesurier," replied the butler, with a diplomatic smile. "She treated him free like."

"As she treats the Major?"

"It would be about that, Mr Hugo."

"Extr'or'nary thing!" gasped the Major.

"You didn't chance to overhear anything?" demanded Hugo.

"No sir," replied the butler, looking him in the face.

"Very well. Thank you, Thomson. You can go."

The servant bowed and silently left the apartment.

"How's that?" snapped Hugo to the Major, as soon as they were left alone.

"Most extr'or'nary thing!" replied that councilor.

"Look here, Major, I will not put up with mysteries. As long as my mother chooses to behave like other people, I'll stand her insolence; but this sort of thing's disreputable, and I'll be no party to it. I'll be at the bottom of the [113] whole affair, or I leave this house and say why."

"Your mother's a very remarkable woman," said the Major with a blink, as if "remarkable" stood for something different.

"That's neither here nor there," said Hugo. "I put it to you; you're a gentleman at least; is this a kind of thing a son should stand? Who is this fellow? What is he after? He's been coming about the house as long as I remember; why do I never meet him? Why am I not introduced? Why are you not? If he's not fit company for us, he's not fit company for her, and there's the short and long of it. And then . . . why is she always in a temper when he's gone? It's like a French novel! That's a fine thing going on in a gentleman's house – a French novel! And now I come to think of it . . . how should he know that you and I were gone to Inveradam for the day . . . unless someone told him in the house? If I thought it was that blackguard Thomson!"

"Doosid civil fellow, Thomson," said the Major.

"Well, so he is, and I don't suspect him, though he was disrespectful – yes, he was! . . . disrespectful tonight. But you see, there's collusion somewhere. Now, Major, what would you do yourself, if you were in my place?"

"I don't know," said the Major.

"O come! Think! What would you do?" [114]

"Upon my honour, I don't know!" said the Major.

"Well, I know," answered Hugo. "Up with you! Come upstairs. I'll have it out at once."

Although the Major would have liked to finish his cheroot, there was nothing for it but to obey. It was a snug place, this of family friend at Tufto Castle, but like all snug places, not without counterbalancing troubles. Between mother and son, he was well broken in. So the cheroot went into the fire, not without the tribute of a sigh, and the pair marched upstairs to the drawing room.

There sat Mrs Lemesurier, sixty-five years old, a tall, beautiful old lady, snuff box in hand. She was what, in Scotland, we call *daft*; she had lived all her life as an aggressive eccentric of the old school, free-tongued, undaunted, a female grenadier; and yet her plump speech and warfaring deportment in society, were not inconsistent with genuine tenderness of soul. In all her flights, although you might stare, you never doubted but she was a lady and a woman. Such dames were not uncommon once in Scotland, but the race is swiftly and unanimously dying out. Looking to what we have instead, I cry, The more's the pity! The Southdown is the plumper animal, but where is the wild savour of the mountain sheep? A man, in old days, would scarce come from courting without scratched [115] hands; but if his wooing prospered, it was a human being that he won.

Hugo marched up to the formidable lady, as it were to a battery of guns.

"There was a fellow here this morning," said he. "You had him to lunch. I want to know his name."

She looked at him squarely with a thrill of anger.

"I want to know his name," he repeated. "It's surely a natural desire."

"Has he been drinking, Heics?" asked the lady.

"Heics," pronounced *hykes*, was her pleasant name for Major Albert Cunningham, H. E. I. C. S., the Tufto family friend. But that gallant officer, well used to similar passages of arms, was studying the "Army List" with passionate abstraction.

"I have not been drinking," answered Hugo, his colour rising a little; "and I beg to direct your attention to the perfectly polite terms in which I have made my request. I call it a request . . ."

"Call it what you please," said the old lady; "it gets no answer out of me!"

"I say, I call it a request at present, and from a desire to show respect . . ."

"Hugo," flashed Mrs Lemesurier, "if there's one more word . . ." Her mouth went awry on her handsome old face, and she [116] took a pinch of snuff with animosity.

"I will not be intimidated," returned Hugo. "I won't live in a house with mysteries. Here is a fellow who comes and goes . . . without a name, with no ostensible business . . . and whenever he comes, he leaves you in the devil's temper. It's not decent; it makes the servants talk; it's what no proper son would tolerate; and I'll have an end to it, or know the reason why."

"Who are *you*?" she cried. "What have you to do here? What's your position that you stamp your foot at me? You're a beggar; you live here on common sufferance like Heics. I put up with you . . . God knows how. And if you don't like me, you may bundle and go!"

"You speak to me so?" said Hugo, "to my father's son."

"Your father was a gentleman; he knew how to conduct himself with ladies!" she retorted. "As for you, Hugo Lemesurier, you've made a fine exhibition of yourself . . . I'd have been ashamed to do it, even before Heics! . . . you're as prying as a housemaid and as rude as a common fiddler. Ah!" she went on, "many a time they told me what trouble I should have with you, and I was too blind to see; but it's years since I've known you in and out; it's years since I wore mourning for all I hoped of you . . . A dull, waspish fellow, and selfish as carrion!" – (This was the height of the wave; the old lady [117] had fired her great guns, her spirit was relieved; and she began to expand onto more general considerations; and by that process, in the ordinary course of these disputes, she might be expected to regain composure rapidly and forget the whole matter before tea.) – "In my time," she went on, "young men were no better than they should have been . . . I daresay that . . . they were always taking too much port and philandering with the maids . . . but at least they had manners and wit. They said good things. You never said one in your life, Hugo Lemesurier, and you'll go to the grave before you do. There was Charlie Cockburn . . . ah, dear me, that was a lad! often I danced with him! Heics, do you remember Charlie?"

"Met him in eighteen hundred and thirty six," returned the Major. Doosid facetious fellow."

"Ah," pursued Mrs Lemesurier. "Ah, that he was! Well, he had been staying at Minewells. . . . But now I think the point of the story is a little too broad for a lady; you can get Carment to tell it you the next time he's here, Heics; ask him for the story of Charlie Cockburn's *splore*; I'll warrant he has not forgotten it. He was a clever, ready lad, Charlie Cockburn, and a great hand at a nickname. There was my dear, good, dead man . . . that's your father, Hugo Lemesurier" (there were tears glistening in her eyes) . . . "well, Charlie called him the [118] Dancing Bear. The Dancing Bear! Did you ever hear the like? The dear man's legs were too thick, you know . . . like Hugo's . . . and he had a vile temper when he was put out, and used to dance . . . as I've seen Hugo."

To any mere spectator, there would have been something pretty and touching in this fidelity of the old lady, as she recalled the absurd peculiarities of her dead husband, and recalled them with unmingled sorrow for his departure. But Hugo was already smothering with rage; and he shared himself in every blow.

"Madam," he cried, "you may insult me to your heart's content; but since you choose to insult my father, I shall leave this house at once."

"By all means," said Mrs Lemesurier, and she rang the bell.

There was a pause, Mrs Lemesurier sitting upright with her nose in the air, Hugo walking viciously to and fro, and the Major once more culling flowers of memory in the garden of the "Army List"; and then Thomson appeared.

"Thomson," said the old lady, in thrilling tones, "you will pack up Mr Hugo Lemesurier's valise, and be sure and don't forget his Bible, and take it to the inn."

The servant bowed, and retired to do as he was told, with perfect, commonplace simplicity; for Hugo not infrequently seceded to the *Mons Sacer* of the village inn. [119] It was no unusual result of a dispute. After a day or two, he would drift back again, no one quite knew how; and the quarrel was tacitly made up.

"And now, Hugo Lemesurier," concluded the old lady, "there is no sense in your waiting here. Thomson will bring down your things. Go, and a better heart to you, and mind and read your chapter."

Hugo retired without a word.

"All this comes of the decline of religion, Heics," said Mrs Lemesurier to the Major as soon as they were alone. "There's that Hugo . . . no more minds the fifth commandment! But he's a fine lad, if he had ballast, and a better temper, and religion. They believe nothing now-a-days. There's nobody but you and me, Heics, left to believe the Christian religion: a pair of old fools like you and me!"

"I never was exactly religious," said the Major.

"No, no more was I," added she; "but I hope I have an interest with God for all that. I read my chapter night and morning, and say my prayers . . . so do you, Heics; don't you?"

"Ye-es," replied the Major, trying to remember when he had said them last.

"And then I believe. O, I've read their books! Colenso . . . a black man! . . . and what not. But I believe."

"I remember in May . . . no, it was June . . . eighteen hundred and sixty-two, meeting a fellow at Buxton . . . he had a beard [120]. . . and he told me all about Joshua stopping the sun and the moon; and, egad, it appears the fellow couldn't have done it! He couldn't have stopped them . . . don't you understand? . . . because of science. Doosid Ingenious!"

"Heics," cried Mrs Lemesurier, in a startling, nasal voice, "do you mean to tell me you disbelieve a miracle?"

"No," cried the Major, to whom this view of his position was both novel and alarming. "No, no," he added, "I believe in miracles of course; but that fellow stopping the sun and moon was a . . . most extr'or'nary thing!"

"That's what a miracle is: an exercise of faith."

"O I hate infidels of course, and radicals; egad, I hate them worse than Napoleon Buonaparty!"

"That's right," said she, taking a pinch of snuff. "The spread of these opinions is incredible. The youth of the country is undermined; lads not out of their teens . . . and what they call girls, now-a-days . . . all thinkers, by their way! This very day . . ."

Mrs Lemesurier paused; an unpleasant reflection had evidently just occurred to her, and her brow contracted. She rang the bell, and asked if Mr Hugo was already gone.

He had been gone some minutes, she was told.

Thereupon she sat silent for a while with a concerned and [121] thoughtful aspect; and then waking up suddenly from this meditation, "Heics," she said, "what was the meaning of Hugo's insolence this evening?"

"He was riled about that fellow," said the Major.

"How?"

"Well, it's a riling thing, don't you understand?"

"And he consulted you, I suppose?"

"Yes, he asked me what I thought."

"A precious couple!" ejaculated Mrs Lemesurier. "And what did you think . . . if that's a fair question?"

"I thought it was a doosid extr'or'nary thing," said the Major.

"I think you're an old wife," retorted Mrs Lemesurier, and she ordered him off to the smoking room.

Chapter IV

Strange Nocturnal Adventures of Hugo Lemesurier

The inn in the village was comfortable enough, for it was a headquarters in the amateur salmon fishery; and it boasted a smoking room, a waiter in dress clothes and a very remarkable scale of charges. To the smoking room, after having briefly announced his arrival at the bar, Hugo made his way. There was but one occupant, Ralph Blackburn, sitting abstractedly in an arm chair, and whistling in a key to which [122] another was hanging by a string. He looked up with a start and, seeing Hugo, rather guiltily pocketed the keys. These two men had never interchanged speech up to that hour; but they knew each other by sight, or by report, and the countenance of each betrayed the knowledge.

Hugo took hold of the back of a chair, and leaning over it in an aggressive attitude, wished Blackburn a fierce "Good evening, sir."

"Good evening," replied the Prophet.

"I am pleased to meet you," continued the other. "I presume you know my name."

"Pardon me," answered Blackburn with a smile. "I do not see the grounds of your presumption."

"Very well, then. I will tell it you. I am Hugo Lemesurier."

"I am glad to hear it," replied Blackburn.

"Why are you glad to hear it? Do you mean anything offensive?" snapped Hugo.

"These phrases are for the adornment of life," returned Blackburn, "not for philosophical accuracy. For instance

. . . you assured me of your pleasure at seeing me; now, I judge by your manner . . . and I fancy the expression was rather negligently used. Yet I suspect you of no offensive meaning."

"I *was* pleased to meet you, Mr . . . you have not yet told me your name, I believe?"

"No," said Blackburn. "I have not. There can be no doubt about [123] it."

"Well."

"Well . . . what?"

"You mean you are not going to tell me?"

"Precisely," said Blackburn.

"I told you mine, sir!"

"You volunteered it," replied Blackburn, "I have not volunteered mine. What is more, this subject is distasteful to me; and I will be forced into no topic under heaven, nor by no man born. Mark me . . . I speak in serene good humour; I am miles from being angry; talk about the weather, or the war, or politics . . . or what you like, except myself . . . and you will not find me backward to reply."

"I was waiting for you there!" cried Hugo. "You admit, almost in so many words, that you have reasons for concealment which apply to me in particular. Do you think I'll sit down under that, sir? I demand an explanation."

"Mr Hugo Lemesurier," said Blackburn; "I think you forget yourself, and I am sure you will regret your petulancy. You might justly demand an explanation, if . . . mark me . . . if I sought to foist myself upon you. But let me remind you . . . that is not the case."

"You foist yourself upon my mother, sir!" cried Hugo.

"Hush!" said Blackburn.

"Hush? Ah! . . . I touch you there! Why hush?" [124]

"Because if I were you," said Blackburn stoutly. "I would not bandy my mother's name in a pot-house brawl of my own seeking. It's not wise; it's not generous; to my mind, it's not decent. You may leave your mother out, young man!"

"I'm in the wrong, am I?" snorted Hugo. "And what are you, sir? You sneak into my house when my back is turned; you eat at my table, though you daren't face me; you poison my mother's mind; and then . . . when I find you, and beard you, and ask a name to call you by . . . I'm a mere, common, pot-house aggressor, and my demand's a pot-house brawl! Is that wise? is that decent? . . . is it simply like a gentleman? You're fond of 'mark me' and 'remind you', and that. Now just mark me . . . and let me remind you . . . if I get my hands on you in my house, I'll take you by the shoulders and march you to the door."

"I hope you would never fail in courtesy to your mother's visitors in your mother's house," said Blackburn.

"You taunt me with my position?"

"O come now, Lemesurier . . . this is not fair," said Blackburn, standing up. "I have done nothing and said nothing, in all my life, that should offend you. I feel perfectly friendly, and if the occasion offered, I should be glad to help you. In the meantime . . . I do my best to leave you alone, and I'll trouble you to do the like by me." [125]

Hugo set his back against the door.

"You don't go out of this until I know your name," he said.

"I ask you to let me pass."

"Tell me your name!"

"You refuse to let me pass?"

"You refuse to tell me your name?"

Blackburn rang the bell.

"Now you see . . . this was very silly," he remarked. "If you care to have a countenance before the waiter when he comes, let me recommend you to sit down. Good night, Lemesurier." And then, the waiter having arrived, he added, "Will you kindly show me to my room?" . . . and was gone.

Hugo remained alone in a paroxysm. Twice he had been rebuffed; his mother had snubbed and insulted him; the anonymous stranger had reproved and outmanœuvred him. Nay, he had even called him a "young man": a pleasant condition in life, but a name which is a smarting and unanswerable insult: a thing which everyone would like to be but none can endure to be called.

"Young man!" thought Hugo. "He's not so much older than myself, confound him!"

He stayed there, grinding under his wrongs, aggravating them, mortifying himself by misrepresentations of his own defeat, the blood singing in his ears, the pulses jumping in his temples . . . in [126] that fever of spirit with which an ill-humoured, proud young donkey accepts the mixture of injustice and rebuke, which is nature's favourite discipline to man. He stayed there, chewing a cigar, stamping about the smoking room, throwing himself violently into chairs and rising up again with indignation; and for anything I know, he might have stayed there all night long, had it not occurred to him, in an evil moment, that he would be still more unhappy in the dark. The attraction of another torture was irresistible. Without a candle, he strode along the passage, entered his bedroom, and leaning his head against the window, looked out into the clear night without moving for perhaps an hour. What he saw, what he heard, he could not have told to save his life; blind indignation filled him, soul and body; he had supped on insult. He had kicked off his boots but he made no more progress with undressing; for bed was hateful to him, and sleep out of the question.

About the end of the hour, however, the noise of a window opening fell upon his ear; he started and stepped back; and next moment the figure of Blackburn crossed, with brisk steps, the gravel space before the inn and disappeared in the direction of Tufto Castle.

Hugo's breath returned to him in a low cry. Surprise and hope cleared his senses of their previous torpor; and his spirit returned. What was the man about? On what midnight business, did he steal abroad? Something shameful, something criminal, [127] beyond a doubt.

"I have him now," thought Hugo. "I have him and can break him like a rush!" And without waiting to put on his boots, as he was, in evening dress and stocking-soles, he threw up the window, leaped out and followed in the track of the unconscious Prophet.

It was chill; a few thin, glimmering clouds flew high up in heaven across the stars; and a wind blew steadily and filled the air with a murmuring of trees and grass. Blackburn walked sharply, whistling in an undertone as he went, and kept his hands in the pockets of his trousers. He passed the gates of Tufto and began to ascend the road, skirting the park walls and looking behind him with brief suspicious glances; but Hugo, rather by fortune than by any skill of his own, continued to follow unperceived. On one point, the two were equal; for Blackburn was shod with some soft slippers, probably of list, which deadened the sound of his footfalls; while his pursuer was almost as well off in a pair of woollen stockings.

At an angle of the wall, the Prophet paused. Hugo well knew the spot; the kitchen road which had hitherto been following the line of the wall, here turned aside and began to cross the park in a wide curve towards the back door of Tufto Castle. Blackburn threw his hat upon the ground and drew something from his [128] pocket. Hugo, ensconced behind a roadside tree, was witness to some strange manœuvres, with the head bent forward and the hands busily engaged behind the neck; but when he next saw Blackburn's face, he could scarce repress a cry. It was black.

"A mask!" thought Hugo, and this new circumstance delighted him at heart. "A mask!" he reasoned. "Ah! the rogue."

Blackburn resumed his hat and searched, right and left, uphill and down dale, with his eyes. Then he stepped back and, in a twinkling, was across the wall.

Although Hugo had dimly expected this, it found him unprepared. For a brace of seconds, he stood at fault. Then, remembering the ground, he saw his advantage, ran some fifty paces higher up the road; and crossed the park wall into the skirts of the plantation.

The starlight, a little veiled by flying clouds, showed him the whole configuration of the park with an obscure distinctness. Tufto Castle, on its mount, stood black against the heavens; the rhododendron clumps and solitary forest trees were like blots upon the gray expanse of lawn; here and there the stream sparkled at a corner. Almost through the middle of his view, lay the kitchen road clearly outlined and strewn with twinkling gravel, bordered on the one hand by a mound and a thicket of rhododendrons and [129] on the other by steep lawns rising to the margin of the wood. Blackburn was walking with some precaution and without a sound to mark his progress, in the direction of the Castle.

Hugo drank in this nocturnal scene with eye and ear; the vast depth of heavens overhead, the grayness, the thin faraway hills, the sound of the wind running among the trees, the bubbling of the stream and a faint but awful rumour of the waterfall from higher up the glen. But his mind fixed itself upon the moving figure. There was his problem; and it was hard to solve. The kitchen road from this point, ran in one steady sweep to the rustic hedge behind the castle. That was Blackburn's path. But Hugo dared not pursue him in the open; he must keep in shelter; he must follow the margin of the pinewoods; and the pinewoods, here running down in promontories, there retreating in bays, drew, as it were, a deeply indented coastline across the dales and shelvings of the lawny slope. To follow this coastline, and at the same time keep alongside of Blackburn on the road, Hugo would have to run at his best pace; and running was no easy matter in a wood of young firtrees and under a strict necessity to silence.

He pulled himself together, and bent his faculties to the task. The trees kept getting in his way; the furzy undergrowth impeded him; here he must crouch, there leap. But [130] Hugo was active, enduring and adroit. It was not for nothing that he had stalked deer and followed otter hounds on foot. Moreover, the wind favoured him, for it blew in a steady gust stronger than usual, and set up a great surf-like noise among the woods; and thus against all odds, he managed to keep up with his quarry on the road.

Blackburn, on his part, continued to advance slowly, still casting comprehensive looks on every side. Whenever he lifted his face towards the woods, Hugo received a new shock. Instead of the familiar brightness of the human countenance, there was a dull, furry substance, absorbing the starlight and making a blot like the rhododendrons on the gray face of the park. It was as if the man had a back to his head all round; and this, as he continued to walk and look about him, gave a strange and chimerical aspect to his gait and figure.

So things continued, until Hugo reached the point where the path from the waterfall cut the woods in two. And here he paused; it was necessary to drop a little behind, before venturing to cross the open. But to his surprise, Blackburn paused at the same moment, and beat his hands together with a faint report. It was doubtless a signal; for immediately, out of the rhododendrons on the other side of the kitchen road, there arose a human figure. For one instant, Hugo supposed him to present his back; the next, [131] he had comprehended: this man, also, was masked. Only two or three words were exchanged, ere the figure once more disappeared among the rhododendrons whence it had arisen, and Blackburn resumed his advance towards Tufto Castle at a somewhat swifter pace.

In spite of his own heart, Hugo felt appalled. A damp covered his brow, and he looked eerily about him. The park was haunted by masks; might not the woods, also, be peopled with the like singular and daunting visitors? He felt himself surrounded, outnumbered, spied upon; and the masks powerfully affected his imagination. A domino in a bright ballroom is an easy phenomenon to confront; but it was a different matter in the clear, cold air and glimmering night: and when the masqueraders, upon some inscrutable design, were concealed among the woods and bushes of a highland park, the business took solemnity from its surroundings. Hugo might reason as he pleased; there was something not quite human in the neighbourhood of these face-less things; he felt a quaking pang at his heart; and stood hesitating on the margin of the clearing.

Then he remembered Blackburn still speeding towards the house; and his manhood came back at a bound.

Falling on his face, he dragged himself laboriously across the open alley of the path; and then forgetting all caution, [132] plunged headlong into the wood upon the other side and ran straight before him for the lowest point. A few paces from the edge, he stopped short with a stifled ejaculation. On the roadway far below him, and just in the jaws of the rustic bridge, four dark figures stood together in a cluster. There was not a face among them; all were masked. Hugo held his breath, and leaning with one hand against a tree, craned forward to observe their movements. One of the figures made a decisive gesture, and the group broke up and began to cross the bridge and ascend the hill towards the back court of Tufto Castle.

"Now for it!" thought Hugo. "What to do?"

And just at that instant of time, he was thrown heavily sideways on the ground, turned swiftly over on his back, and before he could utter a cry, a man's knees were impressed upon his chest and a man's hand was fastened on his throat. The shock was rude; and he must have lost hold upon the thread of his existence; for a moment after, he seemed to return from an incalculable distance, and found himself lying wide-spread upon the ground, his body sorely jarred, and another face-less masquerader crouching over him in the twilight of the woods.

"If you'll hold your tongue," said the mask, "I'll take my hand off your throat." [133]

Hugo nodded; his captor at once released him to the extent proposed; and there was another silence. Hugo looked up through the pines, and saw thin, luminous clouds blowing like moonlit steam across the stars of heaven, so high, so high above in the unscaleable azure that his head went round and round, and his sight failed him, and he sank into another sick and dizzy trance. From this he awoke once more to the claimant reality of the masquerader's knees.

"If I give you my word of honour," he gasped woefully, "not to stir . . . to lie here flat on my back . . . for as long as you tell me . . . will you take your knees away?"

The other agreed, and crouched by him on the pine tassel ready for another spring.

But Hugo meditated no resistance; he felt worse and worse; and being one of those who are easily overcrowed by pain and sickness, a sudden black idea leaped upon him, and his heart expired.

"I am going to die," he moaned.

"My God!" exclaimed the mask, in tones of such profound and unaffected horror and alarm that even the suffering Hugo was affected. "Take some of this," he continued pushing the cup of his flask half filled with whiskey under Hugo's nose and at the same time not ungently raising his head. [134]

"Thank you," went Lemesurier with a dying sigh.

"I say, you know, look here," pleaded the other. "I'm powerful sorry about this. I didn't mean to hurt you, and I couldn't help it, could I? You shouldn't have come here you know."

"I shouldn't walk in my own park?" demanded Hugo, who felt better and perceived his masked assailant to be truly human.

O Ratcliffe! Ratcliffe! ran your mind upon Aunt Jane? Certainly, the position was too great a strain upon his intellectual manhood; he felt a sore need of counsel and moral support; and in the tremor of the moment, gave the single low whistle that should bring Turton to his side.

A light figure, mask on face, came brushing through the trees.

"What's wrong? Hillo, a prisoner of war!"

"He's the owner," whispered Ratcliffe, "and he says he's dying."

"Dying?" repeated Turton. "That's steep. Do you feel badly, sir?" he asked.

"I feel better," answered Hugo dryly.

"Any bones broken?"

"No, I think not."

"Well, then, what's the complaint? How are you dying?" [135]

"I am not dying," said Hugo crossly, for he was ashamed of his weakness and, like a boy as he was, decided to support the dignity of manhood and make a bold appearance even among people he despised. "I did not know what I was saying; I felt sick and shaken, and was hardly conscious."

"Pooh!" said Ratcliffe.

"You're a nice specimen for a bold buccaneer!" Turton thus reproached his feeble-minded fellow sentinel. "You're as soft as dough. If I couldn't be a little more international than that . . . why, hang me . . . I'd be a tutor in a clergyman's family! O Ratcliffe, Ratcliffe, you're weak . . . that's what's the matter with you."

"You'd have gone mad, if you'd been alone with him," retorted Ratcliffe.

"What do you mean to do with me?" demanded Hugo.

"That's it!" said Ratcliffe. "I don't know."

"We must keep you, gentle stranger, till the commodore returns," sang Turton. "But look here . . . let's be friendly . . . let's stick the captive against a tree, and finish the flask. A *fête champêtre* . . . under the moral and intelligent stars. We're a mixed company, but let's be men of the world . . . let's have the joy of garlands and deep goblets. *Vide* the works of Bohn [136] and the immortal dead."

In a twinkling, Hugo was propped against a fir tree, and the two masks were squatted on either hand. Turton, jubilating beyond measure in the absurdity of the position, prepared to do the honours of this unpremeditated feast. Filling some spirits into the cup and raising it towards heaven, he thus opened the proceedings:

"Sir – Holding the deep goblet in one hand, the young man of Baghdad addressed the Unknown Prince with great discretion of language, and after repeating an unprecedented quantity of Arabic verses, begged to have the honour of proposing his highly respectable good health and continued prosperity in his affairs. He then," pursued Turton after having drunk, "fainted several times in succession and lived happy ever afterwards. No, no . . . make yourself at home," he went on, ". . . drain the poisoned chalice . . . don't *gêner* yourself with Us: we're plain, god-fearing people; and we wouldn't harm a fly."

Hugo was by this time as bewildered as a moth among the constellations; this was not what he had been led to expect in life; it was not upon such principles as these, that he looked to see the universe conducted. He drained the whiskey with the air of one committing suicide; and then in a kind of despair "Who, *who* are you?" he implored.

"O no, we never mention it!" sang Turton. "And besides, [137] it's there that the sport comes in. Here we are . . . as happy as Pharaoh or Jeremy Bentham . . . we don't know each other from Adam . . . and we pass the deep goblet with a noble disregard for time, place and circumstance. This it is, O Unknown Potentate, to be Man in the Idea, Noumenal Man! Do you ever reflect, my young friend? Pause, pause in your wild career! Here you are in eternity, as sure as a gun. You're sitting on an idea in the middle of the Absolute! The world's a dream, And here are we, three noumena in a firwood . . . heavens, what glory! . . . who never saw each other before, and never wish to see each other again:

"O what bliss to be a noumenon!
O bid me live, and I will live
Your noumenon to be!"

"What, in the name of fortune, is a noumenon?" cried Hugo.

"No moral science?" asked the Redistributor in horror. "Life, without moral science, is bosh. However," he added, breaking off, "this is not convivial; it's bad form. For my own, I positively dwell among the highest abstractions of metaphysic. It's a solemn, cheerless, imposing destiny . . . but I bear up. And now, look here . . . this little gathering is pure, unmitigated *Arabian Nights*; let's accept the position and tell each other stories. Potentate, lead off." [138]

"What do you mean?" said Hugo. "A story? I will not."

"O come, that's not the way to begin. You ought to start with 'My father was a merchant in Balsorah.'"

"What nonsense you talk!" cried Hugo.

"Lord, have you no imagination?" retorted Turton, "Can't you rise to this colossal situation? All the world's a stage, confound you!"

"Never mind him," growled Ratcliffe. "He always talks nonsense; nobody understands him."

"*Et tu, Brute?* And you, you beast of the field?" cried the Redistributor.

"I say," said Hugo, "you seem rather an ass; . . . but you're not like thieves . . . what are you, once for all? and what are you doing in my park?"

"*Your* park?" cried Turton. "It's no more yours than mine."

Hugo had heard a little too much of this already. "What do you know of that?" he quavered.

"I know rattling well it isn't mine. If it was . . . but then, *ex hypothesi*, it can't be anybody's. Do you mean to say," he went on, rising in manner, that in the presence of the gigantic might and the insulting composure of these natural objects which surround us, you can talk of *you* and *yours*? You? what are you? I deny your [139] existence. I could suppress you . . . at least with the help of the beast of the field . . . like a mere hallucination. And you talk? Young man, young man, this is immoral!"

"Nonsense," returned Hugo. "The Park's mine, and you're interlopers, and I can prosecute you tomorrow."

"If you had any speculative intelligence, I could show you it wasn't yours in three ways. They're mutually destructive, but that doesn't count in Philosophy. The park is not yours, First, because it doesn't exist, Second, because it's God's, Third, as against me, because it's mine."

"I suppose that's why you're here," sneered Hugo.

"O no, I'm here because I choose."

"And I suppose that's why you wear a mask?"

"Suppose it was."

"Do you think that gentlemanly?"

"Look here," said Ratcliffe, "you draw it mild."

"Never mind him," corrected Turton: "he's a duffer."

"I'm a what?" cried Hugo, half leaping up.

"You'll be a dead body, if you don't sit still."

"You insult a man who's in your power? You're a coward. You won't fight me."

"No," said Turton, "I won't. I didn't mean to insult you. I'm as cheery as steam myself. But then you've no sense [140] of humour."

"Am I here of my own free will?"

"O come, I thought you disliked metaphysics."

"I'm in my own place, I tell you," cried Hugo beside himself. "And you'll see what comes of this."

"You needn't have drunk my whiskey," grumbled Ratcliffe.

Two whistles, the signal for a rally sounded close at hand; and next moment four masked figures, carrying a trunk with the greatest difficulty, appeared between the trees and entered the wood.

"A prisoner, commodore," said Turton, with a salute.

"A prisoner?" echoed Blackburn, with unmistakeable concern. He had plainly fallen his whole height at this intelligence. "Let me see him." And he stepped forward. "O, it's you!" he cried.

"Yes. You know me, and I know you. What have you there . . . thief?" hissed Hugo, pointing towards the trunk, which was only dimly visible in the obscurity. "You have robbed my house; you have robbed my mother. O by heaven!" he broke out, "you shall pick oakum for this . . . you and your crew . . . until your fingers ache!"

I will not deny that the Commonwealthers were cast down at this; I will admit on the other hand, that they saw all the colours of the rainbow in a moment; that this large and entertaining [141] existence of free men about upon the world, seemed suddenly to narrow in to the grimy excitement of a Court of Justice and the seclusion of a model jail: horrid transformation! But the calm demeanour of their chief reassured them. He, indeed, seemed totally unmoved by the prisoner's threats.

"That is not the question," he replied. "Is your watch going?"

"Do you want it?" asked Hugo with a sneer and holding it out.

"Not just now," returned Blackburn, with a smile. "My desires are moderate; I only want to know if it's going."

"Why so?"

"O, come now, don't let us make a fight of every word. Presently you will understand; and then it shall be yours to accept or refuse my proposal. Is the thing going?"

"Hang me, if I know what you're coming to! It is not."

"Well, it's twenty minutes past two. Oblige me by setting and winding it up . . . do just oblige me so far. Thanks. Now will you give me your word of honour to remain where you are . . . without disturbance, without seeking in any way to attract attention, as if you were one of the trees . . . until four? I will gladly trust your word."

"O yes," said Turton, "you may. He's quite a gent."

"Now, I begin to understand," said Hugo. "And suppose I [142] say, no?"

"I'll gag you and tie you to that tree, and send a note in the morning to your mother. Take your choice."

There was a long, sour struggle in Lemesurier's mind; and then, "Very well," he said. "You presume upon your numbers. I give my word of honour. But let there be no sort of misconception about the matter; for I'll have you all in the dock or die for it; that's my way. You," to Blackburn, "I know well enough. As for these two," indicating Turton and the Highway, "I can swear to their voices. And you may leave the rest to me . . . I'll run them down."

"You shall hear my voice, too, if you come to that," said Hardy quietly.

"And mine," said Strutt. "This is truly Roman," he added.

Urquhart was not moved, apparently, to say anything.

"Hadn't you better unmask while you're about it?" sneered Hugo. "No? Pack of cads!"

"Up with the swag, my merry men," cried Blackburn. "I follow in a moment." And as the rest marched deeper into the wood, he approached close to Hugo. "One word Lemesurier," said he. "I'm vexed this should have happened, and I hope my friends did nothing rude. But the great point [143] is for you. Do nothing . . . nothing, mind . . . until you've seen your mother. And remember . . . yours will be the loss."

And he followed the others and disappeared among the trees.

Hugo, who was absolutely upright and true to his word, sat him down beside the tree to wait for morning. The tone of Blackburn's last advice had impressed him; he felt little inclination to disobey; it was obvious that underneath all this, lay one of those mysteries which struck him as so undesirable a feature in the life of a country gentleman. Something undoubtedly; but what? What had been all this night's fantastic business around Tufto Castle? Why these masks, this stolen property, this irreconcilable mixture of violence and friendly conduct? And then the mask who spoke nonsense . . . what was he? sane or mad? a thief, a poet, a philosopher? Here were enough thoughts for one young and somewhat narrow head. And meantime the watch was beating seconds in his pocket like a thing of life, the wind was busy in the leaves, the stars stood constant overhead. Hugo shut his eyes to wonder; the covert of his eyelids was agreeable to all his senses; he thought more clearly, and still more clearly, and so clearly at last that he required to think no more, and past events defiled before his memory as by a law of nature; and he saw, without surprise, his mother give her [144] hand to Turton in the dance, and then the robbers all took off their masks to strains of lively music and one and all disclosed the face of Major Cunningham; and then the Major took a live noumenon out of his pocket and handed it, wrapped in a pocket handkerchief, to Hugo; and Hugo in his rage and indignation, started broad awake – and found that another of those great transformations which make up the ages had been carried forward in the theatre of heaven while he slept, and another day begun upon the turning world. He sprang to his feet, like a napping sentry, and looked at his watch. Six o'clock!

Chapter V.

The Dragons in Disorder

[rest of this page blank]

[145]

Explanatory Notes

Title Page The Hair Trunk >

A *trunk* is "a box, usually lined with paper or linen, and with a rounded top, for carrying clothes and other personal necessaries when travelling; originally covered with leather, now often of canvas, painted metal, etc." (*OED*). Horsehair was the most common covering of so-called hair trunks, which by mid-century seem to have been regarded as old-fashioned. In Dickens's *Hard Times* (1854), I, 6, Sissy Jupe, looking for her father, opens and shuts "a battered and mangy old hair trunk." A few years after RLS's *The Hair Trunk* was begun, Mark Twain in *A Tramp Abroad* (1880), ch. 48, writing up his European travels of 1878, has a long comic discussion of a painting that he calls "Bassano's immortal Hair Trunk" – this being, as he says later, Bassano's "Pope Alexander III and the Doge Ziani, the Conqueror of the Emperor Frederick Barbarossa" in the Doge's Palace, Venice. Making fun of art connoisseurs, Twain makes much of the artistic "treatment" of the trunk itself. Hair trunks seem to have been particularly favored for storage, as in the present instance.

Title Page *Sir, said Doctor Johnson, let us make a society.* >

RLS seems to have invented this remark. But he was devoted to Boswell and Johnson. Commenting on his activities now that he had become an Advocate entitled to plead cases before the Scottish Bar, RLS remarked to his friend Charles Baxter in November 1875: "I idle finely. I read Boswell's *Life of Johnson* [and many other works] . . . [and] walk about the Parliament House five forenoons a week, in wig and gown" (Letter 424). The following summer, about a year before he began *The Hair Trunk*, he remarked to Frances Sitwell that he was reading much history and also "Boswell, daily, by way of a Bible; I mean to read Boswell now until the day I die." He added that had also begun "[a] paper called 'A

Defence of Idlers' (which is really a defence of R. L. S.)" (9 July 1876, Letter 438). When that essay was published, as "An Apology for Idlers," in the *Cornhill Magazine*, July 1877 (*Virginibus Puerisque*, 1881), RLS used the following exchange from Boswell's *Life of Johnson* (1791), 26 October 1769, as the epigraph, forgetting or purposely omitting the first occurrence of the word *all* in the quotation:

> BOSWELL: We grow weary when idle.
> JOHNSON: That is, sir, because others being busy, we want company; but if we were [all] idle, there would be no growing weary: we should all entertain one another.

RLS's copy of the first one-volume edition (1848) of J. Wilson Croker's edition (1831) of Boswell's *Life of Johnson*, previously owned by his grandfather Lewis Balfour, was sold as Anderson II, 264, and appeared again in the C. Glidden Osborne sale, Sotheby's, 9-10 May 1949, part I, lot 3. In an essay written but not published during his lifetime, "The Ideal House" (1884), among "eternal books that never weary" RLS listed for the library "immortal Boswell sole among biographers."

Title Page Wo fehlt's nicht irgendwo auf dieser Welt? > Johann Wolfgang von Goethe (1749–1832), *Faust*, Part 2 (1832), Act 1, Scene 2. In the throne room of the Emperor, the various ministers of state complain that they have many burdens, much to labor under. Mephistopheles, as the fool, is asked what he needs and he says that everything is so nice in the domain of the Emperor that he wants for nothing. Pressed, he continues:

> Where isn't there something lacking on this earth?
> There it's this, there it's that, here what's lacking is cash.
> You don't pick money up right off the floor;
> But as deep as it's buried, a wise head can find it.
> Under ancient walls, inside thick veins of ore
> The gold to be had, minted as well as unminted!
> Who is it, you ask, will dig us up this treasure?
> A clever man using the mind that's his from Nature.
>
> - *Faust: Part Two*, trans. Martin Greenberg (1998), Act 1, Scene 2 (The Imperial Palace: Throne Room), lines 278–85

Wo fehlt's nicht irgendwo auf dieser Welt?
Dem dies, dem das, hier aber fehlt das Geld.
Vom Estrich zwar is es nicht aufzuraffen;
Doch Weisheit weiß das Tiefste herzuschaffen.
In Bergesadern, Mauergründen
Ist Gold gemünzt und ungemünzt zu finden,
Und fragt ihr mich, wer es zutage schafft:
Begabten Manns Natur- und Geisteskraft.
- *Faust*, ed. Ernst Merian-Genast (Basel: Verlag Birkhäuser, 1944), 287

RLS omits the third and fourth lines of this comment. RLS first visited Germany with his parents and a cousin on their way home from Mentone in May 1863, when he was twelve. He began learning German in 1865, when he was fourteen, from tutors in Torquay and in Edinburgh, and in July and August 1872 he spent a month in Germany, chiefly in Frankfurt, with Sir Walter Simpson, where they both spent much time developing their command of the language using the celebrated method of H. G. Ollendorff (1803–1865). Among Stevenson manuscript materials at the University of California-Santa Cruz is an unpublished transcription by RLS of the first line of the "Swan Song" from Part 2 of *Faust* ("Wundersam! auch Schwäne kommen") and RLS's 12-line English translation of the song, on pages formerly in a notebook. The handwriting is consistent with a date in the early 1870s; the translation may have been an exercise, or it may be a fair copy derived from a later translation project. In 1883, after the early death of one of his best friends, James Walter Ferrier, RLS recalled to Ferrier's sister that during the 1870s Ferrier had made "a pretty full translation of Schiller's *Aesthetic Letters*, which we read together, as well as the second part of *Faust*, in Gladstone Terrace, he helping me with the German. If nothing else is wanted with it, there is no keepsake I should more value than the MS of that translation. They were the best days I ever had with him, little dreaming all would so soon be over" (RLS to Elizabeth Anne Ferrier, 22 November 1833, Letter 1182). There is no indication that either of these translations survived, except perhaps in RLS's translation of the swan song.

1 in these days of Mr Spencer >
Herbert Spencer (1820–1903) was the great synthetic philosopher of the late-Victorian age, attempting (in the

words of F. C. S. Schiller writing in the 11th edition of the *Encyclopædia Britannica*) "to express in a sweeping general formula the belief in progress which pervaded his age, and to erect it into the supreme law of the universe as a whole."

> His labours coincided in time with the great development of biology under the stimulus of the Darwinian theory, and the sympathizers with the new views, feeling the need of a comprehensive survey of the world as a whole, very widely accepted Spencer's philosophy at its own valuation, both in England and, still more, in America. In spite of all this, however, his heroic attempt at a synthesis of all scientific knowledge could not but fall short of its aim.

When he was a student at the University of Edinburgh, RLS was for a time a great follower of Spencer – chiefly, it would appear, for the support that Spencer's philosophy seemed to give for an ethics that was independent of religion and that took account of modern science. His tutor in Classics and Philosophy during 1872 and 1873, Archibald Bisset, recalled that at that time of their acquaintance RLS had already read Spencer's *Principles of Psychology* (1855), *First Principles* (1862), and *Principles of Biology* (1864–1867). RLS cites Spencer's *Social Statics* (1851) in his essay "John Knox and His Relations to Women" (1874). To his friend and fellow member of the Speculative Society, James Walter Ferrier, RLS himself wrote on 23 November 1873 about a recent meeting: "I am reading Herbert Spencer just now very hard. I got over the fingers at the Spec., the other night. I proposed 'Have we any authority for the inspiration of the New Testament?' as the subject of debate" (Letter 114).
RLS's tutor in classics and philosophy Archibald Bisset also recalled an amusing conversation of the early 1870s between RLS and his father:

> Another time I was walking with father and son out towards Cramond, and the latter had a great deal to say in praise of Herbert Spencer's *Theory of Evolution*. At length, his father said, "I think, Louis, you've got Evolution on the brain. I wish you would define what the word means." "Well, here it is *verbatim*. Evolution is a continuous change from indefinite incoherent heterogeneity of structure and function through successive differentiations and integrations." "I think," said his father, with a merry twinkle in his eyes, "your friend Mr Herbert Spencer must be a very skilful writer of polysyllabic nonsense." (in Rosaline Masson, ed., *I Can Remember RLS*, 1922, 51–52)

RLS's father was much less cordial some years later, when RLS left for the United States without telling his parents, intending to marry – as he eventually did, on 19 May 1880 in San Francisco – Fanny Osbourne, an American woman with two children whom he had met in France. "I see nothing but destruction to himself as well as to all of us," RLS's father wrote to Sidney Colvin on 10 January 1880. "I lay all this at the door of Herbert Spencer. Unsettling a man's faith is indeed a *very* serious matter" (Letter 675).
Of the earlier period, RLS himself remarked twenty years later that Spencer's philosophy was probably less valuable than his intellectual honesty and tone of voice:

> Close upon the back of my discovery of Whitman, I came under the influence of Herbert Spencer. No more persuasive rabbi exists, and few better. How much of his vast structure will bear the touch of time, how much is clay and how much brass, it were too curious to inquire. But his words, if dry, are always manly and honest; there dwells in his pages a spirit of highly abstract joy, plucked naked like an algebraic symbol but still joyful; and the reader will find there a *caput-motuum* of piety, with little indeed of its loveliness, but with most of its essentials; and these two qualities make him a wholesome, as his intellectual vigour makes him a bracing, writer. I should be much of a hound if I lost my gratitude to Herbert Spencer. ("Books Which Have Influenced Me," 1894)

Nevertheless, in *The Hair Trunk* RLS consistently treats Spencer only as the ponderous spokesman for a kind of strenuous, secular high moral seriousness.

2 a place in a tripos > At Cambridge University, *tripos* is the name given to the formal university examinations that are required to earn honours degrees in mathematics, classics, theology, law, history, and other fields. The term is said to come from the fact or legend that at one time the examiner sat on a three-legged stool.

3 the Benthamite Angel of Prudence >
John Stuart Mill greatly regretted that the English philosopher Jeremy Bentham's *Deontology; or the Science of Morality* (1834) "ever saw the light of day" – as it did, edited from miscellaneous unfinished manuscripts, after Bentham's death, by his disciple John Bowring. In Mill's

opinion, Bentham (1748-1832) was, with Coleridge, one of the two Englishmen in the first third of the nineteenth century "to whom their country is indebted not only for the greater part of the important ideas which have been thrown into circulation among its thinking men in their time, but for a revolution in its general modes of thought and investigation." "The father of English innovation both in doctrines and in institutions, is Bentham: he is the great subversive, or, in the language of continental philosophers, the great critical, thinker of his age and country." But, says Mill, in *Deontology* Bentham turns his back on all of the larger questions to focus instead almost exclusively on personal behavior, "and that with the most pedantic minuteness, and on the *quid pro quo* principles which regulate trade" (John Stuart Mill, "Bentham," *London and Westminster Review*, August 1838, rpt. in his *Dissertations and Discussions: Political, Philosophical, and Historical*, 1859).

Bentham's self-proclaimed theme is "the alliance between interest and duty." Prudence, he says, consists of balancing the future against the present and making enlightened choices accordingly, and it will be his aim to show that "to a great extent ... the dictates of prudence prescribe the laws of effective benevolence. . . . A man who injures himself more than he benefits others by no means serves the cause of virtue, for he diminishes the [net] amount of happiness" (*Deontology*, *1*, 177). "Prudence is man's primary virtue. Nothing is gained to happiness if prudence loses more than benevolence wins" (*1*, 189–190).

3 came out a high Wrangler and was made a fellow of the college >

At Cambridge University, intending graduates who passed the tripos in mathematics were not divided into first, second, and third class Honours but were identified as wranglers and senior and junior optimes. Until the practice was abolished in 1907, the highest class, wranglers, were then further identified, in the rank order of their standing in the examinations, as senior wrangler, second wrangler, third wrangler, and so on.

4 Hardy >

RLS may have known the name of Thomas Hardy as the author of *Far From the Madding Crowd* serialized in the *Cornhill*

Magazine in 1874, the year of his own first contribution to the *Cornhill*, "Victor Hugo's Romances" (May 1874), and of *The Hand of Ethelberta* (*Cornhill*, 1875–1876) and *The Return of the Native* (*Belgravia*, 1878). But there is no evidence that he did, or that they were then personally acquainted. It is probably no more than a coincidence that RLS, almost ten years before they first met in 1886, gave the name Thomas Hardy to the mathematician in *The Hair Trunk*.

5 he never condescended to employ his y's and x's on a universe of less than half a dozen dimensions at the least > The mathematics that were needed to extend the vector algebra of complex numbers to geometries with more than two dimensions was developed in the 1840s by Sir William Rowan Hamilton (1805–1865) and extended in the 1860s and early 1870s by Peter Guthrie Tait (1831–1901) and William Kingdon Clifford (1845–1879). This extension of geometry into multiple – in Clifford's work, unlimited – dimensions proved to be crucial in such major scientific formulations as James Clerk Maxwell's equations describing electricity and magnetism, first presented fully in his *Treatise on Electricity and Magnetism* (1873), and in Albert Einstein's general theory of relativity thirty years later. See the note on *quaternions* below (49).

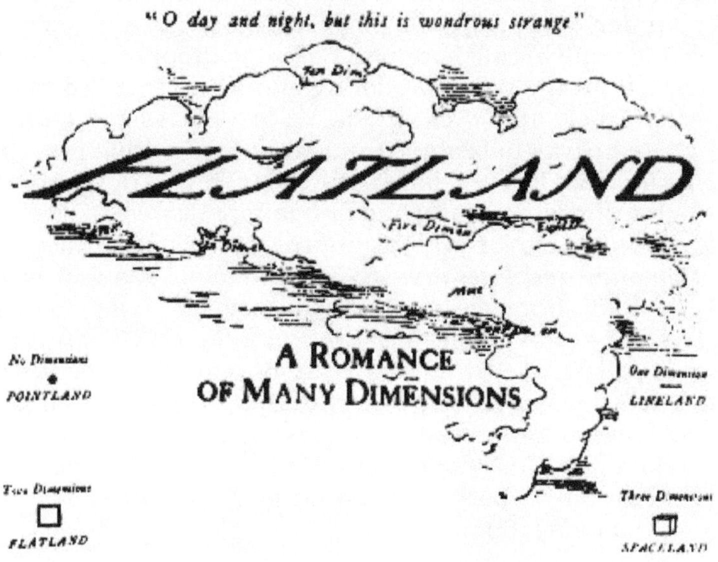

In 1884, only a few years after RLS was writing *The Hair Trunk*, Edwin Abbott (1838-1926), headmaster of the City of London School, and an Honours graduate of Cambridge University in mathematics, classics, and theology, published his sophisticated, amusing, and satirical exploration, *Flatland: A Romance of Many Dimensions. With Illustrations by the Author, A SQUARE.* The reviewer in *The Academy*, 8 November 1884, remarked that "on the whole, the idea is very cleverly worked out, with many happy satiric touches." In the dedication, the author hopes that, inspired by his own story, inhabitants of space "May aspire yet higher and higher / To the Secrets of Four Five or even Six Dimensions / Thereby contributing to the Enlargement of the Imagination / And the possible Development / Of that most rare and excellent Gift of Modesty / Among the Superior Races / Of Solid Humanity."

5 instead of following in the wake of Mr Swinburne and venting his passions in sanguinary, anapestic rhapsodies, > "I got *Atalanta in Calydon* yesterday," RLS wrote to his cousin Bob Stevenson in March 1868 about Swinburne's verse-drama published in 1865. "What a wonderful master of language and measure Swinburne is; and what a pity he is such a sensual brute. All the choruses are splendid: what a power, what cadence, what melody!" (Letter 40). RLS was then seventeen and in the midst of his first year at the University of Edinburgh, and immediately he began planning a verse drama, *Monmouth*, that he and his cousin would write in collaboration. Bob soon dropped out, but RLS completed the play that spring and summer at Edinburgh, Anstruther, and Wick, the latter two places being harbors where he was to begin learning civil engineering first-hand. As he noted years later describing his various youthful flights of poetry, prose, and drama, "in *Monmouth*, I reclined on the bosom of Mr. Swinburne" ("A College Magazine," *Memories and Portraits*, 1887). *Monmouth* was first printed (in 1928) from the manuscript now at Yale (Yale GEN MSS 664, Box 33, Folder 34, Beinecke 6587), but except that it is a melodramatic verse-drama, the indebtedness of RLS's *Monmouth* to Swinburne is, RLS's own comment notwithstanding, slight, as is his use elsewhere of "sanguinary, anapestic rhapsodies" of the sort made famous by Swinburne both in *Atalanta in Calydon* and in *Poems and Ballads* (1866).

5 a poem of some dimensions, from which the unoffending first letter of the alphabet was to be rigorously excluded >
Lipograms – works in which a certain letter is never used – have been written since Classical times. The Spanish writer Lope de Vega once wrote five stories, from each omitting one of the five vowels. For a concise survey, see Tony Augarde, *The Oxford Guide to Word Games* (1984).

5 Dick Turton, commonly called *Turpin,* >
The English highwayman Dick Turpin (1706–1739) was immortalized for Victorian readers in William Harrison Ainsworth's *Rookwood* (1839). Illustrated by George Cruikshank (*example below*), *Rookwood* is the source of the stirring but fictitious tale of Turpin's ride from London to York on his horse Black Bess.

Dick Turpin's story had countless repetitions and developments over the next fifty years, not the least of which was *Black Bess, or The Knight of the Road,* published in 254 weekly parts, 1863–1868, and at 2,028 pages, with a 688-page sequel, possibly the longest penny dreadful ever written.

RLS seems to have first encountered it when he was thirteen, during a holiday stay at Peebles in the summer of 1864, finding in a "deserted chamber" at Neidpath Castle "some half-a-dozen numbers" of the story, which he and his companions took away at once and read "in the shade of a contiguous fir-wood, lying on blaeberries" ("Popular Authors," *Scribner's* Magazine, July 1888; Thistle Edition, 1896). Attributed to Edward Viles, one of the many "giants of the dust" whom RLS celebrated in "Popular Authors," *Black Bess* was probably written at least partly by J. F. Smith, a mainstay of *Cassell's Illustrated Family Paper*, another favorite of RLS's during his childhood.

5 a poll degree >
Cambridge University slang for a "pass" degree, a degree without honours. Traditionally derived from the Greek οἱ πολλοί (*OED*).

6 Ratcliffe (nicknamed The Highway) >

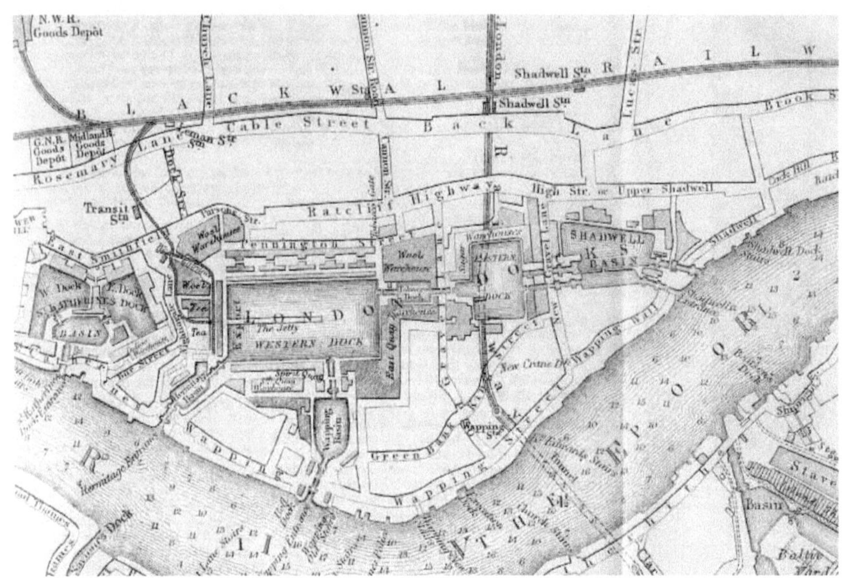

River Thames, with The Docks from Woolwich to The Tower, Longman and Company, 1882 [portion]. University of Texas Perry-Castañeda Library Map Collection: http://www.lib.utexas.edu/maps/historical/thames_river_1882.jpg

The Ratcliffe (or Ratcliff) Highway connecting Smithfield and Shadwell beside the London Docks in East London was notorious for its countless lodging houses, dance halls, and gin shops, all catering to sailors from around the world.

6 Bargee >
a man who has charge of a barge; one of the crew or towers of a barge (*OED*). "I am sure I would rather be a bargee than occupy any position under Heaven that required attendance at an office," RLS wrote in the chapter "On the Willebroek Canal" in *An Inland Voyage* (1878), a book written in late 1877 and early 1878 – at the same time as he was writing *The Hair Trunk* – from the notes of his canoe voyage in Belgium and France with Sir Walter Simpson in September 1876. RLS also recalls conversations during the voyage about a plan that he and Simpson and others put into practice during the following summer, in 1877: to purchased a barge to live on themselves and travel the canals of Europe. They named it after the legendary early medieval martyrdom of innocents associated with St. Ursula, the *Eleven Thousand Virgins of Cologne*, and hired a carpenter in Moret, where the Loing meets the Seine near Grez, to have it rehabilitated to their liking. In August RLS reported to his mother: "The barge is jolly; it is quite far on; and will soon be ready to camp out in" (Letter 479). But the enthusiasm and money ran out, and as RLS notes in his Dedication to *An Inland Voyage*, where he tells the whole story, the barge was eventually sold "by the indignant carpenter of Moret" along with the canoes from the earlier voyage. Will H. Low, who was to decorate the guest room of the barge, has an account of the scheme in his *A Chronicle of Friendships 1873–1900* (1908), 188–193.

6 Hartley Strutt >
Strutt may owe his surname to the English antiquarian Joseph Strutt (1749–1802). Strutt's illustrated account, *The Sports and Pastimes of the People of England; Including the Rural and Domestic Recreations, May Games, Mummeries, Shows, Processions, Pageants, and Pompous Spectacles, From the Earliest Period to the Present Time* (1810), was published in a new edition by Chatto and Windus in 1876, and there were several other reprints at about the same time.

7 underhung >
having the lower jaw projecting beyond the upper, or coming unusually far forward (*OED*).

8 basket-sticks >
basket-stick – a fencing stick with a wicker-work protection for the hand (*OED*); the word *single-sticks* is written on the facing page, in pencil, possibly as an alternative.

8 spelicans >
variant of *spillikins*, a game played with a heap of slips or small rods of wood, bone, or the like, the object being to pull off each by means of a hook without disturbing the rest. (*OED*).

9 Inchmagarrie >
The name is invented. There is no such island. The term *inch* comes from the Scots Gaelic *innis*, meaning *island*, and is common in Scottish place names.

10 seemed to have done pretty well everything and been pretty well everywhere from the bottom of a coalpit to the highest flight of Æronauts, within a trifle of our white-faced neighbour, the Moon >
The first balloon ascents were made in France and then in England in 1783, and by the following year the term *aeronaut* had appeared in print in England to describe the balloonists (*OED*). The great pioneer in Britain was Vincenzo (Vincent) Lunardi (1759-1806). RLS's copy of Lunardi's *An Account of Five Aerial Voyages in Scotland* (London, 1786) bound with Lunardi's pamphlet on his ascent at Liverpool, July 1785, was sold as Anderson II, 293. According to the auction catalogue it is annotated by RLS in pencil: "Very scarce: has all 3 plates." Offprints from the *Edinburgh Encyclopedia* (1788-1830) on "aeronautics" and "aerostation" with the signature of RLS's father were sold as Anderson I, 4. In Poe's "Unparalleled Adventures of One Hans Pfall" (1835) an ascent to the moon is accomplished by balloon, but no such ascents actually occurred or were attempted due to the extreme cold and lack of oxygen at very high altitudes. According to the article "aeronautics" in the 11th edition of the *Encyclopædia Britannica*, from 1862 to 1865, in England, James Glasher made twenty-eight

balloon ascents studying the earth's atmosphere, and in this he was followed in 1867 and 1868 by Camille Flammarion, who made "eight or nine ascents from Paris for scientific purposes," largely confirming Glaisher's results. *Travels in the Air* (London, 1871), translated and edited by Glaisher, describes these undertakings and those of others. Further scientific ascents were few, however, and rarely to very high altitudes. As the *Encyclopædia Britannica* noted: "On the 15th April 1875, H. T. Sivel, J. E. Crocé-Spinelli, and Gaston Tissandier ascended from Paris in the balloon 'Zenith,' and reached a height of 27,950 ft.; but only Tissandier came down alive, and his two companions were asphyxiated. This put an end to such attempts for a time." Low-altitude and tethered balloon ascents were a popular attraction for visitors to the 1867 and 1878 International Expositions in Paris, both of which RLS attended. Toward the end of his historical adventure novel *St. Ives*, unfinished at the time of his death in 1894, RLS introduces the character Byfield, a man described by another character as "an aëronaut. He apes the fame of a Lunardi, and is on the point of offering . . . the spectacle of an ascension" (ch. 25). "If I had known how I was to be connected with him in the immediate future," St. Ives remarks of their actual meeting, in the last chapter that Stevenson himself wrote, "I might have taken more pains" (ch. 30). Completing the novel in 1898, Arthur Quiller-Couch follows up on this remark by having St. Ives make good his escape from Edinburgh in Byfield's balloon the *Lunardi*.

11 Spiers and Pond's Amontillado >
During the 1860s and 1870s, F. W. Spiers (*ca.* 1832-1911) and Christopher Pond (1826–1881), Englishmen who had met in Australia, built a highly successful catering business for railways, theaters, and other public places. Clients included the South Eastern and the London, Chatham, and Dover Railways, as well as the Regent's Park Zoo and the Theatre Royal, Drury Lane. In 1874, Spiers and Pond opened the Criterion Restaurant and Theatre in Piccadilly Circus, London. The bar became a popular meeting place and, in fiction, was the place where Dr. Watson met the friend who introduced him to Sherlock Holmes in Arthur Conan Doyle's *A Study in Scarlet* (1887).

11 bawling P. C.'s >
P. C. – privy councillor –"In the United Kingdom: a body of advisers appointed by the sovereign" (*OED*).

14 the touching missionary hymn . . . "There every prospect pleases, and only man is vile." >
Bishop Reginald Heber (1783–1826), "From Greenland's Icy Mountains" – a hymn that RLS knew well from his mother's support of foreign missions.

> From Greenland's icy mountains, from India's coral strand;
> where Afric's sunny fountains roll down their golden sand:
> From many an ancient river, from many a palmy plain,
> they call us to deliver their land from error's chain.
> What though the spicy breezes blow soft o'er Java's isle;
> though every prospect pleases, and only man is vile?
> In vain with lavish kindness the gifts of God are strown;
> the heathen in his blindness bows down to wood and stone!
> Can we, whose souls are lighted with wisdom from on high,
> can we to those benighted the lamp of life deny?
> Salvation! O salvation! The joyful sound proclaim,
> till earth's remotest nation has learned Messiah's Name.
> Waft, waft, ye winds, his story, and you, ye waters, roll
> till, like a sea of glory, it spreads from pole to pole:
> till o'er our ransomed nature the Lamb for sinners slain,
> Redeemer, King, Creator, in bliss returns to reign.

17 tired of all these Bagmen and Bishops > *bagman* – "a commercial traveller, whose business it is to show samples and solicit orders on behalf of manufacturers, etc. (*Somewhat depreciative.*)" (*OED*).

18 spud > "A digging or weeding implement of the spade type, having a narrow chisel-shaped blade. . . . A digging fork with three broad prongs." The word *spud* was used also colloquially for *potato* in Scotland and Ireland. (*OED).*

18 *coup de tête* > a sensation, a startling and memorable action.

18 Rajah Brooke! >
In the words of the 11th edition of the *Encyclopædia Britannica* (1911), during visits to the islands of the Indian Archipelago in the 1830s the young Englishman James Brooke (1813–1868) was disheartened by the contrast of natural beauty and human savagery that he found there:

In 1830 he made a voyage to China, and during his passage among the islands of the Indian Archipelago, so rich in natural beauty, magnificence and fertility, but occupied by a population of savage tribes, continually at war with each other, and carrying on a system of piracy on a vast scale and with relentless ferocity, he conceived the great design of rescuing them from barbarism and bringing them within the pale of civilization.

James Brooke, First Rajah of Sarawak.
From: Sir Rodney Mundy, *Narrative of Events in Borneo and Celebes, Down to the Occupation of Labuan, from the Journals of James Brooke, Esq.* 2 vols. London: J. Murray, 1848. Vol. 1, facing title page. Ohio University Library Online Resource.

Brooke purchased and equipped a 140-ton yacht, the *Royalist*, and for three years trained its crew of twenty. On 27 October 1838, bound for Borneo, "he sailed from the Thames on his great adventure." Brooke helped put down a rebellion among the Dyak tribesmen and was rewarded with the title of Raja of Sarawak, a title that after some delays was confirmed in 1841.

During the next five years Raja Brooke was engaged in establishing his power, in making just reforms in administration, preparing a code of laws and introducing just and humane modes of dealing with the degraded subjects of his rule. But this was not all. He looked forward to the development of commerce as the most effective means of putting an end to the worst evils that afflicted the archipelago; and in order to make this possible, the way must first be cleared by the suppression, or a considerable diminution, of the prevailing piracy. . . . The pirates were attacked in their strongholds, they fought desperately, and the slaughter was immense. . . . So large was the number of natives, pirates and others, slain in these expeditions, that the "head-money" awarded by the British government to those who had taken part in them amounted to no less than £20,000. In October 1847 Raja Brooke returned to England, where he was well received by the government; and the corporation of London conferred on him the freedom of the city.

For the next twenty years, usually with the support of the British government, Brooke continued his rule in Sarawak and his relentless campaign to suppress piracy. In 1851, however, he was summoned home to answer "grave charges with respect to the operations in Borneo," especially his claiming excessive amounts of head-money. The charges were ultimately declared "not proven" but Brooke was soon afterwards relieved of his governorship of Labuan and the practice of paying head-money was abolished. Upon his death in 1860, he was succeeded as raja by one of his nephews.

19 Navigator Islands >
On 22 June 1875, a little less than two years before he began *The Hair Trunk*, RLS wrote to Frances Sitwell:

> Awfully nice man here tonight. Public servant – New Zealand. Telling us all about the South Sea Islands till I was sick with desire to go there; beautiful places, green forever; perfect climate; perfect shapes of men and women, with red flowers in their hair; nothing to do but study oratory and etiquette, sit in the sun, and pick up the fruits as they fall. Navigator's Islands is the place; absolute balm for the weary. (Letter 398; see also RLS to Elizabeth Fairchild, 1 September 1890, Letter 2249)

The visitor was William Seed (1827–1890), and in New Zealand he held the positions both of Secretary and Inspector of Customs and of Secretary to the Marine Department. In the latter position, Seed was the successor to RLS's mother's older brother James Melville Balfour (1831–1869), who had emigrated to New Zealand in 1863 and was drowned in 1869. On home leave in England after many years, Seed was in Edinburgh in 1875 to consult with RLS's father and uncle David, then the principals of the Stevenson civil engineering firm, on lighthouses and lighthouse administration. Seed stayed with RLS's parents, the discussions extended over several weeks and included a tour of Stevenson lighthouses, and in the following year there began a long business relationship in which the Stevenson firm provided improvements and support for lighthouses all over New Zealand. No doubt Seed was also anxious to see what support there might be for the annexation of Samoa by Britain, a plan that he and others in New Zealand had been urging for some time.

Seed had visited Samoa officially for three weeks in January 1872, and during his visit to Edinburgh in 1875, besides telling RLS about the islands, he left behind a copy of the complete 101-page official report surveying the whole of the South Pacific: *Papers relating to the South Sea Islands, their Natural Products, Trade Resources &c. &c.* (Wellington, 1874; Anderson I, 647). This is no doubt the "New Zealand Blue Book" that in *The Hair Trunk* Blackburn identifies as his main source of information on Samoa (43), and besides detailed statistical and agricultural information it includes Seed's own enthusiastic eight-page account of his visit in 1873. Commenting on the natives personally, Seed gives details that appear likewise in RLS's and Blackburn's accounts:

> The Samoan natives are a fine, tall, handsome race, of a light-brown colour. They are docile, truthful, and hospitable, and are very lively and vivacious. In conversation among themselves and in their intercourse with foreigners, they are exceedingly courteous and polite. They have different styles of salutation, corresponding with the social rank of the persons addressed. . . .
>
> Both men and women frequently wear flowers in their hair,–generally a single blossom of the beautiful scarlet Hybiscus, which is always found growing near their houses. Nature has supplied them so bountifully with food, in the shape of cocoa-nuts, bread-fruit, bananas, native chestnuts, and other wild fruits, and the taro yields them an abundant crop with so little cultivation, that they have no necessity to exert themselves much, and they are therefore little inclined to industry, and probably will never be induced to undertake steady labour of any kind. ("The Navigators Group. Report by Mr. Seed," 13 February 1872, *Appendices to the Journals of the House of Representatives of New Zealand,* 1874, A.-3A.22. Wellington City Libraries.)

RLS himself first arrived in Samoa on 7 December 1889 at the end of his second South Seas charter, on the trading schooner *Equator*. His plan then was to stay in Samoa only long enough to gather material for his book on the South Seas and then to continue by regular steamer to Australia and then to England. But in January 1890 he bought slightly more than 300 acres in the hills above Apia, made arrangements to have a small house built there, and at the end of September RLS and his wife Fanny began what he called their "laborious, destitute and delightful existence in the woods" at Vailima (RLS to Lloyd Osbourne, 10 October 1890, Letter 2258). This was in the small house later known as Pineapple Cottage, since demolished, not the much larger house known as Vailima that he built and added to in the years following and that still stands in Samoa.

19 "They have leprosy in the South Sea Islands, have they not?" inquired Hardy.
"Not in Navigator," replied Blackburn. "In the Sandwich group I believe they have something of the kind, but not in Navigator." >
Leprosy, now known as Hansen's Disease, was, and remained, all but unknown in Samoa. In Hawaii – the Sandwich Islands – the disease was known as early as the 1840s, but it was not a major problem until a sudden and rapid increase of cases in the 1860s and early 1870s. In 1866 the Hawaiian government established an isolation settlement on the island of Molokai, and by the end of the 1874 more than 1,100 persons "without distinction of rank or nationality" had been sent there, of whom about 700 were then living. Among other sources in Britain, RLS might have seen these and other comments on leprosy in Hawaii in the article by David Wedderburn, "Maoris and Kanakas," *Fortnightly Review*, 127 (June 1877), 798–800. It was to the settlement on Molokai that Father Damien Joseph De Veuster (1840–1889) came in 1873, but his work there was not well known until the mid-1880s. RLS's friend Charles Warren Stoddard (1843–1909), whom he first met in San Francisco toward the end of 1879 or early in 1880, visited the settlement in early October 1884 and in *The Lepers of Molokai* (1885) made much of the fact that Father Damien had now contracted the disease. RLS himself visited in May 1889, six weeks after Damien's death. His impassioned defense, *Father Damien: An Open Letter*

to the Reverend Doctor Hyde of Honolulu, was published in Sydney in March 1890. See Gavan Daws, *Shoal of Time: A History of the Hawaiian Islands* (1968), and *Holy Man: Father Damien of Molokai* (1973).

20 after a photograph by Sarony & Co >
Napoleon Sarony (1821–1896) was a flamboyant, eccentric, and popular New York photographer who also worked in Britain. He was noted for his striking portraits of actors and actresses including Adah Isaacs Menken (1865) and Edwin Booth (*ca.* 1875). Sarony popularized the cabinet-card format, 4 inches by 6½ inches. He was said to pay his sitters the highest fees of any photographer, and he sold thousands of copies of his most popular photographs. Sarah Bernhardt (1880), Lilly Langtry (1882), and Oscar Wilde (1882) were among his later subjects. See Barbara McCandless, "The Portrait Studio and the Celebrity," in Martha A. Sandweiss, ed., *Photography in Nineteenth-Century America* (1991), 63–71, and Ben L. Bassham, *The Theatrical Portraits of Napoleon Sarony* (1978).

21 It combines Dumas, and *The Coming Race*, and Herbert Spencer >
The Coming Race (1871) was published anonymously in 1871 and went through eight editions by 1873. Written by Edward Bulwer-Lytton (1803–1873), it is an early work of science fiction with elements of satire and social criticism. A young American finds a highly advanced civilization of human-like creatures called the Vril-ya living below the surface of the earth in complete harmony, equality, and happiness. They have done this by achieving (in the words of the narrator's principal guide) "the extinction of that strife and competition between individuals, which, no matter what forms of government they adopt, render the many subordinate to the few, destroy real liberty to the individual, whatever may be the nominal liberty of the state, and annul that calm of existence, without which, felicity, mental or bodily, cannot be attained" (ch. 15). They have also discovered and achieved mastery of a powerful "all-permeating agency" called vril.

21 ruffling >
making a great show, swaggering, proud (*OED*).

22 would have done honour to Prince Rupert's cavaliers >
Prince Rupert, Earl of Holderness and Duke of Cumberland (1619–1682), was the nephew of Charles I. He was defeated by Cromwell at the Battle of Marston Moor, near York (2 July 1644), and the decisive Battle of Naseby (14 June 1645) – in both instances largely because of the poor discipline of his officers and troops.

22 *rasade* or Willie-waucht >
a glassful, a big drink, as in the next-to-last verse of Burns's "Auld Lang Syne" (1788):

And there's a hand, my trusty fiere!
And gie's a hand o' thine!
And we'll tak a right guid-willie waught,
For auld lang syne.

24 for an old song >
for a song, a traditional phrase meaning *for practically nothing.* Not long before he began *The Hair Trunk*, RLS used the phrase as the title of his first published short story, "An Old Song," published anonymously in *London* in four weekly installments, 24 February–17 March 1877. Byron also uses the phrase: "The cost would be a trifle – an 'old song'" (*Don Juan* [1821], XVI, 59).

29 "You may smile," he said, turning upon them and smiting his bosom theatrically, "but there's something Here which Responds to these Orbs!" >
[unidentified]

30 had his pulses steadied and all his pegs screwed up, like those of Quarles' Theorbo, from notes higher. >
RLS echoes the second and third lines of "The Invocation" in Francis Quarles, *Emblems, Divine and Moral, Together with Hieroglyphicks of the Life of Man* (1634): "Scrue up the heightned pegs / Of thy Sublime Theoboroe foure notes higher." The *theorbo*, a large archlute or bass lute, is shown in the facing illustration. Years later, in Samoa, RLS twice echoed these same lines in letters – even mentioning Quarles by name. On 21 April 1893, writing to his mother of family matters, he says that in one case he plans to tell a polite lie, but that this may help him: "The need to be untrue might screw the pegs of my sublime theorbo one quarter

tone higher" (Letter 2561). On 10 June 1893 RLS described *The Ebb-Tide*, then just completed, as "a dreadful, grimy business in the third person; where the strain between a vilely realistic dialogue and a narrative style pitched about (in Quarles's phrase) 'four notes higher' than it should have been, has sown my head with grey hairs; or – if my head escaped, my heart has them" (RLS to Edmund Gosse, 10 June 1893, Letter 2585).

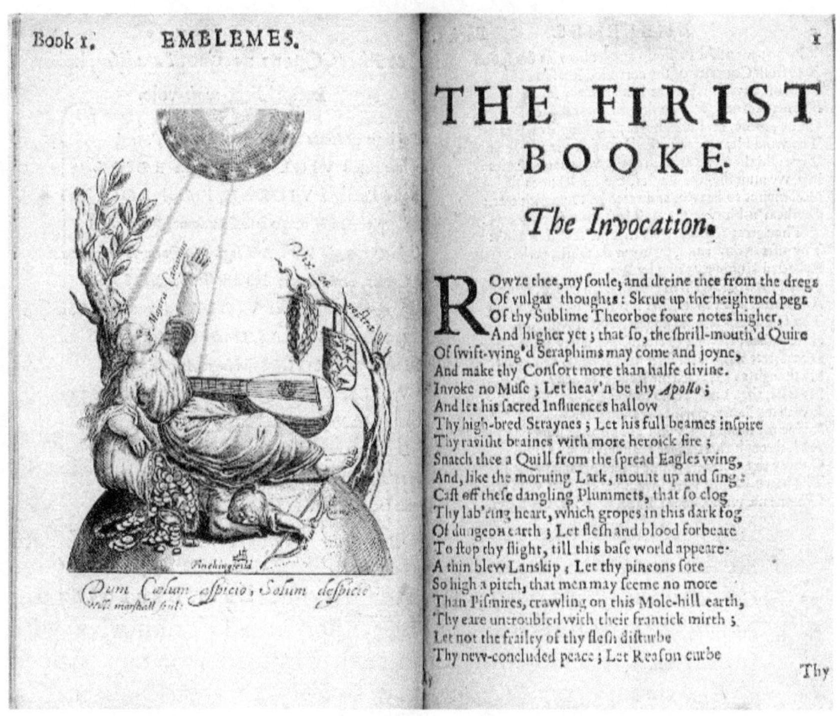

Book I. EMBLEMES.

1

THE FIRIST

BOOKE.

The Invocation.

ROwze thee, my soule, and dreine thee from the dregs
Of vulgar thoughts: Skrue up the heightned pegs
Of thy Sublime Theorboe foure notes higher,
And higher yet; that so, the shrill-mouth'd Quire
Of swift-wing'd Seraphims may come and joyne,
And make thy Consort more than halfe divine.
Invoke no Muse; Let heav'n be thy *Apollo*;
And let his sacred Influences hallow
Thy high-bred Straynes; Let his full beames inspire
Thy ravisht braines with more heroick fire;
Snatch thee a Quill from the spread Eagles wing,
And, like the morning Lark, mount up and sing:
Cast off these dangling Plummets, that so clog
Thy lab'ring heart, which gropes in this dark fog
Of dungeon earth; Let flesh and blood forbeare
To stop thy flight, till this base world appeare·
A thin blew Lanskip; Let thy pineons sore
So high a pitch, that men may seeme no more
Than Pismires, crawling on this Mole-hill earth,
Thy eare untroubled with their frantick mirth;
Let not the frailty of thy flesh disturbe
Thy new-concluded peace; Let Reason curbe

Thy

"The Invocation," Francis Quarles, *Emblems, Divine and Moral, Together with Hieroglyphicks of the Life of Man* (1634).
From: The English Emblem Book Project of the Penn State University Libraries' Electronic Text Center.
http://emblem.libraries.psu.edu/qu00_1.htm

34 mess >
"[a] serving of food; a course; a meal"(*OED*).

34 Harvey's Sauce >

"Sauces . . . were made commercially starting in the 1760s. One of the first big sellers was Harvey's Sauce, a mixture of wine, anchovies and both mushroom and walnut ketchups. It had been created by a London innkeeper named Peter Harvey, whose sister, Elizabeth Lazenby, sold her own sauce, Lazenby's Anchovy Essence. Eventually there were hundreds of sauces on the market, the most durable being Worcestershire (1838), which mixes anchovies with tamarind, vinegar and some real, Chinese-type soy sauce." – Charles Perry, "A Mystery Begins in the Backyard ... Barbecue sauce, ketchup, steak sauce – where do they come from?" Los Angeles *Times*, 31 July 2002.

34 the Sieyès of the Ideal Commonwealth >
Emmanuel Joseph Sieyès (1748–1836), best known as the Abbé Sieyès from his high position in the Church, was the most important constitutional theorist of the French revolution. His pamphlet *Qu'est-ce que le tiers état?* (1789), greatly helped the goal of convening of the National Assembly as a single body, where Sieyès then did much to shape the various constitutional declarations that were

its result, especially in the two or three years after 1789. Sieyès survived the decade of turmoil that followed, mostly by keeping many of his views to himself, but he continued to be closely involved with the government and with intrigues to change it. According to J. H. Rose writing in the 11th edition of the *Encyclopædia Britannica,* Sieyès was displeased with the constitution of 1795 and began to work secretly to replace it. "The death of Joubert at the battle of Novi, and the return of Bonaparte from Egypt marred his schemes; but ultimately he came to an understanding with the young general. . . . After the *coup d'etat* of Brumaire [9 November 1799], Sieyès produced the perfect constitution which he had long been planning, only to have it completely remodelled by Bonaparte." Sieyès not long afterwards retired from government service altogether.

35 Publicist >
"[a]n expert or writer on the law of nations or international law" (*OED*).

37 blague >
"pretentious falsehood, 'humbug' (*OED*).

37 the errors of the Phalanstères >
The French utopian philosopher Charles Fourier (1772–1837) promoted the idea of self-contained communities of 1,600 people living in specially constructed buildings called *phalanstères.* None was ever built in Europe, however, because Fourier was never able to raise the money that was needed for their construction.

39 the Beast of the Field Class >
beasts of the field is a common Biblical expression, for example in Psalms 8:7, 50:11, and Isaiah 56:8-10.

39 *connubium* >
connubium describes a marriage that is valid under Roman law in that it confers upon the children the rights of the father. "The right of entering into a valid civil marriage . . . is called the Jus Conubii. The Jus Conubii belonged only to Roman citizens; the cases in which it at any time existed between parties not both Roman citizens, were exceptions to the general rule. 'Roman men citizens,' says Ulpian

(*Fragm.* 5, 4, 11), 'have *connubium* with Roman women citizens (Romanae cives); but with Latinae and Peregrinae only in those cases where it has been permitted. With slaves there is no *connubium*'" – *A Dictionary of Greek and Roman Antiquities*, ed. William Smith *et al.* 3rd ed. 2 vols. (1890-1891), *1*, 138. See also the annotation of "*vi, clami vel precario*" (58).

42 Tea – the temperance Blue Ruin >
"*Blue Ruin.* Gin. Called *blue* from its tint, and *ruin* from its effects" (Brewer).

43 rigmarole >
"language or discourse characterized by elaboration or (excessive) length . . . rambling or incoherent speech or writing" (*OED*).

48 Monaco or Saxon >
By "Saxon" must be meant one of the many casinos then popular in Saxony and other regions in present-day Germany, but the exact reference is unclear. On 4 November 1890, RLS wrote to E. L. Burlingame, his principal contact at Scribner's, that he was thinking of writing some essays of reminiscence, for instance one that might draw on "my long experience of gambling places" (Letter 2269). He mentions Bad Homburg, which he visited with his parents in May 1863, when he was twelve, as well as Wiesbaden, Baden-Baden, and "old Monaco and new Monte Carlo." In the outline of an essay that he must have begun shortly thereafter, "Random Memories: An Onlooker in Hell," RLS adds Frankfurt and Leipzig, and in the opening paragraph he recalls vividly the to him unforgettable sound of the "continuous ringing of counted money on the tables of a gaming house" (quoted from the incomplete 2-page manuscript in the National Library of Scotland in Letter 2269, n. 3). On 12 February 1863, two months before their visit to Bad Homburg, the Stevensons, then staying in Mentone, had all gone over to Monaco to look at the new casino then just getting underway as a major enterprise thanks to the new concessionaire Vincent Blanc, formerly the concessionaire at Bad Homburg. The area was re-named Monte Carlo in 1866 and gained much from the completion of the railroad through from Nice to Ventimiglia in 1868. At the end of December 1873 RLS stayed ten days

in a quiet hotel there with Sidney Colvin but he would not visit the casino, from an abhorrence of gambling for money. An unpublished manuscript by RLS consisting of 9 folio leaves, 10 pages of text, contains the beginning of a story headed (or possibly titled) "Prologue: At Monte Carlo" (Yale GEN MSS 664, Box 33, Folder 796, Beinecke 6588). It describes the aimless doings of a young man called John Masters in the Casino at Monte Carlo. He meets a mother and daughter, the latter a heartless young girl called Emmeline. At the State University of New York, Buffalo, are three manuscript leaves by RLS formerly in a notebook probably from the early 1870s. The first is headed "The Prologue" and has the beginning of a story about a young man called John Carton. He is adrift in the world but there is no mention of a casino. The other two leaves have notes from Hobbes's *Leviathan*. This may be an earlier draft of the story that was resumed as "Prologue: At Monte Carlo." In a story written on the yacht *Casco* in 1888, "The Enchantress" (Yale GEN MSS 684, Box 9, Folder 159; first published, *Georgia Review*, Fall 1989) RLS used the name Emmeline and the same character type of a heartless young woman. No doubt indebted to the earlier story or stories, "The Enchantress" also begins with the hero losing the last of his money in a casino, this time at Royat.

49 Quaternions >
Quaternions are mathematical expressions that describe complex numbers with multiple dimensions. RLS could have read about them in Professor Peter Guthrie Tait's *An Elementary Treatise on Quaternions* (1867), in Tait's collaboration with Professor Philip Kelland, *Introduction to Quaternions, with Numerous Examples* (1873), or in Tait's article on the subject in the 9th edition of the *Encyclopædia Britannica* (1875) – the edition to which RLS himself contributed the entry on Béranger and prepared an essay on Burns, which was rejected.
During the four years that RLS studied engineering at the University of Edinburgh, November 1867-April 1871, Tait (1831-1901) was his professor in Natural Philosophy. Kelland (1808–1879) taught him mathematics during his first two years. "No man's education is complete or truly liberal who knew not Kelland," RLS remarked. "There were unutterable lessons in the mere sight of that frail old clerical

gentleman, lively as a boy, like a kind of fairy godfather, and keeping perfect order in his class by the spell of that very kindness. . . . Kelland's class I attended, once even gained there a certificate of merit, the only distinction of my University career" ("Some College Memories," *Memories and Portraits*, 1887). Tait was a close friend of RLS's father and often visited the Stevenson family home at 17 Heriot Row in Edinburgh. Beinecke 2590, at Yale, is a copy of Tait's *Lectures on Some Recent Advances in Physical Science with a Special Lecture on Force*, 2nd ed. (1876), inscribed by Tait to Thomas Stevenson.

Quaternions had been invented by the Irish mathematician Sir William Rowan Hamilton (1805–65) in 1843. As he wrote to Tait in 1868:

> To-morrow will be the 15th birthday of the Quaternions. They started into life, or light, full grown, on [Monday] the 16th of October, 1843, as I was walking with Lady Hamilton to Dublin, and came up to Brougham Bridge, which my boys have since called the Quaternion Bridge. That is to say, I then and there felt the galvanic circuit of thought close; and the sparks which fell from it were the *fundamental equations between i, j, k; exactly such* as I have used them ever since.

Tait's contribution was in working out the physical applications of quaternions, and his work directly benefited James Clerk Maxwell in developing the four partial differential equations describing electricity and magnetism (now known as Maxwell's equations) first presented in 1864 and developed fully in Maxwell's *Electricity and Magnetism* (1873). As Maxwell had written to William Thomson, later Lord Kelvin, in 1871:

> You should let the world know that the true source of mathematical methods as applicable to physics is to be found in the Proceedings of the Royal Society of Edinburgh. The volume- surface- and line-integrals of vectors and quaternions and their properties as in the course of being worked out by Tait is worth all that is going on in other seats of learning.

Also during the early 1870s, William Kingdon Clifford (1845–1879) extended Sir William Hamilton's insights in a more purely mathematical direction. Clifford held the chair of Mathematics and Mechanics at University College, London, and became a Fellow of the Royal Society in 1874. Although his mathematical work was not widely known or published in collected form until after his early death in 1879, Clifford was a brilliant public lecturer on general scientific topics, including the nature of perception, conscience, and thought. Stevenson knew him as a fellow-member of the Savile Club. See my comments in the Introduction.

50 why do half-pay captains go to Dinan and the Touraine? . . . why, we might perhaps retire at sixty . . . to New Cross! >
Until 1871, when the selling of commissions was made illegal, British army officers who wished to retire either sold their commissions or accepted a retainer of half their pay, in return for which they remained nominally still available for service. Dinan is in Brittany, on the river Rance. The Touraine region is in the Loire Valley. The appeal of both was cheap living and a mild climate. New Cross is in southeast London, near Greenwich, and was among the many suburbs developed during the last half of the nineteenth century.

50 pennywise hucksters in England >
huckstering - petty trafficking; sordid dealing; haggling (*OED*).

53 *cock-shot* >
"*colloq.* Anything stuck up as a convenient mark for missiles" (*OED*). In his essay "Talk and Talkers" (1882; *Memories and Portraits*, 1887) "Cockshot" is the name that RLS gives to his friend Professor Fleeming Jenkin.

54 Monte Cristo, Gold Bug, St. Mark in Facino Cane >
Alexandre Dumas, *Le Comte de Monte Cristo* (1844–1846); Edgar Allan Poe, "The Gold-Bug" (1843); Honoré de Balzac, "Facino Cane" (1836). Although *Le Vicomte de Bragellone* (1847–1850) was his favorite and was the subject of his essay "A Gossip on a Novel of Dumas'" (*Memories and Portraits*, 1887), RLS knew the other romances as well. In *Le comte de Monte-Cristo* (1844), Edmond Dantès uses the treasure hidden by Cardinal Spada on the island of Monte Cristo to right the wrongs of many years standing.
RLS writes of his debt to "The Gold-Bug" in his account of the genesis and writing of *Treasure Island*. The map was "the chief part of my plot," he says.

For instance, I had called an islet *Skeleton Island*, not knowing what I meant, seeking only for the immediate picturesque; and it was to justify this name that I broke into the gallery of Mr. Poe and stole Flint's pointer. ("My First Book: *Treasure Island*," 1894)

In both stories, the arrangement of a skeleton reveals the location of the treasure. RLS reviewed J. H. Ingram's edition, *The Works of Edgar Allan Poe* (1874–1875), in *The Academy*, 2 January 1875, but he said nothing about "The Gold-Bug" except to mention it as among only seven stories of Poe's that could be recommended without hesitation. Nor did he mark or underline anything in "The Gold-Bug" in his review copy, now in the New York Public Library.

Balzac's short sketch tells the story of an 82-year-old Italian musician named Facino Cane. Cane now lives in Paris and has been blind for more than fifty years. He says that he is descended from Marco Facino Cane, Prince of Varese, and that during a period of imprisonment in Venice he found in his cell an inscription, in Arabic, directing him to two loose blocks at the base of the cell wall that gave access to a secret passageway dug by a former prisoner. After a month's continued excavation, Cane breaks through into the Secret Treasury of the Venetian Republic – a storehouse of unbelievable wealth. He and his jailer made off with two thousand livres weight of gold as well as diamonds, Cane says, but unfortunately only the jailer knew the exact location of the cell and he has since died. Cane is confident, however, that if the narrator accompanies him to Venice they can find the treasure again. Cane himself dies not long after telling the story, with the Venice trip still unmade.

RLS's enthusiasm for Balzac can be dated as early as 28 March 1872, when he wrote to Charles Baxter of his pleasure reading the *Droll Stories* (Letter 96). According to an acquaintance of the time, during the early 1870s RLS was according to a female acquaintance at the time "fascinated by Balzac, steeped in Balzac," so much so that on one occasion he lectured her at great length the subject (Flora Masson, in Rosaline Masson, ed., *I Can Remember RLS*, 1922, 127–128). Nearly two dozen volumes of Balzac owned by RLS are at Yale, many of them marked. Hippolyte Taine's essay on Balzac in his *Nouveaux essais de Critique et d'histoire* (2nd ed., 1866; Beinecke 2588) is the only essay in the copy that RLS owned that is marked, with pencil lines in the margins beside many passages. Inside the back cover of RLS's copy of Edward Arber's reprint of James VI of Scotland's *The Essayes of a Prentise, in the Divine Art of Poesie* and *A Counterblaste to Tobacco* (1869; Robert Louis Stevenson Museum, St. Helena, California) is a list by RLS, probably of intended essays, no doubt made during the early or mid-1870s:

V. Hugo
W. Blake
Scott and Balzac.
M. Taine's ~~Art~~ Philosophy of Art.

58 "Herbert Spencer has incidentally exposed that prejudice," replied Hardy. "It is the young who ought to be considered . . . the coming generation who should be treated with respect." >
[unidentified]

58 *vi, clami vel precario* >
Justinian I (482–565), *Pandects*, Book XLIII, Title 17, Uti possidetis: *nec vi nec clami nec precario* – a legal formula in Roman law listing alternative ways (by violence, clandestinely, or under a precarious title) of gaining control of territory. Since the seventeenth century, the concept has been applied in international law to mandate the continuance of traditional or administrative boundaries at the end of a war or other conquest or when colonies are formed or dissolved. Having given up civil engineering after four years, RLS began law classes at the University of Edinburgh on 3 November 1871, studying Civil Law under Professor James Muirhead and Public Law under Professor James Lorimer. On the back of RLS's official class certificate, Lorimer wrote that RLS "[a]ttended very regularly, did the work of the department well, and obtained the third place in honours" (Anderson II, 566; see also RLS to Lorimer, 12 July 1875, Letter 404, requesting a duplicate certificate). Roman law is the foundation of Scottish law, and RLS's copy of *The Institutes of Justinian With English Introduction, Translation, and Notes by Thomas Collett Sandars, M.A.* (4th ed., 1869) is now held as Beinecke 2546; the advertisements are dated March 1871. To be admitted as an Advocate, RLS was required to write a short commentary, in Latin, on a title in Justinian. His was on *Pandects*, Book XLI, Title 9, on the distinction between "Pro Dote" and "Pro Suo" as these definitions apply to a person's state before and after

marriage (MS., National Library of Scotland). He passed his final examinations on 14 July 1875 and two days later was admitted Advocate, the equivalent of a barrister in England. Except for a couple of courtesy briefs, he never practiced.

60 where Alan Gregor found the tongs >
included as early as 1737 in Allan Ramsay's *A Collection of Scots Proverbs,* "Ye fand it where the Highland-man fand the tangs," and used in a song by Walter Scott, "Donald Caird's Come Again" (*Albyn's Anthology,* 1816; *The Gentleman's Magazine,* March 1818), "Donald Caird finds orra things / Where Allan Gregor fand the tings", where it is annotated as "at the fireside." The expression actually refers to theft. Andrew Harrison, ed., *Scottish Proverbs* ("New Edition," 1881), 147, glosses it as follows: "At the fireside. Said to those who having stolen something say they found it." Stevenson used the phrase again in *David Balfour / Catriona* (1893), ch. 8, as among the insulting comments made to David Balfour by Lieutenant Hector Duncansby, "a gawky, leering Highland boy": "'Tit you effer hear where Alan Grigor fand the tangs?" said he. / "I asked him what he could possibly mean, and he answered, with a heckling laugh, that he thought I must have found the poker in the same place and swallowed it."

60 *soi-disant* >
self-styled, would-be.

61 a thirst that from the soul dost rise >
Ben Jonson (1573–1637), "To Celia" ("Drink to me, only, with thine eyes").

63 'Varsity Boat >
University Boat. Both *'varsity* and *varsity* are short terms for *university.* First held at Henley-on-Thames in 1829, the Oxford and Cambridge Boat Race has been held since 1845 on the Thames between Putney and Mortlake, generally in late March, annually since 1856 except for the war years in the twentieth century. Huge crowds of spectators line the riverside and the bridges.

64 Balzac's conspiracy of thirteen >
L'Histoire des treize, three short novels characterized by

George Saintsbury as "a collection in the more extravagant romantic manner" (*Encyclopædia Britannica*, 11th ed.). These are *Ferragus, chef des Dévorants* (1833), *La duchesse de Langeais* (1833), and *La Fille aux yeux d'or* (1834–1835). According to Balzac's preface to *Ferragus*, the "thirteen" were members of a secret society supposedly known only to one another:

Thirteen men were banded together in Paris under the Empire, all imbued with one and the same sentiment, all gifted with sufficient energy to be faithful to the same thought, with sufficient honor among themselves never to betray one another even if their interests clashed; and sufficiently wily and politic to conceal the sacred ties that united them, sufficiently strong to maintain themselves above the law, bold enough to undertake all things, and fortunate enough to succeed, nearly always, in their undertakings; having run the greatest dangers, but keeping silence if defeated; inaccessible to fear; trembling neither before princes, nor executioners, not even before innocence; accepting each other for such as they were, without social prejudices, – criminals, no doubt, but certainly remarkable through certain of the qualities that make great men, and recruiting their number only among men of mark. That nothing might be lacking to the sombre and mysterious poesy of their history, these Thirteen men have remained to this day unknown; though all have realized the most chimerical ideas that the fantastic power falsely attributed to the Manfreds, the Fausts, and the Melmoths can suggest to the imagination. To-day, they are broken up, or, at least, dispersed; they have peaceably put their necks once more under the yoke of civil law, just as Morgan, that Achilles among pirates, transformed himself from a buccaneering scourge to a quiet colonist, and spent, without remorse, around his domestic hearth the millions gathered in blood by the lurid light of flames and slaughter. (trans. Katharine Prescott Wormeley, 1895)

64 Gaboriau's M Lecoq >
In his police novels of the 1860s, Émile Gaboriau (1832–73) created an important archetype of the modern detective story. His hero is a young policeman named Lecoq, who appears in *L'Affaire Lerouge* (1865-66), *Le crime d'Orcival* (1866), and *Monsieur Lecoq* (1868). In English translation, the second of these novels, under the title *The Orcival Murder*, was serialized as the *feuilleton* in the short-lived weekly *London*, 22 September 1877 through 1 June 1878. It was followed in this place by RLS's "Latter-Day Arabian Nights," seven linked stories first published in seventeen

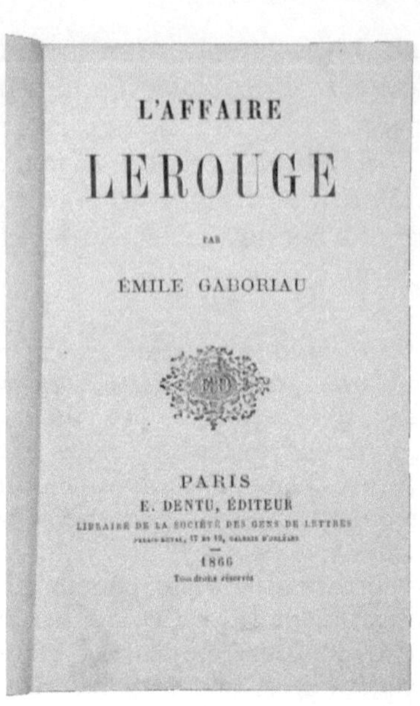

L'AFFAIRE

LEROUGE

ÉMILE GABORIAU

PARIS

E. DENTU, ÉDITEUR

LIBRAIRE DE LA SOCIÉTÉ DES GENS DE LETTRES

1866

Émile Gaboriau, L'Affair Lerouge. Paris: E. Dentu, 1866.
Bloomington by Gaslight: Sherlock Holmes in the Lilly Library
http://www.indiana.edu/~liblilly/holmes/

weekly installments in *London*, 8 June–26 October 1878, stories that were re-titled *New Arabian Nights* when they were collected, with others by RLS, in two volumes in 1882. Stevenson was a great fan of Gaboriau's, and as I have noted in the Introduction, in "The Story of the Young Man in Holy Orders" in "Latter-Day Arabian Nights" RLS has Prince Florizel recommend Gaboriau (not altogether seriously) as a source of knowledge of the world. Two copies of novels by Gaboriau owned by RLS are at Yale, both published in the 1870s, as are five by his rival and successor Fortuné Du Boisgobey, two published in the 1870s, the others in the 1880s. All are in French, in which language RLS was both fluent and literate from his early teens.

65 prigging >
"petty theft, pilfering" (*OED*).

66 The other four, like the followers of Cortez, "Looked at each other with a wild surmise." >
Keats, "On First Looking Into Chapman's Homer" (1816).

69 swell mobsman >
"The swell mobsmen were experts [in picking pockets] who mingled inconspicuously with the well-to-do people they robbed. Prosperous-looking, often 'square rigged' (dressed in a decorously conservative style), easy and leisurely in their bearing, these virtuosos . . . might take twenty or thirty pounds in a good afternoon" – Kellow Chesney, *The Victorian Underworld* (1970; Pelican Books, 1972), ch. 5, "Gonophs, Footpads, and The Swell Mob," 167. For the phrase "a member of the swell mob," *OED* cites, among others, Mayhew, 1862: "'Mobsmen', or those who plunder by manual dexterity."

70 "It is a woman's letter," said Urquhart. "I can see by the crossing." >
To send as much news at the least possible expense in postage, the practice of *crossing* letters arose. When a page was finished, it was rotated ninety degrees and the letter-writer continued, writing at a right angle to (across) what had been written already. That this was not done in business letters is probably why Urquhart concludes that the letter is a woman's.

70 mare's nest >
"*To find a mare's nest* is to make what you suppose to be a great discovery, but which turns out to be all moonshine" (Brewer).

72 "till the red flag by inches is torn from the mast" >
here attributed to Milton but actually from a song by William Kennedy, "The Pirate's Serenade", *Fitful Fancies* (Edinburgh: Oliver and Boyd, and London: Geo. B. Whittaker, 1827), 146-148. The first three of the five verses are:

> My boat's by the tower, my bark's in the bay,
> And both must be gone ere the dawn of the day;
> The moon's in her shroud, but to guide thee afar,
> On the deck of the daring's a love-lighted star;
> Then wake, lady! wake! I am waiting for thee,
> And this night, or never, my bride thou shalt be!
> Forgive my rough mood; unaccustomed to sue,
> I woo not, perchance, as your land-lovers woo;
> My voice has been tuned to the notes of the gun,
> That startle the deep when the combat's begun;

And heavy and hard is the grasp of a hand,
Whose glove has been, ever, the guard of a brand.
Yet think not of these, but, this moment, be mine,
And the plume of the proudest shall cower to thine;
A hundred shall serve thee, the best of the brave,
And the chief of a thousand shall kneel as thy slave;
Thou shalt rule as a queen, and thy empire shall last
Till the red flag, by inches, is torn from the mast.

A version set to music by John Thomson appeared almost immediately, also in 1827.
If he needed a reminder of it, RLS could have found the text in James Grant Wilson, *The Poets and Poetry of Scotland*, 2 vols. (1876), II, 216. He reviewed the first volume of this collection in the *Academy*, 12 February 1876; his review copy of this first volume, with many marked passages, is in the Robert Louis Stevenson Museum, St. Helena, California. His copy of the second volume was sold as Anderson I, 704. Stevenson quotes another line from "The Pirate's Serenade" in *The Ebb-Tide* (1894), Chapter VII, "The Pearl Fisher": "'For my voice has been tuned to the note of the gun, That startles the deep when the combat's begun,' quoted Attwater, with a smile, which instantly gave way to an air of funereal solemnity."

72 Bishopsgate Station >
Bishopsgate Station was the original (1840–1875) London terminus of the Great Eastern Railway, serving Cambridge and East Anglia. A new passenger station of this name was built adjacent to the original one in 1872, on the line to the new Liverpool Street Station nearby, then under construction; when the Liverpool Street Station became fully operational on 1 November 1875, the original Bishopsgate Station was converted to a Goods Depot. The new passenger station built in 1872 remained in service until it was destroyed by fire in 1964.

73 tricks of illumination of which Hassad is the only master >
Untraced and possibly invented by RLS, the reference is no doubt meant to bring to mind the *Arabian Nights* – stories that he greatly admired and had known since childhood. "Out of all the years of my life, I can recall but one home-coming to compare with these," he wrote about coming home with sheets for Skelt's juvenile drama when he was

a child. This was coming home to his grandfather the Rev. Lewis Balfour's home at Colinton Manse before or not long after his ninth birthday:

> . . . the night when I brought back with me the *Arabian Entertainments* in the fat, old, double-columned volume with the prints. I was just well into the story of the hunchback, I remember, when my clergyman-grandfather (a man we counted pretty stiff) came in behind me. I grew blind with terror. But instead of ordering the book away, he said he envied me. Ah, well he might! ("'A Penny Plain and Twopence Coloured,'" 1884; *Memories and Portraits*, 1887)

The two most popular English translations in the mid-nineteenth century were by the Rev. Edward Forster, with engravings from paintings by Robert Smirke (1802), and by Edward William Lane, illustrated from designs by William Harvey (1839–1841). RLS is probably remembering the one-volume edition of Forster's translation, xvi + 1032 pages with 600 engravings, London: Willoughby & Co, 1852–1854, Glasgow: Griffin & Co., 1854. Although it is not "double-columned" in the strict sense, such an impression is created by the narrower-than-usual pages (5 inches wide) and the fact that every page is enclosed in a single-rule border. The book is about 3 inches thick and about 10 inches high.

In "A Gossip on Romance" (1882; *Memories and Portraits*, 1887) RLS refers to a class of stories in which "character and drama [are] omitted or subordinated to romance." He continues:

> There is one book, for example, more generally loved than Shakespeare, that captivates in childhood and still delights in age – I mean the *Arabian Nights* – where you shall look in vain for moral or for intellectual interest. No human face or voice greets us among that wooden crowd of kings and genies, sorcerers and beggarmen. Adventure, on the most naked terms, furnishes forth the entertainment and is found enough.

In "The Ideal House" (1884), an essay written but not published during his lifetime, RLS listed for the library among "eternal books that never weary" the *Arabian Nights* "and kindred stories, in Weber's solemn volumes." This compilation consists of the *Arabian Nights* and two additional volumes of tales: *Tales of the East, Comprising the Most Popular Romances of Oriental Origin; and the Best*

Imitations by European Authors: With New Translations, and Additional Tales, Never Before Published, ed. Henry Weber, 3 vols., Edinburgh: J. Ballantyne and Co. 1812. Weber's compilation was a favorite of Sir Walter Scott's as well, and Weber also served for a time as Scott's amanuensis. Hassad's "tricks of illumination" are not described in any of Weber's additional tales, however. See also the notes on "the young man of Baghdad addressed the Unknown Prince" (137) and "a merchant in Balsorah" (139).

73 a sort of Birmingham majesty >
RLS may be thinking of the sweeping changes in local government – and, with them, major public works and slum clearances – made in pursuit of the so-called "civic gospel" in Birmingham during the late 1860s and 1870s, especially during the terms as mayor of Joseph Chamberlain (1836–1914) from 1873 to 1876. See Asa Briggs, "Birmingham: The Making of a Civic Gospel," ch. 5 in his *Victorian Cities* (1963; Pelican Books, 1968), 184–240.

74 one of those new mechanical pianos trampled through "Spring, Gentle Spring" >
Barrel-and-pin type mechanical devices for pressing down the keys of a piano or organ were common street entertainments by the 1870s, but RLS probably has in mind the players driven by continuous paper rolls of the type shown by the Glasgow-born American John McTammany (1845–1915) in St. Louis in July 1875 and by three other manufacturers at the Centennial Exposition in Philadelphia in 1876. Although McTammany filed a caveat for a patent in 1877, others were much more successful than he was in exploiting and developing the device over the next several years. Technical problems also had to be solved and the first fully automatic piano was not marketed until 1899.
"Spring! Gentle Spring!" was a very popular tune by Jules Rivière (1819–1900) from the spectacular operetta *Babil et Bijou,* which ran for eight months at Covent Garden in 1872. As Rivière himself remarked in his autobiography, *My Musical Life and Recollections* (1893): "*Spring! Gentle Spring!* became so popular everywhere, that when it got on all the street organs, not a few among my friends declared that they should owe me an eternal grudge for having produced it."

74 apron >
"the leather covering for the legs in a gig or other open carriage" (*OED*).

74 manicoloured >
seemingly an RLS coinage meaning *many-coloured.*

75 coup d'œil >
"A view; glance; prospect; effect of things in the mass" (Brewer).

75 the lusts of the flesh and the pride of life >
"For all that is in the world, the lust of the flesh, and the lust of the eyes, and the pride of life, is not of the Father, but is of the world" (1 John 2:16).

77 Chromolithographs, gaudy and egregious; coloured supplements to the illustrated papers representing young persons gathering apples and feeding poultry >
Lithography was invented during the late 1790s by Alois Senefelder (1771-1834) and was quickly developed by him as a practical commercial process to compete with engraving. Color lithographs were first printed in Paris in 1816 by the rival printers Lasteyrie and Engelmann, but even after much development the process was time-consuming and its use was mostly in costly scientific and art books. In 1837, however, Englemann and his son patented a successful commercial process that they called *chromolithographie*, a fore-runner of today's four-colour lithography. The invention of the steam-powered rotary press by Richard M. Hoe (1812-1886), and its use for high-speed commercial printing beginning in 1847, was followed in 1850 by Hoe's adaptation of the rotary press for chromolithography using the Englemann process. This made mass-production of chromolithographs easy and cheap, and by 1860 dozens of firms in England were producing colour labels, advertising posters, and reproductions of works of art done originally in other media. It was objected that compared to color lithography done by hand using multiple stones the results were garish – "gaudy and egregious" to use RLS's phrase – but *chromos*, as they were soon called, were immensely popular throughout the second half of the nineteenth

century, especially those depicting historical, foreign, and sentimental domestic scenes such as those that RLS mentions.

77 an original Manet in the last stage of impressionalism > RLS spent the winter of 1873–1874 at Mentone, on the French Riviera, and in April 1874, on his way home to Edinburgh, he spent three weeks in Paris visiting his cousin Bob, who was continuing his art studies there. On 15 April 1874, during RLS's stay, the first of the exhibitions by the artists who in their third exhibition of 1877 accepted the name impressionists opened at 35, Boulevard des Capucines. The exhibition ran for a month, but there is no indication that RLS or Bob attended.

Édouard Manet (1832-1883) did not have any paintings in the first impresssionist exhibition, but he did exhibit in the later ones and was at all times a major influence upon his younger contemporaries. RLS was much taken with Manet's work and wanted to buy Manet's painting of a young woman in a pink peignoir standing beside a parrot. Some years later, in a letter to his cousin Bob, 9 October 1883, he remarked about this painting: "by mere vivacity and variety of facture, the public may be cheated into admiration; Manet's cock and lady that I wanted to buy, is the game; or etching as a parallel for the best sort" (Letter 1158).

Manet's painting is now known as "Young Lady in 1866" and is in the Metropolitan Museum of Art, New York. It was first shown in the Salon of 1868, at which time one critic wrote of Manet that "he has borrowed the parrot from his friend Courbet and placed it on a perch next to a young woman in a pink peignoir. These realists are capable of anything!" Most critics ignored the subject, however, to ridicule Manet's "present vice . . . a sort of pantheism in which the head is esteemed no more than a slipper." After the Salon of 1868, the painting was bought from Manet by Durand-Ruel, but it does not seem to have been exhibited again until the sale by Ernest Hoschedé, Hôtel Drouot, Paris, June 6, 1878, no. 44, when it was titled "Femme au Perroquet" and sold for Fr 700 to Henri Hecht. As this was the day before RLS and Fleeming Jenkin left for Paris, where Jenkin was to be a juror in the International Exhibition, RLS acting as his secretary, he must have seen (and wished to buy) the painting privately some time before. Annotating

RLS's letter to his cousin Bob in 1883, Ernest Mehew notes: "In conversation with the artist John LaFarge at Vailima in October 1890, RLS took 'some credit for having recognised the value of Manet, the so-called impressionist, on his first sight of a painting by him' (La Farge, letter in *New York Times*, 30 December 1894)." But it remains unknown just when this might have been.
The term *impressionism* was first applied, in French, to the loosely-associated group of painters by a journalist reviewing the first exhibition, taking it from the title of Claude Monet's *Impression, Soleil levant.* The earliest instance in the *OED* illustrating the word *impressionism* in the artistic sense in English is eight years later, in *The Athenaeum*, 10 June 1882. Henry James is cited for the term *impressionist* in a comment on the 1876 exhibition ('Parisian Festivity', New York Tribune, 22 April 1876, rpt. Parisian Sketches, 1876). The term *impressionalist*, used of artists, is cited to the New York Nation, September 1876, but Stevenson's term *impressionalism* (possibly his own coinage) does not appear in the OED except in philosophical writings.

78 compresses >
compress – "*Surg[ery].* A soft mass of linen, lint or other material formed into a pad, which, by the aid of a bandage, can be made to press upon any part" (*OED*).

78 Mr Pater . . . and the works of Paul de St Victor >
In the essays themselves and in the "Preface" and "Conclusion" of the collection of his essays of the late 1860s and early 1870s titled *Studies in the History of the Renaissance* (1873), Walter Pater (1839-1894) articulated a view of art and literature – and of life – that prized above all the sensations and emotions stirred in the individual viewer or reader by the work itself. "Not the fruit of experience, but experience itself, is the end," he wrote in the "Conclusion" of the collection. "A counted number of pulses only is given to us of a variegated, dramatic life. How may we see in them all that is to be seen in them by the finest senses? How shall we pass most swiftly from point to point, and be present always at the focus where the greatest number of vital forces unite in their purest energy?" Pater's views were soon taken up, by Oscar Wilde among others, as the credo of an "aesthetic" approach to art and life – an approach that

was at the same time intense, passionate, and engaged, yet detached, composed, and indifferent.

Paul Bins, Comte de Saint-Victor (1827–1881), known as Paul de Saint-Victor, was a leading theatre, art, and literary critic in France from the 1850s until his death in 1881. He was noted especially for his ornate prose style. Saint-Victor was one of the three contributors (the others were Théophile Gautier and Arsène Houssaye) to the collection of essays, *Les dieux et les demi-dieux de la peinture* (1864). RLS's copy of Saint-Victor's collection, *Hommes et dieux, études d'histoire et de littérature* (1867; 4th ed., 1872) is at Yale. He may also have known the collection *Barbares et bandits, la Prusse et la Commune* (1872).

According to the 11th edition of the *Encyclopædia Britannica*, "Saint-Victor's critical faculty was considerable, though rather one-sided. He owed a good deal to Théophile Gautier, but he carried ornateness to a pitch far beyond Gautier's."

From: *Le Second Empire, 1851-1870*, sous la direction d'A. Dayot. Flammarion, n.d. Online: http://membres.lycos.fr/goncourt/IllustrBio/Album/stvictor.htm

78 to give Cook's tourists a sense of historical continuity and their own peculiar blessedness as Englishmen of the nineteenth century >

UK National Archives Learning Curve Exhibition. Victorian Britain: A Happy Nation? http://learningcurve.pro.gov.uk/victorianbritain/

In June 1841, Thomas Cook (1808-1892) organized the first railway trip for the general public, a special train from Leicester to Loughborough and back for 570 attendees at a temperance conference. The fare was 1s. It was a great success, and Cook soon branched out into organized pleasure excursions in the British Isles. His tours to the Crystal Palace Exhibition in 1851, for example, attracted 165,000 customers. By the mid-1860s Cook was arranging travel almost everywhere in Western Europe and, after the United States Civil War ended, to North America, beginning in 1866. By 1869, trips to Palestine were being offered. Trips to Egypt and the Nile began the following year with the appointment of Cook's son

John Mason Cook (1834–1899) as the government's manager of passenger traffic on the Nile. The younger Cook became a partner with his father in 1872, from which date the firm was known as Thos. Cook and Son.

78 The trick of looking upon things and apartments, as a whole >
RLS was much taken with the painter's technique of squinting to reduce the visibility of details and to highlight the whole. He begins an early essay, "Cockermouth and Keswick" (1871), as follows: "Very much as a painter half closes his eyes so that some salient unity may disengage itself from among the crowd of details, and what he sees may thus form itself into a whole; very much on the same principle, I may say, I allow a considerable lapse of time to intervene between any of my little journeyings and the attempt to chronicle them." His most memorable statement on the technique is in "A Humble Remonstrance" (1884), the essay that led to his friendship with Henry James:

> Man's one method, whether he reasons or creates, is to half-shut his eyes against the dazzle and confusion of reality. . . . . Life is monstrous, infinite, illogical, abrupt and poignant; a work of art, in comparison, is neat, finite, self-contained, rational, flowing and emasculate. . . . A proposition of geometry does not compete with life; and a proposition of geometry is a fair and luminous parallel for a work of art. Both are reasonable, both untrue to the crude fact; both inhere in nature, neither represents it. ("A Humble Remonstrance," 1884; *Memories and Portraits*, 1887)

79 with a crop for all corn >
willing to eat or to like everything indiscriminately; a Scottish proverbial expression.

79 billiard-marker >
"a person who marks the 'points' made by each player, and keeps account of the progress of the game" (*OED*).

79 chiffonier >
"[a] piece of furniture, consisting of a small cupboard with a top made so as to form a sideboard" (*OED*).

79 the Apollo Belvedere >
A Roman copy, in white marble, of a large statue of Apollo (7 ft 4 in high, 2.24 m) created by the Greek sculptor Leochares

between 350 and 325 B.C. It was found in present-day Italy in 1489 and was not long afterwards placed in the Vatican garden Cortile del Belvedere, where it remains today under the care of the Vatican Museums. It was greatly admired by the German art historian Johann Joachim Winckelmann (1717-1868), who wrote of it at length in his *Geschichte der Kunst des Alterthums* (1764) as among the finest expressions of classical art and culture – a view that continued throughout the nineteenth century. It was among the many works of art, later returned, that Napoleon captured and sent to Paris during his Italian campaigns.

80 “gentlem . . . Mr. Purray . . . expected ’ome” >
the spelling is probably intended to indicate the landlady’s pronunciation.

80 one of the meanest devices of modern art – a portable billiard table >
[unidentified]

81 about the time of the Handel Festival >

When the Great Exhibition closed in Hyde Park in October 1851, the Crystal Palace was taken apart and rebuilt on Sydenham Hill in Norwood, Kent, south of London. In 1857, in 1859 for the centenary of Handel's birth, and in late June every three years after that until 1926, the week-long "Triennial Handel Festival" was held at the rebuilt Crystal Palace, featuring performances of *The Messiah* (Monday), various selections (Wednesday), and *Israel in Egypt* (Friday), all with a huge organ, thousands of singers and orchestral musicians, and audiences normally around 20,000. A *carte de visite* souvenir of the 1865 festival boasts of "four thousand performers" and shows the organ, the orchestra, and the huge chorus.

Raymond Mander and Joe Mitchenson, eds., *Victorian and Edwardian Entertainment From Old Photographs* (1978), item 42.

On Monday 22 June 1874, during the month, 13 June – *ca.* 11 July, that they shared lodgings at Abernethy House, Mount Vernon, Hampstead (the house still stands, at the corner of Mt. Vernon and Holly Place, and is marked with a plaque) Stevenson and his friend Sidney Colvin attended the performance of the *Messiah* in the Fifth Triennial Handel Festival. See RLS to his mother, 23 June 1874, Letter 284:

"I was at the *Messiah* yesterday; the crowd was nasty." A month earlier, a writer in *The Athenæum*, 9 May 1874, 641, had looked forward enthusiastically to the event:

> The Sacred Harmonic Society will now be actively engaged in preparing for the Grand Handel Festival next June, in the Crystal Palace. Triennially, in the vast 'Sydenham Glass-House,' are the majestic strains of Handel heard with an executive of 4,000 artists, vocal and instrumental; and whatever may be the narrow-minded notions of those Handelians who think that the oratorios of the master-mind should be heard only with the limited number of singers and players of his day, there are stupendous effects achieved in the Palace execution which were never before dreamt of. If old Handel could rise from his grave to hear them, he would be as enthusiastic in his eulogy as Meyerbeer was when he listened to the choruses in the 'Israel in Egypt' with sensations of awe and delight, which he said he had never before experienced. [Meyerbeer attended the second Handel Festival in 1859.]

CRYSTAL PALACE.—HANDEL FESTIVAL WEEK.

CALENDAR for WEEK ending JUNE 27, 1874.

MONDAY, June 22.—First Day of Great Handel Festival.—Performance of the 'MESSIAH.'

TUESDAY, June 23.—Ordinary Attractions.

WEDNESDAY, June 24.—Second Day of Handel Festival.—SELECTIONS from 'SAUL,' 'ACIS and GALATEA,' 'UTRECHT JUBILATE,' &c.

THURSDAY, June 25.—Performance of SHAKSPEARE'S 'MUCH ADO ABOUT NOTHING.' GREAT FIREWORK DISPLAY by Messrs. C. T. Brock & Co. GARDEN FETE.

FRIDAY, June 26.—Last Day of Handel Festival.—'ISRAEL in EGYPT.'

SATURDAY, June 27.—Production of Verdi's Opera, 'BALLO in MASCHERA.' Madame Ida Gilliess-Corri and Miss Blanche Cole, Miss Lucy Franklein, Messrs. Nordbloem, Aynsley Cook, &c.

Monday, Wednesday, and Friday, 7s. 6d.; or by Admission Tickets purchased before each day, 5s. Tuesday and Thursday, 1s. Saturday, 2s. 6d. Guinea Season Tickets admit on every day during the week.

GREAT HANDEL FESTIVAL, MONDAY, WEDNESDAY, and FRIDAY next, June 22, 24, and 26. 4,000 Performers. Conductor, Sir MICHAEL COSTA. The Musical Arrangements under the Direction of the Sacred Harmonic Society.

GREAT HANDEL FESTIVAL.—Solo Artists: Mdlle. TITIENS, Madame Sinico, Madame Otto-Alvsleben, and Madame Lemmens-Sherrington; Madame Trebelli-Bettini and Madame Patey; Mr. Sims Reeves, Mr. Cummings, Mr. E. Lloyd, Mr. Kerr Kedge, and Mr. Vernon Rigby; Signor Foli, Signor Agnesi, and Mr. Santley. Solo Organist, Mr. W. T. Best; Organist, Mr. Willing.

GREAT HANDEL FESTIVAL.—MONDAY, June 22.—MESSIAH.—Mdlle. TITIENS, Madame Sinico, Madame Trebelli-Bettini, and Madame Patey; Mr. Sims Reeves, Mr. Kerr Gedge, and Mr. Vernon Rigby; Signor Agnesi and Mr. Santley. Orchestra and Chorus of 4,000 Performers. Conductor, SIR MICHAEL COSTA.

GREAT HANDEL FESTIVAL.—WEDNESDAY, June 24.—SELECTION from Handel's SACRED and SECULAR WORKS.—Mdlle. TITIENS, Madame Lemmens-Sherrington, Madame Trebelli-Bettini, and Madame Patey; Mr. Sims Reeves, Mr Cummings, Mr. Edward Lloyd, and Mr. Vernon Rigby; Signor Agnesi and Mr. Santley.—Selections from 'Saul,' 'Jephthah,' 'Susanna,' 'Utrecht Jubilate,' 'Acis and Galatea,' Ode to 'St. Cecilia's Day,' 'Alexander's Feast,' 'Semele,' 'Samson,' and 'Joshua.' Orchestra and Chorus of 4,000 Performers. Conductor, SIR MICHAEL COSTA.

GREAT HANDEL FESTIVAL.—FRIDAY, June 26.—ISRAEL IN EGYPT.—Madame LEMMENS-SHERRINGTON, Madame Otto-Alvsleben, and Madame Patey; Mr. Sims Reeves, Mr. Kerr Gedge, Signor Foli, and Mr. Santley. Orchestra and Chorus of 4,000 Performers. Conductor, SIR MICHAEL COSTA.

The Athenæum, 20 June 1874, 813.

The soloists in the Sixth Triennial Handel Festival, 25–29 June 1877, when RLS was beginning *The Hair Trunk*, included well-known opera stars such as Adelina Patti, Emma Albani, and Helen Lemmens-Sherrington. By 1883, the total had grown to 4,000 singers and 4,441 orchestral players. "[N]o composer has suffered so much from pious misinterpretation and the popular admiration of misleading externals," the 11th edition of the *Encyclopædia Britannica* grumbled in 1911, citing first among these "the burial of Handel's art beneath the 'mammoth' performances of the Handel Festivals at the Crystal Palace." A history of the first thirty years appeared as "The Handel Festival," *The Musical Times*, 1 July 1900, 461-463.

81 Doctor Kenealy looks a plenipotentiary every inch of him: so noble and so replete! >
Dr. Edward Vaughan Hyde Kenealy (1819-1880), an Irish-born barrister, Q. C., and bencher of Gray's Inn, was chief counsel to the so-called Tichborne Claimant in a criminal trial of unprecedented duration, 23 April 1873 – 28 February 1874. In an equally long civil trial, 10 May 1871 – 6 March 1872, it had been decided that the Claimant was not the long-lost Sir Roger Tichborne, heir to an immense fortune in Hampshire. In the criminal trial that followed, he was held to be in fact Arthur Orton, a butcher born in Wapping who had emigrated to Australia.
The affair had begun in 1865, with the answering of an advertisement placed on behalf of Tichborne's mother searching for her son, to the effect that her son was living in the remote village of Wagga Wagga, New South Wales, 240 miles from Sydney. In the words of Mark Twain, who followed the case avidly and eventually visited Wagga Wagga during a visit to Australia in 1895:

> It was out of the midst of his humble collection of sausages and tripe that he [the Tichborne Claimant] soared up into the zenith of notoriety and hung there in the wastes of space a time, with the telescopes of all nations leveled at him in unappeasable curiosity – curiosity as to which of the two long-missing persons he was: Arthur Orton, the mislaid roustabout of Wapping, or Sir Roger Tichborne, the lost heir of a name and estates as old as English history. We all know now, but not a dozen people knew then; and the dozen kept the mystery to themselves and allowed the most intricate and fascinating and marvelous real-life romance that has

ever been played upon the world's stage to unfold itself serenely, act by act, in a British court by the long and laborious processes of judicial development. (*Following the Equator*, 1897, ch. 15)

Almost ten years later, the Claimant was at length convicted of perjury and sentenced to fourteen years imprisonment. Kenealy's extreme behaviour during the criminal trial, abusing witnesses, the judge, and opposing counsel and insisting that his client was the victim of a conspiracy, led to his chastisement by the judge and words of reprimand even from the jury. He was, however, undaunted by his client's conviction or by his own disbarment soon afterwards, and during the rest of the 1870s Kenealy continued his campaign of abuse and advocacy. "[H]e sought to elevate his own and his client's grievances to the level of matters of national concern, founded the Magna Charta Association to avenge them, perambulated the country, delivering a characteristic lecture on the Tichborne trial (which was printed)," published a widely-circulated, scurrilous popular newspaper called *The Englishman* devoted to the cause, and stood successfully for Parliament, where he then introduced, without success, bills attempting to secure his client's claims (*DNB*).

Leslie Ward ("Spy"), "The Claimant's Counsel," in *Vanity Fair*, 1 November 1873.

Kenealy wore a full black beard, and he was caricatured by Leslie Ward ("Spy") as "The Claimant's Counsel" in *Vanity Fair*, 1 November 1873. In *The Hunting of the Snark* (1876), begun in 1874, Lewis Carroll clearly draws upon the affair for "The Barrister's Dream." He followed the criminal trial with interest and noted the verdict and sentence in his diary. He devised an anagram of Kenealy's name as "Ah! We dread an ugly knave!" and had to dissuade his brother from sending Kenealy a copy of *The Hunting of the Snark* (see *Letters*, I, 208, 247). In Henry Holiday's illustration, the Barrister is clearly Kenealy. See Martin Gardner, ed., *The Annotated Snark* (1962), 75–77, and the cartoon in *Punch*, 1875, vol. 68, p. 91, cited there. RLS's only mention of the affair, at the time, is to confess to Frances Sitwell "a malicious joy in the incarceration of Mr Whalley" (30 January 1874, Letter 229). Annotating this letter, Ernest Mehew explains that Whalley, "a Liberal MP for Peterborough and an ardent supporter of the Tichborne Claimant, was fined £250 for contempt of court on 23 January while the Tichborne trial was in progress. He refused to pay the fine and spent the night in prison; he was released the next day when his sister paid the fine." Twenty years later, RLS recalled a favourite phrase of Solicitor-General John Duke Coleridge in his cross-examination of the Tichborne Claimaint during the criminal trial, "would it surprise you to know" – a phrase that was "for a long time afterwards a catchword in London" – Douglas Woodruff, *The Tichborne Claimant: A Victorian Mystery* (1957), 198. RLS's comment was as follows: "And do you know – or I should rather say, can you believe – or (in the famous old Tichborne trial phrase) would you be surprised to learn, that all you have read of Vailima – or Subpriorsford, as I call it – is entirely false, and we have no ice machine, and no electric light, and no water supply but the cistern of heaven, and but one public room, and scarce a bedroom apiece?" (RLS to Elizabeth Fairchild, 25 March 1892, Letter 2395).

In the *DNB* account it is noted that in 1850, when he was twenty-nine, Kenealy "was prosecuted by the guardians of the West London Union for punishing with undue severity Edward Hyde, his natural son, aged 6 (*Morning Chronicle*, 13 May 1850)." There is no reason to think that RLS knew this, or that if he did, it was to make some oblique reference to Kenealy that he gave the same name to Mr. Hyde in *Strange Case of Dr. Jekyll and Mr. Hyde* (1886).

Detailed accounts, from a near-contemporary perspective, appear in the *Encyclopædia Britannica*, 11th ed., in the entries for Kenealy and for The Tichborne Claimant. Douglas Woodruff, *The Tichborne Claimant: A Victorian Mystery* (1957), and Rohan McWilliam, *The Tichborne Claimant: A Victorian Sensation* (2007), are detailed modern accounts. Michael Roe, *Kenealy and the Tichborne Cause: A Study in Mid-Victorian Populism* (1974), discusses the great popular sentiment in favour of the Claimant during and after the trials.

81 affable archangel >
Milton, *Paradise Lost*, VII.41, describing the archangel Raphael.

82 Jack Sheppard was a thief but he never told a lie >

Jack Sheppard. From: University of Michigan "Eighteenth-Century England" Web Resource http://www.umich.edu/~ece/student_projects/bonifield/burglary.html

The English robber Jack Sheppard (1702–1724) was hanged at Tyburn on 16 November 1724 and memorialized at the time in various works including *A Narrative of all the Robberies, Escapes, &c., of John Sheppard* (1824), an account that was probably written by Daniel Defoe.
As with Dick Turpin, it was William Harrison Ainsworth who gave Jack Sheppard new life for the Victorians. Ainsworth's *Jack Sheppard* began its serial run *in Bentley's Miscellany* (then edited by Charles Dickens) in January 1839, and for four months it ran together with the closing chapters of *Oliver Twist.* Illustrated by George Cruikshank, *Jack Sheppard* was published in book form in October 1839 and sold initially three thousand copies a week, eclipsing even *Oliver Twist.* By the end of October there were also eight theatrical versions running in London.
In 1859, George Augustus Sala complained that the idea that Jack Sheppard never told a lie was the creation of one of the dramatists: "At a West-end theatre, was produced the only immoral version of an immoral (and imbecile) 'Jack Sheppard,' which is, even now, vauntingly announced as being the 'authorised version' – the only one licensed by the Lord Chamberlain; and in that 'authorised version' occurs the line, 'Jack Sheppard is a thief, but he never told a lie,' a declaration than which the worst dictum of howling Tom Paine or rabid Mary Wolstoncraft was not more subversive of the balance of moral ethics." – *Twice Round the Clock, or The Hours of the Day and Night in London* (1859), 272, quoted in Lee Jackson, "The Victorian Dictionary" (online: http://www.victorianlondon.org/publications/sala-18.htm).

83 [Calvin] was reluctantly compelled to burn some of his fellow creatures in the interests of moderation >
RLS no doubt refers to the arrest for blasphemy and the trial and execution by burning alive of Michael Servetus (1511–1553). According to the 11th edition of the *Encyclopædia Britannica*: "It can be justly charged against Calvin in this matter that he took the initiative in bringing on the trial of Servetus, that as his accuser he prosecuted the suit against him with undue severity, and that he approved the sentence which condemned Servetus to death." The decision was widely approved, however, and Coleridge is perhaps right in his *Notes on English Divines* (collected 1853) that the

death of Servetus was not "Calvin's guilt especially, but the common opprobrium of all European Christendom."

84 take our pets in the twig >
take them as we find them; *twig* means "condition, state, fettle; esp. in the phrases *in (prime, good) twig*" (*OED*).

84 "People propose geometry on a large scale for the inhabitants of the moon," suggested Blackburn. > In the novel by Jules Verne known in English as *From the Earth to the Moon Direct in Ninety-Seven Hours and Twenty Minutes* (Paris, 1865), Impey Barbicane, President of the Gun Club in Baltimore, Maryland, reviews previous speculations by way of preparing the membership for his proposal to launch a projectile to reach the moon. He reviews and dismisses a number of speculative works, and then turns to one recent practical suggestion, from Germany:

> "So much for those expeditions," he continued, "which I consider purely literary, since they provide no serious means for establishing relations with the luminary of the night. But I should add that some practical minds have tried to enter into serious communication with the moon. Several years ago, a German geometrician suggested that a team of scientists be sent to the steppes of Siberia. There, on the vast plains, they would set up enormous geometric figures, outlined in luminous materials, among others the square of the hypotenuse (vulgarly called 'the ass's bridge' by the French). Every intelligent being, the geometrician maintained, would comprehend the scientific meaning of that figure. The Selenites, if there are any, will indicate they have understood by responding with a similar figure. Once communication is established, it should be easy to create an alphabet that will make it possible to converse with the inhabitants of the moon. This is what the German geometrician suggested, but his plans have never been carried out, and until now there has been no direct link between the Earth and her satellite." (ch. 2; in *The Annotated Jules Verne: From the Earth to the Moon*, trans. Walter James Miller, 1978, 12; Miller notes that the geometrician was Karl. F. Gauss, 1777–1855, also a distinguished astronomer, and that the idea of outlining the figures in luminous materials actually came from another German astronomer, Joseph J. von Littrow, 1781–1840)

In *The Academy*, 3 June 1876, RLS enthusiastically reviewed *From the Earth to the Moon* and seven other novels by Jules Verne in English translation collected under the title "Jules Verne's Stories" (London: Sampson Low, 1876):

"Of human nature it is certain he [Verne] knows nothing; and it is almost with a sense of relief that one finds in these days a good trotting horse of an author who whistles by the way and affects to know nothing of the mysteries of the human heart. . . . He has the knack of making stories to a nicety. He is as full of resources as one of his own heroes; his books are as accurately calculated as the lines of the *Nautilus*, or the partition-breaks of the projectile."

85 lefty-handedly >
inappropriately or anomalously; left-handed in this sense means "[a]mbiguous, doubtful, questionable" (*OED*); RLS's variant version is not recorded in the *OED*.

87 "you leave all your jugs and snuff-boxes lying around loose.
–88 It appears you and your landlady are not on international terms?" >
in other words, they are on friendly terms, with no need to guard against pilfering. Probably this is a recollection of Blackburn's comment earlier: "International policy has been, is, will be, and must be, treacherous in council, ruthless and deadly in execution" (59). Turton later uses *international* in opposition to the word *weak* (136).

89 alternate strips of bright sea and bars of dark chersonese >
chersonese – a peninsula, originally the Thracian peninsula west of the Hellespont (*OED*).

92 it soon led them among plantations of fir >
"One thing in life calls for another; there is a fitness in events and places. . . . Something, we feel, should happen; we know not what, yet we proceed in quest of it. It is thus that tracts of young fir, and low rocks that reach into deep soundings, particularly torture and delight me. Something must have happened in such places, and perhaps ages back, to members of my race; and when I was a child I tried in vain to invent appropriate games for them, as I still try, just as vainly, to fit them with the proper story" ("A Gossip on Romance," 1882; *Memories and Portraits*, 1887).

90 striking up the march of the Connaught Rangers >
The 88th Regiment of Foot, "The Devil's Own," was a fierce regiment raised in 1793 in the Western province of Ireland,

Connaught, comprising the counties Galway, Mayo, and Roscommon. It was for a time commanded by the Duke of Wellington. It was disbanded in 1922, when the Irish Free State was created. Another name for this famous march is the "Garryowen."

90 Capting >
as on manuscript p. 109, the spelling is probably meant to indicate Turton's pronunciation of *captain.*

91 the road rang below their consonant feet >
consonant – "[i]n agreement, accordance, or harmony" (*OED*).

91 a lusty view hulloah. >
view-halloo – "the shout given by a huntsman on seeing a fox break cover" (*OED*). The most recent citation in the *OED* is from the end of the ninth paragraph of *Dr. Jekyll and Mr. Hyde* (1886):

> All at once, I saw two figures: one a little man who was stumping along eastward at a good walk, and the other a girl of maybe eight or ten who was running as hard as she was able down a cross street. Well, sir, the two ran into one another naturally enough at the corner; and then came the horrible part of the thing; for the man trampled calmly over the, child's body and left her screaming on the ground. It sounds nothing to hear, but it was hellish to see. It wasn't like a man; it was like some damned Juggernaut. I gave a view-halloa, took to my heels, collared my gentleman, and brought him back to where there was already quite a group about the screaming child.

During the walking tour that he took in Cumberland 1871 and described a year or two later in the essay "Cockermouth and Keswick," RLS may have heard the popular song "D'ye ken John Peel" and the line in its chorus "Peel's view holloa would wake the dead" – probably neither for the first nor for the last time:

> Do ye ken John Peel with his coat so grey?
> Do ye ken John Peel at the break of day?
> Do ye ken John Peel when he's far, far away
> With his hounds and his horn in the morning.

Chorus

Twas the sound of his horn brought me from my bed
And the cry of his hounds has me oftimes led
For Peel's view holloa would wake the dead
Or a fox from his lair in the morning.

Written in the 1820s by John Woodcock Graves about his friend, the Cumberland farmer and hunter John Peel (1776–1854) to an 18th-century tune, in 1869 it had been given a new musical setting by William Metcalf – whose version then enjoyed great popular success in the 1870s.

91 like a fat terrier in the huff > *huff* – "[a] fit of petulance or offended dignity caused by an affront, real or supposed; esp. in phr. *in a huff, to take huff*" (*OED*). Stevenson and his father were both very fond of dogs. The conversation here between Turton and Blackburn anticipates in some respects RLS's essay "The Character of Dogs" (1884; *Memories and Portraits*, 1887).

92 Mulagh Creigh > an imaginary name; translated from the Scots Gaelic, it would mean "top of the rock or crag".

93 caller > "fresh and cool; well-aired" (*OED*).

95 who would not cry with Burns that it was worthy of a grace as long as my arm? > Burns, "To a Haggis" (1786):

Fair fa' your honest sonsie face,
Great chieftain o' the puddin'-race!
Aboon them a' ye tak your place,
Painch, tripe, or thairm:
Weel are ye wordy o' a grace
As lang's my arm.

95 conslaught > seemingly a variant spelling by RLS of *onslaught*; not recorded in the *OED*.

95 but ae bed, forbye mines > only one bed, except for mine.

95 a wheen strae > a little bit of straw.

95 halesome > wholesome.

96 kye > cows.

96 kirn > churn.

96 haugh >
"[a] piece of flat alluvial land by the side of a river, forming part of the floor of the river valley" (*OED*).

96 haw an' little >
nothing of the slightest value; "[u]sed as a type of a thing of no value. *Obs.*" (*OED*).

98 only Guinness who can brew good stout >
Arthur Guinness (1725-1803) began brewing stout (porter) at St. James's Gate, Dublin, in 1759; forty years later, in 1799, it became the firm's only product. Writing to Sidney Colvin, 19 February 1893, aboard the S. S. *Mariposa* en route to Auckland and Sydney, RLS commented: "Fanny ate a whole fowl for breakfast to say nothing of a tower of hot cakes. Belle and I floored another hen betwixt the pair of us and I shall be no sooner done with the present amanuensing racket than I shall put myself outside a pint of Guinness. If you think this looks like dying of consumption in Apia I can only say I differ from you" (Letter 2542). RLS's comment was first published in the *Vailima Letters* (2 vols., 1895) and for many years was used in Guinness advertising, for example in the *New Yorker*, 4 April 1936; *Time*, 6 April 1936; and *Punch*, 10 August 1955.

99 The unwearied sun >
Joseph Addison (1672–1719), "The Spacious Firmament on High":

> Th' unwearied Sun, from day to day
> Does his Creator's Pow'r display
> And publishes to every Land
> The Work of an Almighty Hand.

100 "no sorrow in his song" >
John Logan (1748–1788), "To the Cuckoo": "Thou hast no sorrow in thy song, / No winter in thy year."

100 jolly chanticleer ... dame Partlet >
RLS no doubt knew the beast fable of Chanticleer and Pertelote from Chaucer's "The Nun's Priest's Tale." His copy

of *Poetical Works of Geoffrey Chaucer Edited with a Memoir by Robert Bell*, 6 vols. [vol. 4 lacking in this set], London: Charles Griffin, n.d. [187-], is in the Lockwood Memorial Library, State University of New York-Buffalo.

101 mutch >
"[*Scottish*] A night covering for the head" - "[a] nightcap" (*OED*).

101 ornamental shooting boxes >
shooting box – "a small country house in or adjacent to a shooting locality used as a residence while shooting" (*OED*).

102 in a kind of antitype of the old myth of the escalcade of Heaven and the resounding ruin of the Titans >
According to Hesiod, *Theogony* (*ca.* 700 BC), 617-744, Zeus and his followers overthrew Cronos and the Titans as rulers of the universe in a battle of tremendous ferocity:

> The boundless sea rang terribly around, and the earth crashed loudly: wide Heaven was shaken and groaned, and high Olympus reeled from its foundation under the charge of the undying gods, and a heavy quaking reached dim Tartarus and the deep sound of their feet in the fearful onset and of their hard missiles. So, then, they launched their grievous shafts upon one another, and the cry of both armies as they shouted reached to starry heaven; and they met together with a great battle-cry.
>
> Then Zeus no longer held back his might; but straight his heart was filled with fury and he showed forth all his strength. From Heaven and from Olympus he came forthwith, hurling his lightning: the bolts flew thick and fast from his strong hand together with thunder and lightning, whirling an awesome flame. The life-giving earth crashed around in burning, and the vast wood crackled loud with fire all about. All the land seethed, and Ocean's streams and the unfruitful sea. The hot vapour lapped round the earthborn Titans: flame unspeakable rose to the bright upper air: the flashing glare of the thunder stone and lightning blinded their eyes for all that they were strong. Astounding heat seized Chaos: and to see with eyes and to hear the sound with ears it seemed even as if Earth and wide Heaven above came together; for such a mighty crash would have arisen if Earth were being hurled to ruin, and Heaven from on high were hurling her down; so great a crash was there while the gods were meeting together in strife. Also the winds brought rumbling earthquake and duststorm, thunder and lightning and the lurid thunderbolt, which are the shafts of great Zeus, and carried the clangour and the warcry into the midst of the two hosts. An horrible uproar of terrible strife arose: mighty

deeds were shown and the battle inclined. But until then, they kept at one another and fought continually in cruel war. And amongst the foremost Cottus and Briareos and Gyes insatiate for war raised fierce fighting: three hundred rocks, one upon another, they launched from their strong hands and overshadowed the Titans with their missiles, and hurled them beneath the wide-pathed earth, and bound them in bitter chains when they had conquered them by their strength for all their great spirit, as far beneath the earth as heaven is above earth; for so far is it from earth to Tartarus. (Theogony, trans. G. Evelyn-White, in *Hesiod: The Homeric Hymns and* Homerica, Loeb Classical Library, 1914, lines 677-721)

103 a large and handsome modern edifice called Tufto Castle >
The name Tufto may recall Lieutenant-General George Tufto in Thackeray's *Vanity Fair* (1848). Becky Sharpe's husband Rawdon Crawley is Tufto's aide-de-camp.

103 vineries >
vinery – "[a] glass house or hot-house constructed for the cultivation of the grape-vine" (*OED*).

104 Xanadu >
Coleridge, "Kubla Khan" (1798), ultimately from Samuel Purchas's *Purchas his Pilgrimage* (1613), where the place is called Xamdu.

104 Mountains of the Moon >
In the Roman geographer Ptolemy's *Geographia* the source of the Nile River is said to be the *Lunaes Montes* or Mountains of the Moon, a group of snow-capped mountains in equatorial Africa. Probably these are the mountains known today as the Ruwenzori (or Rwenzori) Range, first described in detail by Henry Morton Stanley, *In Darkest Africa* (1890), chapters 28-31. The highest of the peaks is Mt. Stanley, 16,763 ft (5,109 m).

104 bedizened and coquettish policies of the great house >
bedizened – [d]ressed up with vulgar finery; *policies* – enclosed, landscaped areas or grounds (*OED*).

105 the bottom of a sort of devil's punch bowl >
the term *devil's punch bowl* is applied to natural bowls or amphitheatres of many kinds. Among these is the Devil's Punch Bowl, Hindhead Commons, near Godalming, Surrey

– now a National Trust property – but there is no evidence that RLS ever visited it or even that he knew about it.

106 Tufto Castle is not the sort of house in which we should expect to find a Werther; but wherever there are lazy people, there will be sluggish livers; and wherever there are sluggish livers, sad thoughts and melancholy aspirations are sure to be in vogue. >
RLS shared the prevailing disdain for the hero of Goethe's *Die Leiden des jungen Werthers* (1774), generally known in English as *The Sorrows of Young Werther.* In a letter to Elizabeth Crosby, July 1873, he mentions "Werther and his sham sorrows" (Letter 128). See also his comments in letters to Mrs. Sitwell, 8 and 9 September 1873, Letters 137-138.

106 a little cockney dependency of the cockney castle, the last outpost of Birmingham >
see the note on "Birmingham majesty" (90).

108 braced from top to toe >
braced – "strained, strengthened, girt, etc." (*OED*).

109 Capting >
as on p. 90, the spelling is probably meant to indicate Turton's pronunciation of *captain.*

110 skulk >
"to move in a stealthy or sneaking fashion, so as to escape notice" (*OED*).

110 "Doosid remarkable woman," said the Major >
doosid is a humorous usage of the slang term *deuced* meaning "plaguy, confounded; 'devilish'; expressing impatient dislike, or as a mere emphatic expletive" (*OED*).

111 Major Albert Cunningham, H. E. I. C. S. >
Honourable East India Company's Service. Until 1858, when as a result of the Indian Mutiny of 1857 the East India Company's administrative and military control of India was assumed by the Crown, the Honourable East India Company's Service comprised the top administrative level of the civil service in India. This group was replaced by the Indian Civil Service.

111 Furlough >
regularly scheduled home leave.

111 the white feather >
to show the white feather is to show cowardice.

111 The Buffs >
The Third (or East Kent) Regiment of Foot, known from their uniform facings as the Buffs, was raised in 1572 and served often in India.

112 *Gwalior* >
Gwalior is a major city in north India noted especially for its fortress on a high rock in the middle of the city. There does not seem to have been a ship so named in the East India Company service, however.

112 cuddy >
"a room or cabin in a large ship abaft and under the round-house, in which the officers and cabin-passengers take their meals" (*OED*).

114 Inveradam >
there is no such place; in Scots Gaelic, *inver* means loch or river mouth and is very common in place names, the best known of which is the name of the town of Inverness.

116 passages of arms >
passage of arms – "an exchange of blows by armed opponents, an encounter; also fig. a controversial bout" (OED).

116 studying the "Army List" >
"The broad outline of an army officer's career can be discovered fairly easily by using the Army List. . . . The first official army list was published in 1740." Army Lists appeared annually from 1754 to 1879 and monthly beginning in 1798. The monthly lists were "arranged by regiment, but also give some idea of where the regiment was. Officers of colonial, militia and territorial units are included, along with the regular army." – United Kingdom National Archives, Research Guides: The Army Lists.

118 Minewells >
invented by RLS: there is no such place.

118 *splore* >
"A frolic, merrymaking, revel, carousal," also "[a] commotion or disturbance; a skirmish or encounter; a scrape" (*OED*, with citations from Burns and Scott in both senses).

120 the fifth commandment >
"Honour thy father and thy mother: that thy days may be long upon the land which the Lord thy God giveth thee" (Exodus, 20:12).

120 "O, I've read their books! Colenso . . . a black man! . . . and what not. But I believe." >
John William Colenso (1814–1883), English bishop of Natal, in 1862 published *The Pentateuch and Book of Joshua Critically Examined*, the first of seven commentaries that he published through 1879 under the collective title *Critical Examination of the Pentateuch* (1862–1879). Colenso stated his general conclusion in the first chapter:

> that the Pentateuch, as a whole, cannot possibly have been written by Moses, or by any one acquainted personally with the facts which it professes to describe, and further, that the (so-called) Mosaic narrative, by whomsoever written, and though imparting to us, as I fully believe it does, revelations of the Divine Will and Character, cannot be regarded as *historically true.*

His reason for so believing, Colenso insisted,

> is not that I find insuperable difficulties with regard to the *miracles*, or supernatural *revelations* of Almighty God, recorded in it, but solely that I cannot, as a true man, consent any longer to shut my eyes to the absolute, palpable, self-contradictions of the narrative.

These self-contradictions had become apparent to him translating the Bible into Zulu, especially through the naive but sincere and obvious questions asked by his African assistants. When the first volume was published, Colenso immediately became the center of a storm of controversy, and though his opponents were largely successful in preventing him from preaching in England, he remained active in Natal and actively championed the rights of the Zulu natives among whom he worked as a missionary and whose questions had first led to his own research. It is perhaps this last association that connects him in Mrs. Lemensurier's mind with "a black man."

120 a fellow at Buxton . . . he had a beard . . . and he told me all
–121 about Joshua stopping the sun and the moon; and, egad, it appears the fellow couldn't have done it! He couldn't have stopped them . . . don't you understand? . . . because of science. >

Buxton is a popular spa town in Derbyshire developed during the eighteenth and nineteenth centuries by the Dukes of Devonshire as a rival to Bath. The Biblical passage is as follows: "Then spake Joshua to the Lord . . . and he said in the sight of Israel, Sun, stand thou still upon Gibeon; and thou, Moon, in the valley of Ajalon. And the sun stood still, and the moon stayed, until the people had avenged themselves upon their enemies. . . . So the sun stood still in the midst of heaven, and hasted not to go down about a whole day" (Joshua 10:12–13). In his Preface to *The Pentateuch and Book of Joshua Critically Examined* (1862), Bishop Colenso remarked in reply to another commentator that "every natural philosopher will know to be wholly untenable" the idea that such a miracle might be accomplished if both the earth's travel around the sun and its rotation on its axis were suddenly stopped. But if this were to occur, Colenso says, "a man's *feet* would be arrested, while his *body* was moving at the rate (on the equator) of 1,000 miles an hour . . . so that every human being and animal would be dashed to pieces in a moment, and a mighty deluge overwhelm the earth unless all this were prevented by a profusion of miraculous interferences." Nor would the earth's stopping have any effect upon the moon's motion around the earth. No source is known to me of the scientific arguments (such as they are) that impressed Major Cunningham. Probably there was no such source, Stevenson's reference being to discussions of this sort generally.

128 list >

a type of cloth used for borders or edges (*OED*).

134 overcrowed >

overcrow – "[to] crow or exult over; to triumph over; to overpower" (*OED*, with citations from Spenser; Scott, who mentions Spenser; and Borrow, *The Bible in Spain* [1843]).

135 Hillo, >
thus in MS., probably to indicate the pronunciation.

136 keep you, gentle stranger, till the commodore returns >
[unidentified]

136 *fête champêtre* >
a rustic festival.

136 let's have the joy of garlands and deep goblets. *Vide* the
-137 works of Bohn and the immortal dead >
As he does briefly here, in a letter to Charles Baxter, 3 March 1872, Letter 95, signed R. L. Stevenson Bohn, RLS parodies the clumsy and literal style of the popular translations of Greek and Latin classics published by Henry George Bohn (1796–1884). "The name of Bohn is principally remembered for the important *Libraries* which he inaugurated: these were begun in 1846 and comprised editions of standard works and translations, dealing with history, science, classics, and archaeology, consisting in all of 766 volumes. . . . It had been one of Bohn's ambitions to found a great publishing house, but, finding that his sons had no taste for the trade, Bohn sold the *Libraries* in 1864 to Bell and Daldy, afterwards G. Bell & Sons" (*Encyclopædia Britannica*, 11th ed.). Among the Bohn translations that RLS owned is vol. 1 of *The Tragedies of Euripides, Literally Translated or Revised, with Critical and Explanatory Notes by Theodore Alois Buckley* (London, 1871; Anderson, I, 227). In a notebook that RLS was keeping in 1873–1874, "Bohn's Cribs" is among the titles in a list of projected essays (Notebook A 265A, Yale GEN MSS 684, Box 1, Folders 37-39).

137 the young man of Baghdad addressed the Unknown Prince >
As with RLS's later reference to the "merchant of Balsorah" (139), the reference is probably generic. There is no tale specifically about a young man in Baghdad and an Unknown Prince, even in Henry Weber's three-volume *Tales of the East* (Edinburgh: James Ballantyne, 1812), which includes tales in addition to those in the *Arabian Nights* strictly so called. See also the note on "tricks of illumination of which Hassad is the only master" (73).

137 don't *gêner* yourself >
don't worry yourself.

137 "O no, we never mention it!" >
An adaptation of the title and first line of the sentimental parlor ballad by the prolific Thomas Haynes Bayly (1797–1839), "Oh! No! We Never Mention Her."

Oh! no! we never mention her,
Her name is never heard;
My lips are now forbid to speak
That once familiar word.

In 1891 RLS echoed the song again in the deed of gift of his birthday, 13 November, to Annie Ide, who had been born on Christmas Day, stating "that I, the said Robert Louis Stevenson, have attained an age when, O, we never mention it, and that I have no further use for a birthday of any description" (RLS to Henry Clay Ide, 19 June 1891, Letter 2328).

138 as sure as a gun >
"beyond all question, to a dead certainty" (*OED*).

138 O what bliss to be a noumenon! / O bid me live, and I will live / Your noumenon to be!" >
Robert Herrick, "To Anthea, who may command him any thing":

Bid me to live, and I will live
  Thy Protestant to be:
Or bid me love, and I will give
  A loving heart to thee.
A heart as soft, a heart as kind,
  A heart as sound and free,
As in the whole world thou canst find,
  That heart Ile give to thee.
Bid that heart stay, and it will stay,
  To honour thy decree:
Or bid it languish quite away,
  And't shall doe so for thee.
Bid me to weep, and I will weep
  While I have eyes to see:
And having none, yet I will keep
  A heart to weep for thee.
Bid me despaire, and Ile despair,
  Under that *Cypresse* tree:
Or bid me die, and I will dare
  E'en Death, to die for thee.
Thou art my life, my love, my heart,

The very eyes of me:
And hast command of every part,
To live and die for thee.

RLS's copy of Herrick's *Hesperides: The Poems and Other Remains . . . Now First Collected*, ed. W. Carew Hazlitt, 2 vols., London: John Russell Smith, 1869, is now held as Beinecke 2536. RLS has marked many passages in pencil and in the index has marked the titles of 51 poems. Writing in November 1883 to Edmund Gosse on Gosse's *Seventeenth-Century Studies*, then just published, RLS remarked: "Your Webster is not my Webster; nor your Herrick my Herrick. . . . They are two of my favourite authors: Herrick above all: I suppose they are two of yours . . . and we can but agree to differ" (Letter 1176). RLS uses the surname Herrick for one of the protagonists in *The Ebb-Tide* (1894).

138 "What, in the name of fortune, is a noumenon?" >
According to the philosophy of Immanuel Kant (1724-1804), behind every perception – every *phenomenon* – is the thing, in itself, as it really is. This is a separate philosophical entity without tangible attributes, called a *noumenon*. "[There is] a realm of objects which, in opposition to the *phenomena* of our relative and limited experience, may be called *noumena* or things-in-themselves. The *noumenon*, therefore, is in one way the object of a non-sensuous intuition, but is more correctly the expression of the limited and partial character of our knowledge." – *Encyclopædia Britannica*, 11th ed.

139 a merchant in Balsorah >
The port, now known as Al Basrah or Basra, at the head of the Persian Gulf and at the confluence of the Tigris and Euphrates rivers. It was from Balsorah that Sinbad departed on his voyages in the *Arabian Nights*. As with RLS's earlier reference to "the young man of Baghdad" addressing "the Unknown Prince" (137), the reference is probably generic. There is no tale specifically about a merchant in Balsorah, even in Henry Weber's three-volume *Tales of the East* (1812), which includes tales in addition to those in the *Arabian Nights* strictly so called. See also the note on "tricks of illumination of which Hassad is the only master" (73).

139 All the world's a stage >
Shakespeare, *As You Like It*, II.vii.147.

139 *Et tu, Brute?* >
Shakespeare, *Julius Caesar*, III.i.87.

140 duffer >
"[*Colloquial*] [a] person who proves to be without practical ability or capacity; one who is incapable, inefficient, or useless in his business or occupation; the reverse of an adept or competent person. Also more generally, a stupid or foolish person" (*OED*).

143 cads >
cad – "[a] fellow of low vulgar manners and behaviour. (An offensive and insulting appellation)" (*OED*, with a note suggesting that it is Victorian university slang derived from usages at Eton and Oxford).

144 the covert of his eyelids >
Covert is a variant spelling of *cover*. "*[U]nder (the) cover of*: (*lit.* and *fig.*) under the protection or shelter of" (*OED*).

• • • • •

Textual Notes

Most of the changes that Stevenson made in the fair-copy manuscript of *The Hair Trunk* – as he wrote it out in ink or afterwards, in pencil or possibly in ink – have been assimilated into the text of this edition without comment, as if the manuscript were being set in type for publication. Only when a change has seemed to me clearly a change of intention or desired effect, or in some other way to shed light on Stevenson's intentions or his actual or potential satiric targets, is notice taken of it in these Textual Notes. As is sometimes the case in other notebooks and books owned by Stevenson, a list of page numbers is written in pencil on the first leaf inside the front cover of the first notebook, probably by him. There are twelve such page numbers, and they correspond to pages in the first fifty-eight pages on which changes or comments are made, also in pencil. (Changes in pencil appear on later pages, too, but there is not a list of them.) As the text, including deletions and changes, is otherwise entirely in ink, the changes and comments in pencil must have been made at a time later than the original copying. Other changes, in ink, may have been made at any time.

Table of Contents or The Ideal Commonwealth >
written at an angle, rising to the right, suggesting that the sub-title was not originally included on this page

Table of Contents The Disciples >
replaces an earlier version of this chapter title: A pack of young Fools

1 The Ideal Commonwealth >
written heavily in ink to replace by over-writing possibly as

many as two other subtitles, one of them being “The Hairy Portmanteau,” a phrase which is also changed in pencil at the end of the first chapter

1 The Disciples >
this chapter title is written in pencil to replace the earlier version, written in ink: A Pack of Young Fools

4 eccentric >
RLS’s variant spelling *ex-centric*, which he uses twice in *The Hair Trunk*, is recorded in the *OED* as used in an 1803 edition of Henry Mackenzie’s *The Man of Feeling* (1771) and adjectivally as late as 1875. All other nineteenth-century examples about people rather than physical position in the OED use the spelling *eccentric*.

6 It was difficult to understand . . . But his silence seemed to make disciples. >
this comment about Ratcliffe is added on the facing page

8 whiskey >
RLS uses the Irish (and American) spelling throughout *The Hair Trunk*; the usual Scottish spelling is *whisky*. In *Kidnapped*, (1886), he uses the word twice, and in both instances the manuscript and the first book-form edition agree in the spelling ‘whiskey’ (middle of ch. 25, ‘In Balquidder’; fifth paragraph from the end of ch. 26, ‘We Pass the Forth’).

9 Hair Trunk >
changed in pencil from: Hairy Portmanteau

13 an estate in the West Highlands. >
originally followed by an additional sentence, later deleted in pencil: Bloated plutocrats and sinecurists, one and all!

15 answered Turton. >
originally continued as follows: “Stamen and Pistil,” he added, with a manly gesture. . . . That’s about the sum of my endowments. I could have taken first class honours on the Hermaphrodite Plants, ’tis true, from the natural curiosity of the subject. But I think poorly of the Vegetable Kingdom as a whole. It doesn’t form a racy study.

15 Hardy laughed . . . >
written in the margin opposite this paragraph: all this in Herbert Spencer

15-16 Flesh and Blood cannot support so violent a change. >
originally this paragraph was continued as follows, with the words *see* and *feel* both deleted, without a replacement, with the word *person* deleted and replaced by *man*, and eventually the whole continuation deleted: And any one of us who is fool enough to try it, will [see] [feel] the force of my remarks when he comes to his death bed. And for another thing, a [person] man cannot willingly divest himself of his liberty.

16 piping >
originally: sickening

16 physically incapable >
originally this sentence was continued with a colon and the following words: . . . I repeat the words; physically incapable; you other fellows mayn't be, but I am . . . physically incapable

20 children >
the word *children* is queried on the facing page and replaces, in pencil, the earlier phrase: Feudal Castles

21 *The Ideal Commonwealth!* >
underlined twice in the manuscript

21 Prince Rupert's cavaliers. >
originally followed by the following additional words, all later deleted; the words in square brackets seem to have been deleted as the sentence was being written: And it was noticeable that each, as each set down his empty glass, he reached out mechanically for the bottle, and proceeded to replenish it with that [indifference to any proportion between the ingredients and that] gay [liberty] confidence which is peculiar to the dwindling night. Alone of the party, Strutt preserved some appearance of calm – not that he failed to

23 Finding therefore a difference between himself and all his companions, >
followed originally by this additional phrase, later deleted in pencil: which was really due to his cold heart,

29 knees >
originally: mortal tabernacle

29 something Here which Responds to these Orbs!" >
the capital letters are written in pencil over the lower-case versions in ink

35 Secret Police >
written in pencil to replace the earlier phrase: Fine Arts

35 gasping with brown sherry >
originally: gasping and helpless with brown sherry

35 like a cheap print, or something in a novel, don't you know?" >
-36 originally continued as follows: "Here was this man of the world . . . this *viveur* . . . this mathematician . . . chock full of brown sherry, too . . . giving the responses in a rich thrilling baritone, with a kind of far-away look in his eyes, as if his happy childhood were passing before him! By George, I was almost affected to tears!"

36 a practice common to the vast majority of the human race. >
originally followed by two additional sentences: "As for prayer . . . a man is surely very silly to neglect so agreeable a practice . . . not to put it higher. It prevents remorse," he added, in the rich thrilling notes alluded to by Turton, ". . . it is so mollifying to the conscience."

40 a statesmanlike measure! >
originally followed by this sentence: Did I not say I had the soul of a Publicist?

46 with the air of a chairman taking votes. >
originally continued as follows, with the word *thrust* replaced by *put* and the whole continuation later deleted: and [thrust] put his hands into the arm holes of his waistcoat.

50 Now, if we can raise funds to go . . . >
the Yale draft begins with this sentence, with the word *tin* used instead of *funds*

50 "My dear Mr. Strutt" . . . >
in the Yale draft, this paragraph lacks the references to retired military men: "Permit me, Mr. Strutt," replied

Blackburn. "With the same capital, we might be a firm of hucksters in England, while we can live like kings in Navigator."

53 social free-lances. >
in the Yale draft, this sentence originally continued with a comma after the word *free-lances* and what would appear to be two different attempts to provide more detail, both of them later deleted: which comprises (as Turton might have said) the landscape painter begins at the door of the gin palace to end in the Royal Academy

53 I can imagine almost any number of consecutive vestrymen
-54 . . . men enough to substitute their own. >
in the Yale draft, this passage reads as follows, with the words in square brackets deleted: [I can figure to myself Mr] I think I can see Mr Herbert Spencer tarred and feathered by an [unruly] congregation of landscape painters. I can imagine a vestryman weeping on the neck of Mr Herbert Spencer, much more readily than a landscape painter. And whether it is regarded as a compliment or the reverse, it may be said that the [whole] New Gospel is likely to remain a dead letter for the outcast and unruly.

54 substitute their own. >
originally continued as follows: Not much logic show of logic is required for such an audience, but a great effusion of generous and inconsequential sentiment or on occasion; a bright and vague

55 an Ideal Commonwealth in Navigator Islands. >
in the Yale draft, this phrase reads: an Ideal Commonwealth in the South Sea Islands.

58 "Damn Herbert Spencer!" cried Turton >
in the Yale draft, Turton's response is as follows: "If you think I've cut the Bible, to take up with Herbert Spencer," cried Turton, in a fury ". . . if you think I've refused one set of authorities, and a very good set too . . . to bow down in the prime of my youth, before a confounded Natural Science man, if you imagine for a moment, Mr Hardy . . ."

59 imported epidemics, civilisation advances with gigantic strides. >
in the Yale draft, this sentence originally ended as follows, with the words in square brackets deleted: [civilised diseases] imported epidemics, and God's blessing as they say, [the inferior race dwindles and disappears like some burning flax before the advance of the superior] civilisation advances with gigantic strides.

59 imperfect hand-mirrors, literally by the ship load. >
in the Yale draft, this sentence ends with the word *hand-mirrors* and the following words deleted in continuation after a semicolon: so as not only to hasten the disappearance of the aborigine, but Civilisation looks on advances

59 Morality . . . is civil and never international. >
in the Yale draft, the word *personal* is used instead of the word *civil*

61 Nobody . . . has a better right to it than we ourselves. >
originally followed by this additional sentence: I am aware that that must sound strange; but I swear to you, so it is.

61 The Prophet looked about him with a grand air . . . >
-62 this paragraph is not present in the Yale draft

62 "Shall we wear masques?" . . . "I could shed tears!" >
in the Yale draft, these three paragraphs appear twice, in two different versions, at the foot of the page numbered 8 and at the top of the un-numbered page. The second version is followed in the notebook, a fact that suggests that in writing the first version RLS started anew at the top of a new page but forgot to delete the first version at the foot of the previous page. This first version originally began: "So much the better!" cried Turton. "Shall we wear masks?" It was then changed to: "Shall we wear masks?" asked Turton. The next two paragraphs are as follows, with the words in square brackets deleted:
"Upon my soul, I think we had better," replied Blackburn.
"[Why man] I've worn masks at school . . . when there was no use for it . . . often and often," answered Turton; "and I never tasted a purer order of pleasure in my life. [To] But to wear them in solemn earnest . . . to go after a real treasure,

with a real loaded pistol in my right hand . . . I assure you, Blackburn, I never dared to hope for such an intoxicating moment."

62 so strong was my vocation. >
originally followed by: I own I'm pining for moonlight adventure, escapades

65 "Will you do me the favour to walk twice or thrice round the quadrangle with me, Mr Strutt?" he asked. >
originally continued as follows: "I have something to add which may affect your determination."

68 You're a humbug," answered Turton. >
originally followed by: "I understand that."

69 twittered occasional comments >
originally: twittered an accompaniment

71 a sheet of paper >
originally: a ragged sheet of paper

75 just let him see a town!" >
originally followed by: And Turton threw up his hand with an elegant gesture.

BOOK II

89 Across the Forest >
this chapter title replaces the deleted title "Tufto Castle," which RLS then used for the title of the second chapter

89 The road turned and wound . . . >
this sentence is added on the facing page

91 strange and inspiring >
originally: full of solemn glee

93 It's no verra grand; >
MS. lacks the word *grand*, possibly intentionally to suggest shyness; the whole phrase is used on p. 95, however

98 the sails of a mill >
originally: only the sails of a mill

98 voice >
originally: chatter

98 chronic >
originally: an overweening

98 or something else? >
originally followed by the beginning of a sentence, later deleted: Or am I really what I seem to be, a definite, free

100 The voice of the waterfall . . . to the frosty stars. >
this sentence is added on the facing page

100 “no sorrow in his song” >
changed by RLS from the original wording, which was not in quotation marks: not a shade of sorrow in his song

100 repinings >
originally: regret

102 throned above calamity >
originally: set above all calamity

102 gloom and glimmer in the changeful phases of a highland climate >
originally: gaze steadfastly abroad from their gorges

102 charioting >
originally: hurrying

110 British >
replaces the partly-written but then deleted word: Englis

112 That Fellow . . . Fellow . . . That Fellow >
all of the capital letters are written in pencil over the lower-case versions in ink

114 Doosid >
originally: Very

114 collusion somewhere. >
originally: collusion somewhere. Collusion!

115 savour >
originally: flavour

115 if his wooing prospered >
originally: when his wooing was complete

116 pronounced >
the manuscript reading, perhaps intentionally, is: pronounce

117 and go!" >
originally followed by an additional sentence: Your back will be a cordial!"

117 fine >
originally: bonny

117 you're as prying as >
originally begun: you've shown the curiosi[ty]

118 Major. >
originally: Major promptly.

119 now I think the point >
originally: now I come to think of it, the point

118 broad >
originally: gross

118 He >
originally: Aye, he

119 and be sure and don't forget his Bible, >
inserted above the completed line

119 he shared >
originally: he came in for

121 incredible >
originally: positively incredible

121 undermined >
originally: quite undermined

122 riling >
originally: doosid riling

123 snapped >
originally: demanded

125 my position?” >
originally: my beggary?”

126 and unanswerable >
inserted above the completed line

128 “I have him and can break him >
this remark is preceded by the deleted word: “Revenge

128 kept his hands in the pockets of his trousers. >
originally: looking behind him with brief, suspicious glances.

128 woollen >
originally: thick woollen

129 the rogue.” >
changed in pencil from: the rogue means mischief!”

132 spied upon; >
originally: spied upon; he suspected every shadow

132 night; and when >
originally: night; the thing took solemnity from its surroundings; and when

133 lowest point. >
originally followed by the beginning of an additional sentence, with both of the words in square brackets deleted: This lowest point, or farthest outpost of plantation, on the side of Tufto Castle [ran] [lay] far down the hillside

134 so high, so high above >
thus in the manuscript, possibly an unintended repetition

136 clergyman’s family! >
this sentence was originally continued as follows, with the words in square brackets deleted and then undeleted before

the whole was finally deleted in favor of the present wording: [. . . and play the flute at night beside the lake] . . . and say grace when the parson was from home

137 with Us >
the upper-case letter U is underlined twice in the manuscript

138 “Life, without moral science, is bosh.” >
originally: “My young friend, your education has been neglected.”

140 this is immoral!” >
originally: you cut me to the heart!”

140 “You insult a man >
originally: “That’s nice conduct, isn’t it . . . to insult a man

141 O by heaven!” >
originally preceded by: Thief! thief!

142 existence of free men about upon the world, >
thus in the manuscript, consecutively in the main flow of the text; RLS may have decided to say *upon* rather than *about* the world but failed to delete his first thought; the phrase as it stands, however, has a certain logic and thus may be intentional; I have not emended it

143 “No? Pack of cads!” >
originally: “Very well. You see you are a pack of cads!”

144 The tone of Blackburn’s last advice had impressed him >
originally: Something in the tone of Blackburn’s last communication inclined him

144 he felt little inclination to disobey >
this phrase is preceded by the following deleted words: and as the old lady was

• • • • •

www.ingramcontent.com/pod-product-compliance
Lightning Source LLC
Chambersburg PA
CBHW060803310726
48980CB00002B/218
9781846220500